No Regrets

Rebecca Deel

Copyright © 2018 Rebecca Deel

All rights reserved.

ISBN: 1985856697
ISBN-13: 978-1985856691

DEDICATION

To my husband, who constantly amazes me.

ACKNOWLEDGMENTS

Cover by Melody Simmons.

CHAPTER ONE

"Everybody down on the ground. Now."

Sasha Ingram froze. Screams rang out in the normally quiet building. The terror on the teller's face convinced Sasha this wasn't a joke. Her bank in idyllic Otter Creek, Tennessee was the target of a robbery.

She'd waited ten minutes later than normal to deposit Perk's revenue for the day, hoping to have another one-sentence conversation with a certain black ops soldier who didn't return for his usual second cup of coffee today. If Sasha had gone to the bank on time, she wouldn't be here now.

"Did you hear what I said, lady?" a second male voice said. "Get on the ground." He punctuated his point by jabbing something hard into Sasha's back and shoving her to the floor in front of teller row.

She fell on her hands and knees, her dark hair swinging forward and obscuring her vision. A heavy weight settled on her back and shoved Sasha flat, keeping her pinned there like a bug. "Hey!"

"Shut up."

Sasha frowned. "Get off me, you oaf. I can't breathe."

"You won't be breathing at all if you don't close your trap and do what we tell you," he growled, his voice sounding like he'd eaten a bowl of gravel for breakfast.

She turned her head enough to see the second robber. He was dressed in black from head to toe, including the iconic ski mask covering his face and the gun in his hand. Assuming these two bozos didn't become twitchy and kill all the bank's occupants, the police would need some kind of description to catch the criminals. Her description wouldn't help them catch anyone. In fact, the operative she'd been mooning over the last few months wore the same thing every day sans the mask. He filled his clothes out better than these guy, though.

The first robber threw a sack to the teller. "Fill it up. Hurry." He practically danced in place, reminding Sasha of a nervous rabbit.

"Please don't hurt me." The teller's voice quivered.

"No talking. Just do what we say and nobody will be hurt." A moment later, Rabbit tossed another bag to the second teller, an older woman whose eyes burned with fury. "Same for you, lady. Hurry up."

When the tellers finished, the goon still holding Sasha down with his foot asked his partner, "What about the vault?"

"No time," Rabbit snapped. "We did what we're supposed to do. Let's go."

Tires screeched outside the bank. Both robbers cursed.

Sasha raised her head enough to peer through the window and saw flashing lights in the front. Thank goodness. One of the bank employees must have triggered a silent alarm. Since the police station was across the square, the officers had responded fast.

"What are we going to do?" Gravel asked.

"We got what we came for. We just need a little insurance."

Insurance? Sasha's stomach knotted. She had a horrible feeling she knew what his statement meant. Glancing around the interior revealed she was the only customer in the bank at the moment. The rest of the occupants were employees.

"You're coming with us," Gravel said, waving his gun at the young teller who had deposited Perk's proceeds for the day.

"No, please." The teller sobbed. "Don't take me. I have two little girls at home."

The man holding Sasha down shifted his weight and grabbed the girl by the arm. "You either come with us, or I'll shoot you where you stand."

Her shrill screams filled the room as the petrified woman struggled to free herself.

"We don't have time for this," Rabbit said, glancing nervously out the front door. "Let's just go."

"We have to follow the plan," Gravel said.

One moment Sasha was on the floor. The next, she found herself on her feet, a hairy arm across her throat and her back pressed against Gravel's chest.

"We'll take the mouthy one." He shoved one of the money bags in her hands and propelled her down the back hallway.

"You won't get away with this."

"Shut up." His hold on her neck tightened, making it hard to breathe much less talk. "Be smart, lady. Play nice and you might live another hour."

Rabbit peered carefully out the back door, then motioned for his partner to bring Sasha. Though she dragged her heels, Sasha didn't have leverage. Gravel had several inches of height on her. He simply moved her along at a faster clip. Once through the door, he shoved her into the backseat of the waiting car and pushed her to the floor, once again holding her in place with his booted foot.

"Give me the bag," he ordered. When she complied, he pitched that bag and the second one on the alley asphalt and slammed the door shut. "Go," he ordered his partner.

The men had tossed the money and kept her? Why rob the bank if you didn't intend to keep the cash? She hoped these yahoos weren't crazy because crazy didn't bode well for her getting out of this in one piece.

Car tires squealed as Rabbit raced from the alley. Men shouted for the driver to stop. Shots rang out and car windows shattered. The two robbers cursed, but Rabbit didn't slow down.

He groaned. "I'm hit."

"How bad?" Gravel demanded.

"I don't know. It hurts bad."

"Can you make it to the house?"

"I think so."

"If you can't, find a safe place to stop and I'll take over."

"You should give up now," Sasha said. "Your friend needs medical help."

"I told you to keep quiet." A second later, the robber slammed the butt of his gun on the side of her head and Sasha's world went dark.

She woke to the sound of two men arguing. For a moment, she couldn't place them. Memories of the robbery and being abducted flooded her mind. Great. She was still in the hands of the two would-be robbers.

Sasha opened her eyes to slits and saw nothing. Pulse pounding in her throat, she opened her eyes wider, strained to see anything and breathed a sigh of relief when she noticed a sliver of light.

Because the bank robber had slammed the butt of his gun on the side of Sasha's head, she had a blinding headache to go along with a world-class case of nausea.

Pain in her shoulders and side registered. Sasha tried to adjust her position and discovered her hands were bound behind her back. She flexed her hands and while the binding moved with her, she didn't create more room to slip her hands free. Zip ties, maybe. Giving up on freeing herself for now, she concentrated on exploring her dark prison.

Carpet fibers tickled her fingers as she maneuvered into a sitting position. She gritted her teeth as her stomach pitched and rolled. Although she hated being in the dark, in this instance darkness was good. She didn't want to know how much worse her headache would be if the lights were on.

Sasha scooted until her back was pressed against a wall. No windows and the room felt small. A closet?

She needed to escape, but from the sound of the men's voices, they might be in the next room. Instinct told her remaining quiet would be her best option. She didn't want to antagonize the bank robber who already proved willing to hurt her without a qualm.

When Sasha shifted to take pressure off her shoulders, her hands brushed against her back pocket. She stilled. Her cell phone was still in her pocket. Since she wore a heavy sweater with a long hem, the robbers had missed it.

She twisted her hands to one side and wiggled her phone from her pocket. The instrument dropped to the carpeted floor. She waited to see if the men noticed the small noise. The argument continued unabated.

Calling for help would be easier if her hands were in front of her body. Sasha thought about the logistics for a moment. She scrunched into a tight ball and inched her body through the circle of her arms. When she finished, Sasha leaned against the wall a moment to catch her breath.

Feeling around for her phone, she scooped it up and crawled as far from the door as possible. Sasha tapped in her code and turned to face the corner, hoping to dampen the sound of her voice. If the robbers caught her with the phone, there was no telling what they would do to her.

She frowned as her finger hovered over the keypad. How would she tell the police where she was? She'd been unconscious when she was transported inside. Perhaps the police could track her phone signal.

Sasha dialed 911.

"911. What is the nature of your emergency?"

"My name is Sasha Ingram. I'm being held hostage. I need help."

"Where are you?"

"I don't know. They knocked me out. I woke up in a closet."

"I'm notifying the police chief. Stay on the line, Sasha, and remain quiet. We'll find you."

"Tell them to hurry."

A minute later, a deep voice filled her ear. "Sasha, it's Ethan. Can you talk to me?"

"For now."

"How many kidnappers are we dealing with?"

"Two men." The argument in the other room continued and the only voices she heard were the two men who took her from the bank.

"Armed?"

"Handguns. One of them is injured."

"Do you know how bad?"

"No. The other one knocked me out."

"Are you injured?"

"Massive headache where the guy hit me with his gun."

"Do you have any idea where you are?"

"I wish. They shoved me onto the floor of the backseat before one robber knocked me out. How will you find me, Ethan?"

"Stay calm, Sasha. Don't antagonize them. Keep the phone on and with you. We'll track your signal. If they take you out of the closet, pay attention to your surroundings. Help us out with clues if you can without putting yourself in danger. When help arrives, go to the ground as fast as you can."

"Yes, sir."

The sudden silence on the other side of the door made Sasha's skin crawl. The floor creaked as someone approached.

"Someone is coming."

"Hang on. We will find you."

Sasha grabbed the phone and shoved it into her pocket without ending the call. She believed Ethan would find her. The question was, would he find her in time to save her life?

CHAPTER TWO

Today was the day. Cade Ramsey's stomach tightened into a knot at the thought of asking the beautiful coffee shop owner to go to dinner with him. He swallowed hard as he scaled the climbing wall on Personal Security International's obstacle course for the final leg of the training session with his team. He sidled over the top, leaped to the ground, and sprinted to the finish line where his team leader, Trent St. Claire, waited with the stop watch.

Cade routinely faced down insurgents, built and defused bombs as the EOD man for his team, all without breaking a sweat. Looking into Sasha Ingram's sparkling eyes, he became a tongue-tied idiot and the butt of his teammates' jokes.

He couldn't wait any longer to make his move. A couple trainees and one Fortress operative had hit on her in the past two weeks. If he didn't find a way to talk to her, Cade would lose his chance. One thing he would never do was poach on another man's territory.

He crossed the finish line and bent over at the waist, sucking in much needed air as his teammates surged past him.

Trent scribbled down their times on his clipboard. "Good time."

"But?" Liam McCoy, the team's sniper, glanced up from his sprawl on the ground.

"We can do better. We have to do better."

Simon Murray, Liam's spotter, sent Trent a wry smile. "How did I know you were going to say that?"

"He's right." Matt Rainer, Bravo team's medic, dragged in a deep breath and straightened to face the rest of them. "We might be roughed up from the last mission, but we can't let the trainees outshine us. We'd never hear the end of it."

Roughed up? Cade scowled. Every one of them had wounds from their latest rescue mission in Ecuador. They'd gone into the jungle to free a handful of missionaries from guerrillas out to make a name for themselves in the world of terrorism. The guerrillas might have been ill trained, but they had been well armed and unafraid to waste bullets. Each member of Bravo had come away from Ecuador with bullet or knife wounds. At least all the missionaries had been liberated without injuries to them.

"Are we finished here?" he asked Trent.

"Got a hot date?" Liam teased. "Oh, wait. You can't have a hot date because you can't talk to the woman of your dreams."

Cade frowned as his teammates dissolved into peals of laughter. "All right. Laugh it up, guys. I need to shower. I have stuff to do." A certain woman to track down.

"Hit the showers," Trent said. "Check in with me before you take off for the night. PT first thing tomorrow morning at 6:00 sharp."

Good-natured groans filled the air as Cade and his teammates headed for the instructors' locker room. Fifteen minutes later, all of them assembled in the hall. Trent ran down his observations for the training session, pointing out places where they could improve their time and work better as a unit.

Before he finished, his cell phone signaled an incoming call. Trent frowned at the screen. "Wait," he told his team, then answered the call. "St. Claire." His frown deepened as he listened, gaze locking with Cade's. "Where, Ethan?"

His leader's fierce expression made Cade's muscles tense. Whatever Trent was hearing from Otter Creek's police chief wasn't good. A glance at his teammates showed their attention had sharpened to mission-ready focus.

"Do you have a lock?" A pause. "Give me the number. Murphy can track the phone signal long before you obtain legal permission. I'll text you the info as soon as we have it." He ended the call, his attention on Cade. "The bank in Otter Creek was robbed. The two men took a hostage. Ethan needs a SWAT team. Since Durango is on a mission, we're on call."

Cade's nape prickled. "Who is the hostage?"

"It's Sasha."

He'd known, and yet the news hit him like a physical blow. Matt grabbed his shoulder to steady Cade when he stumbled back. "How long have the robbers had her?"

"Almost an hour."

"Breathe," Matt murmured. "You won't be any good to her if you can't function."

Those words snapped him out of the daze. He clenched his hands and straightened with a short nod. "I'll call Zane."

"The rest of you suit up. We need to roll as soon as Z points us in the right direction."

Cade paced the hallway as his call went through to Zane Murphy, Fortress Security's tech and communications guru. If anyone could find Sasha, it was Zane. The former Navy SEAL was scary good at his job. More alphabet government agencies than Cade could name wanted to hire Z. He refused all offers, preferring to stay with Fortress.

"Yeah, Murphy."

"It's Cade Ramsey. Need a favor, fast."

"Name it."

He rattled off Sasha's cell phone number, a number engraved in his memory. Just because he hadn't used it yet didn't mean he wasn't prepared. "Ping the signal and pinpoint a location. Hostage situation." He hesitated a second, then said, "It's Sasha, Z. A bank holdup gone wrong. She was taken."

"Might take me a couple minutes."

"Hurry." Cade's voice broke. Tracing a phone signal took time, but he feared it was time Sasha didn't have. The bank robbers must be desperate to take a hostage. How long would they keep her with them, alive and unhurt?

"Hold." Keys clicked in the background. He heard Zane talking to someone, his voice muffled. More keys clicking.

Cade berated himself for being a coward and not pursuing a relationship with the coffee shop owner sooner. The possibility he was too late and would lose his chance forever gutted him. No more. He wasn't waiting any longer. Of all people, he knew life was short and could end in the blink of an eye.

"Got her. I'll text the address and send the link to your email. I have another call coming in, but I'll keep an eye on her signal. If the location changes or stops, I'll let you know." And he was gone.

Cade glanced at the address, scowled. Other side of the county. Great. More delays in reaching Sasha.

Trent strode from the locker room, dressed in black fatigue pants, long-sleeved t-shirt, bullet-resistant vest, Ka-Bar on one thigh, his Sig strapped to the other, a rifle in one hand and his Go bag in the other. "Anything?"

He told Trent the address Zane had sent. "Sound familiar?"

"Farm country. Not much out there." He inclined his head toward the locker room. "Get your gear. Suit up on the way."

Cade raced inside, grabbed his Go bag and equipment bag. The thought of having to use explosives to reach Sasha made his jaw clench. So many things could go wrong, all of them ending with Sasha's blood spilling on the floor. Unacceptable. He couldn't lose her before he had a chance to know her.

When he sprinted from the building, two of the team SUVs were idling at the entrance. Cade dove into the shotgun seat of the lead SUV with Trent behind the wheel.

Bravo's leader floored the accelerator as Cade shut the door. Matt leaned over the seat, grabbed Cade's Go bag, and handed him the gear he needed to protect himself and his teammates.

As he strapped on weapons and yanked on his vest, he asked Trent, "Any news?"

"Ethan and Nick Santana are en route, two minutes ahead of us."

"They know not to engage, right?"

Trent slid him a look.

"Stupid question. Ignore it." Ethan Blackhawk had been an Army Ranger, like Cade. The police chief was the best of the best with a reputation that still made the rounds of discussion in Special Forces circles. Ethan knew how to utilize his best assets and right now that was Bravo team.

"He and Nick will do reconnaissance and set up a perimeter."

"Does he know if Sasha's all right?" When Trent hesitated, Cade's head whipped his direction, frozen in the act of shoving his Ka-Bar into place. "Trent?"

"She talked to Ethan for a couple minutes. They had locked her in a closet. A few minutes ago, one of the men dragged her out."

Every muscle in his body tightened. "And?" If they had hurt Sasha, those men would be lucky to survive the night.

"One of the robbers is injured. The other one wanted Sasha to help the injured man."

"Did she?"

"Couldn't. Apparently, one of them had clubbed her on the head with his weapon during the escape. When the uninjured robber dragged her out of the closet, she barfed."

Oh, man. He dragged a hand down his face. He could imagine how that went over.

"Probably has a concussion," Matt said.

"What happened?" Cade asked.

"Ethan said the clown who wanted the help slugged Sasha. He heard her cry out in pain. She fell against something and hasn't made another sound. The uninjured robber is cursing a blue streak."

Cade's closed his eyes for a few seconds, fighting to regain control. He shoved his knife deep into the sheath, imagining it going deep into the gut of the man who hurt Sasha. Grabbing his Sig, he checked that his weapon was ready, slid it into the holster on his thigh, then positioned his backup piece in the ankle holster. He loaded extra magazines for both weapons even though he doubted that much fire power would be necessary. A couple of two-bit thugs wouldn't stand a chance against Bravo team. Still, he wasn't taking chances with Sasha's life.

After shrugging into his long-sleeved shirt, he grabbed his phone and checked the signal connecting his team to Sasha. Still in the same place. Did that mean she was there as well or just her phone? Cade wanted to barf himself at the possibility the men had found her phone and left it behind when they relocated to another place, one Bravo team wouldn't be able to find before it was too late to save her life.

CHAPTER THREE

Bravo team's SUVs stopped one-quarter mile from the target address, and Cade bailed out along with his teammates. They each shrugged on their packs.

"Grab your gear and let's move." Trent signaled for his team to activate their comm systems. Cade and his teammates made sure the comm systems were in working order as they ran silently toward the appointed location to meet Ethan and Nick. Each of them had backup headgear in case of malfunctions.

The mission clock ticked in Cade's head along with a burning need to find Sasha. He used the first to help him focus and ruthlessly controlled the second. Rushing inside the place Sasha was held without a plan would endanger her, himself, and his teammates. Bravo team was the best he'd ever worked with. He trusted them with his life. He could trust them with Sasha's. Yet he still fought a pitched battle to maintain discipline.

Bravo team climbed a small rise and spotted Ethan and Nick hunkered down behind an outcropping of rocks. Although Cade and his unit didn't make any noise as they approached, the police chief turned and motioned to them.

"Sit rep," Trent said.

"Two tangos inside, both armed with handguns. One is injured, shot during the escape from the bank. He's in the back bedroom, east corner, second floor, and alert enough to hold onto his weapon. The second one closed the drapes not long ago."

Cade couldn't wait anymore. "Sasha?"

"In the same bedroom. No visual on her in the last few minutes. The other man is pacing back and forth, keeping watch on the surroundings. He never leaves the house, but he's constantly checking the area and his phone."

"His phone?" Simon looked puzzled. "Why hasn't he left Sasha and bugged out with his buddy?"

"He's waiting for someone to contact him," Nick said. The Otter Creek police detective, and Ethan's brother-in-law, never took his gaze from the farm house several hundred yards from their location. "Nothing else makes sense."

"He's a fool," Liam said. "He can't handle an injured partner and an injured hostage. Better to wait for the phone call while they're on the move."

"What's the layout of the house?" Trent asked.

Ethan grabbed a stick and drew on the ground, pointing out windows and doors. "There's a wraparound porch on the first floor and a balcony off the master bedroom on the west corner of the second floor. The second robber does a circuit of the upstairs windows every ten minutes or so. He starts in the bedroom with his partner, then makes his way down the hall toward the master bedroom before going to the bedroom windows at the front of the house. Once he finishes the circuit, you'll have a few minutes before he starts another round."

"Tight," Simon commented.

"We can distract him," Nick said. "Try to start a conversation with him."

"No." Cade's tone was brusque. "We can't take the chance he'll hurt Sasha again. He'll know we tracked her somehow."

Trent slid Cade a look.

Although holding his tongue galled him, Cade knew better than to defy his team leader. Trent would tear a strip off his hide if he didn't close his trap.

"No conversation," Ethan agreed. "However, we can still provide a distraction. How long do you need to set your plan, Trent?"

"Five minutes."

A nod from the police chief. "We'll be ready. Go in from the back. Nick and I will be out front. I need at least one of these guys alive. This isn't a simple bank robbery gone wrong." With that cryptic statement, he and Nick disappeared into the trees that enclosed the property on three sides.

Trent crouched in front of Ethan's drawing. "Here's what we're going to do." He laid out the plan, pointing out the best points of access. "Cade, you and Matt take the balcony. We already know of two injuries. You'll need Matt with you. Liam, Simon, set up here and here. If these guys slip past us, take them down. Non-lethal shot unless you have no choice. I'll come in the kitchen door and make sure we don't have any nasty surprises. Questions or suggestions?" At the head shakes, he said, "Move into position. Cade."

He pivoted, impatient with yet another delay. "Sir?"

"Make sure your head's in the game."

"Yes, sir." He ran to catch up with his teammate.

Cade and Matt circled to the tree cover on the left side of the house and worked their way toward the back of the property. When they were ready, Cade activated his mic. "In position," he murmured, his gaze fixed on the balcony. He didn't want to use a grappling hook, afraid the noise might attract attention despite Ethan's distraction. Doable with a boost from the medic, then he'd lower a rope for Matt.

At that moment, he heard a loud argument start up between Ethan and Nick, both of them slurring words, sounding like two drunks arguing over who would get the next drink from the bottle.

"Cade, Matt, go," Trent whispered in the comm system.

Weapons up and ready, they crossed the backyard, staying in the shadows as long as possible before surging over the last ten yards of open space. Thankfully, no shots rang out. Simon and Liam had their backs, but Cade wanted an unannounced approach for Sasha's safety.

He holstered his Sig and signaled Matt to give him a boost. The medic crouched, hands forming a cradle. Seconds later, Cade clambered over the wooden rail, shrugged off his pack, and dropped a rappelling rope. While Matt climbed to the balcony, Cade kept his weapon trained on the door in case Ethan's distraction backfired.

"One minute," Trent murmured.

Cade chafed at the delay. He sucked it up and counted off the seconds in his head. His team leader needed that time to get into position himself. While they waited for Trent's command to execute the rest of the plan, Cade turned the French door's knob. Locked. He grabbed his lock picks and went to work. Another thing they didn't know was whether or not the house was wired for explosives.

The lock gave. He glanced over his shoulder at Matt and nodded. They were ready to go as soon as Trent gave the word.

His team leader's voice came over the comm. "Execute."

"Copy."

Cade motioned for the medic to move back a step and turned the knob. Weapon up, he nudged the door open wide enough to slip into a darkened room. Light from the hallway gave enough illumination so he and Matt didn't stumble into furniture and give away their presence in the house.

At the doorway, he pressed his back to the wall and peered down the hall. Clear. Didn't know how long that would last so they needed to move. He motioned for Matt to follow him. Weapons tracking, they cleared each room in silence.

As they approached the bedroom where Sasha and the injured robber were last seen, they heard a fury-filled voice swearing at the commotion from Ethan and Nick.

"If they'll move along, I'll give them my bottle of Jack Daniels," a thready voice whined. "Can't you get rid of them?"

"No one's supposed to know we're here, you idiot."

"They're drunk, man. They won't remember nothing."

A snort. "You remember stuff that happens when you're drunk as a skunk."

"Come on. We got to get rid of them before Wes calls."

"Shut up," hissed the second man. "No names."

"She's not going to tell no one."

Cade edged closer to the room, his hand tightening on the Sig's grip.

"I need help, man."

"We got our orders. Can't move until we get the word."

He frowned. Orders? What was going on?

"First floor is clear," Trent said. "Moving to cut power now."

Cade moved close enough to see the robber pacing in a mirror on the bedroom wall. A slight shift in position and he saw the injured man's sneaker-covered foot as he lay sprawled on the bed. Unfortunately, he couldn't see Sasha's position in the room.

He turned and told Matt the position of the two men via hand signals.

"Going dark in three, two, one." The electricity kicked off.

Cade slid his NVGs in place and the area in front of him lit up in green.

"Hey, what's going on?" the injured robber asked. "Did a breaker blow?"

"Zip it. Something's wrong."

By the time he finished his statement, Cade and Matt were inside the room on opposite sides of the doorway. Sasha was unmoving near the window, too close to the bank robber for Cade's peace of mind. A good shooter wouldn't miss at that distance.

"Put down your weapons." Cade targeted the man he was certain had hurt Sasha. The robber's face twisted into a mask of fury. "Last chance. Put down your weapon."

One gun clattered on the floor. "Don't shoot. I'm hit. I need help."

"On your stomach," Matt ordered.

The injured man groaned as he complied.

The second robber shouted curses as he swung the barrel of his weapon toward Sasha.

Cade squeezed the trigger of his Sig. The tango dropped, partially covering Sasha. The injured man yelled as Cade flung the second robber away from Sasha. He checked for a pulse, didn't find one. Ethan was not going to be happy.

He kicked the downed robber's gun away and turned to Sasha, activating his mic. "Targets secured. Lights." Cade and Matt took off the NVGs before Trent turned the electricity on.

Light flooded the room.

Cade sucked in a breath when he saw Sasha. Oh, man. Her cheek was already starting to bruise where the clod's fist had slammed into her face. He pulled out his Ka-Bar and sliced the restraints from her wrists. "Matt."

"Keep an eye on this one."

He swiveled on one foot, his Sig pointed at the blubbering robber with his hands cinched behind his back, whining that he hadn't meant to hurt anybody.

The medic knelt beside Sasha and began to check her over as feet pounded up the stairs toward the bedroom.

"It's Ethan and Nick," the police chief warned from the hall before he entered the room. He took in the room at a glance, inclining his head toward the man on the floor in an unspoken question.

Cade shook his head. "I didn't have a choice. He turned the gun toward Sasha."

Nick pulled out his handcuffs. "Ambulance is on the way. I've got this one."

Those words released Cade to focus on what was most important to him. He handed Ethan his Sig, grip first. "You'll need this."

"Thanks. I'll need a statement from you and Matt."

"You know where I will be. Come find me."

"Is Bravo scheduled for deployment?"

"Not while Durango is out of the country," Trent said as he walked into the room.

"Good enough. I'll need statements from the rest of you as well."

"We'll make ourselves available."

Matt sat back. "I think it's safe to move her out of here. No broken bones. She'll need to go to the hospital. They'll want to keep her overnight at least."

"Take her downstairs to wait for the ambulance," Ethan said. "She doesn't need to wake up to this." He motioned toward the dead bank robber.

The medic shifted out of the way to make room for Cade.

He crouched and cradled Sasha in his arms. She couldn't weigh more than a buck twenty. Cade maneuvered her carefully through the doorway and downstairs.

In the living room, he laid her on the sofa, figuring she would be more comfortable there although he was reluctant to release her. Cade brushed strands of her hair away from her face. Sasha Ingram was even more beautiful up close, bruised or not.

She stirred, moaned.

"Sasha, you're safe now."

The coffee shop owner jerked at the sound of his voice. "It's Cade. You're safe."

"You found me."

"I would have torn this county apart to find you." Simple truth.

"The men?"

"Not a problem anymore."

The growl of a siren cut off abruptly.

He stood, turned to unlock the door for the EMTs when a soft hand caught his.

"Don't go," she murmured, her eyes squinting up at him.

"I need to let the EMTs inside." He hurried to unlock the door and admitted the men. "Upstairs, last door on the right. Gunshot victim."

"What about her?"

"I'll transport her myself." Cade didn't want Sasha in the same ambulance with the bank robber. He returned to Sasha, crouching beside her. "As soon as Matt comes down, we'll take you to be checked out."

"Hate hospitals."

He grinned. "Who doesn't?"

A ghost of a smile curved her lips.

Two minutes later, his team medic came downstairs with his mike bag. "Ready?"

Cade nodded. "Stay with her. I'll bring the SUV."

Matt tossed him a key fob. "Trent will hitch a ride to the hospital."

He squeezed Sasha's hand. "I'll be back in five minutes." As he ran out the door, he heard the medic asking Sasha routine questions. True to his word, he returned by the five-minute mark, parking the SUV where the ambulance had been.

Matt grabbed his mike bag and stepped aside. "I'll ride in the backseat with Sasha. You drive."

Cade wanted to argue, but nodded in agreement. Sasha was injured, maybe more seriously than first appearance. He wanted her to have medical care for the twenty-minute ride to the hospital.

He lifted her in his arms and carried her to the SUV.

"I could have walked," she muttered.

Doubtful. "Indulge me." He settled her with care along the backseat. Matt climbed in and knelt on the floor as he dug into his medical bag. While his friend shook a chemically-activated cold pack, Cade slid behind the wheel and put the SUV in gear. The sooner a doctor checked Sasha over the better.

As he sped through the county toward Memorial Hospital, Cade thought over the conversation he overheard between the robbers. Ethan was right. This wasn't a simple bank robbery gone wrong. The uppermost concern in his mind, though, was whether Sasha was safe or if this was just the beginning of something more dangerous to the woman who fascinated him.

CHAPTER FOUR

Sasha flinched as Dr. Anderson shined a bright light into her eyes. "Come on, Doc. Have some pity."

The white-haired physician who was a town favorite chuckled and continued to antagonize her headache. Finally, he turned off the pen light and moved back a step. "Well, my dear, I'm happy to say you only have a concussion. No signs of bleeding in the brain. How does your head feel?"

"As though I've been listening to hard rock music at full volume for a week, thank you."

"On a scale of one to ten, how bad is your headache?"

"One hundred."

He patted her hand. "I'll have the nurses give you medication for the pain. The medicine will make you sleepy."

She doubted that. Unless the drugs knocked her out, she wouldn't be sleeping. All Sasha wanted to do at the moment was crawl into a dark cave until the light sensitivity faded and the headache eased. "When will you release me?"

"Anxious to leave us so soon?"

"Do you blame me?"

"If there are no complications, you can expect to sleep in your own bed tomorrow night, Sasha. You would be wise to have someone cover for you at the coffee shop for a couple days at least, although I will miss seeing you behind the counter."

Right. She employed several part-time college students. None could stay from open to close. "I'll try."

"There's a young man in the hall who's anxious to see you. Are you able to see a visitor while I find an orderly to take you to your room for the night?"

Sasha's cheeks grew hot. Was he talking about Cade? "Sure."

"I'll see you tomorrow morning, my dear." He left the examination room.

After a low-voiced conversation in the hall, a tap sounded on the door frame and a tall, broad-shouldered man walked into the room.

Sasha squinted against the bright lights. A second later, the overhead light went off and she breathed a sigh of relief. "Thanks."

"No problem."

Disappointment spiraled through her. Her visitor was Cade's teammate, Matt. "I thought you would have gone home by now."

Matt dragged a chair close to her bedside and sat. "I'll be here for a few more hours. How's the head?"

"Hurts. Concussion."

"Still nauseated?"

She smiled a little. "How did you know?"

"No color in your face and nausea is a common side effect of concussions. Once you're set up in a room, I'll find an ice pack for you and some ice chips. Both will help."

Made sense that Matt would stay with her. He was a medic, after all. She couldn't help but be disheartened because Cade had left. She'd hoped the elusive, quiet operative might be inclined to stay since he'd managed to say more than one sentence to her at the old farm house where Bravo rescued her.

An orderly steered a wheelchair through the doorway.

"Here's your ride." Matt helped her from the bed and into the wheelchair. "Give the lady a smooth ride, Tom," he said.

"We don't have far to go, Ms. Ingram. We'll take the elevator up two floors and be there before you know it."

"Thanks."

Tom was right. The ride took no more than five minutes, thank goodness. By the time she climbed into the hospital bed in her room, Sasha was feeling sick again.

She dragged in a shaky breath. "Might be a good idea to find the ice pack, Matt."

He handed her a small plastic tub. "Use that if you have to. Don't leave the bed, Sasha. You're weaker than you realize. I'll be back in a minute."

Sasha settled deeper into the pillow, tugged the blanket up higher, and closed her eyes, praying the nausea passed soon. The last thing she wanted to do was vomit in front of a friend even if he was a medic.

A light tap sounded on the door and someone walked inside. Too tired and head hurting too bad to peek, she murmured, "You found the ice pack fast."

"Sasha."

Her eyelids flew up. She stared into the brown eyes of the operative she'd been mooning after for months. "Cade. I thought you left."

"I'll leave the hospital when you do."

"But I'm staying overnight. Dr. Anderson insisted."

"Okay." He moved a chair to her bedside and sat.

Sasha noticed he was still wearing his work gear. Good grief. The man was loaded down with weapons. "How did you walk into the hospital with all that obvious hardware?" His smile caused her heart to skip a beat. Good thing she didn't have a heart monitor on. She would have brought all the nurses running into her room for sure because of Cade's killer smile.

"Fortress Security operatives are cleared to carry weapons on hospital grounds. We're in the building often."

Matt returned with two ice packs in hand. He tossed one to Cade who snatched it in mid-air. "Left side of her head." The medic placed the other ice pack behind Sasha's neck. Cade pressed the second pack to the knot on her head.

She sighed, relief immediate. "Thanks."

"The nurse will be in soon to give you pain meds and something for the nausea." Matt sat in a chair at the foot of the bed although he turned the chair so he could also watch the door.

"Is something wrong?" she asked Cade.

"Precaution."

"Could you be any more cryptic?"

His eyes twinkled. "Yes."

She rolled her eyes as Matt laughed. "How did Bravo team find me?"

"Tracked your phone signal."

"Wow. Four words at once. Just can't shut you up, Cade."

This time, both men laughed.

Oh, man. Cade had the best laugh. Deep, rich, sexy. Yeah, she was smitten.

"All right, Sassy. I deserved that."

Sassy? Despite how horrible she felt, Sasha liked that nickname. It meant Cade had noticed her enough to give her one.

Another tap on the door brought both men to their feet, hands on their guns. When the door opened, a nurse walked in with a cart loaded with equipment to take her vitals and a small plastic cup with two pills.

Cade and Matt relaxed.

"Hi, Grace," Matt said. "What are you doing on this floor?"

"I left the ER long enough to volunteer to check on my favorite coffee maker. How are you feeling, Sasha?"

She smiled at the blond nurse who was married to Bravo team's leader. "Lousy, thanks. My head feels like it's going to explode any minute."

"Understandable. You took a good knock to the head. I'm glad you're all right." Grace handed the small cup to Sasha along with a soft drink. "You don't have to drink all of this, but the carbonation will help dissolve the meds faster."

Good enough for her. Sasha took the pills, aware of Matt returning to his seat and Cade holding the ice pack to her head again. Something was up with that, more than the terse comment from Cade about taking precautions. Precautions against what? According to Cade, the bank robbers weren't a problem anymore. From their behavior, though, the two men were on guard duty.

Is that the only reason Cade was staying? Duty? Man, she hoped not. She didn't want to be a job to Cade Ramsey.

"How bad is the headache?" Grace asked after she finished noting all Sasha's vitals.

"I told Dr. Anderson it was one hundred on a scale of one to ten."

The nurse squeezed her shoulder. "The meds will help. I'll turn the overhead light off, but you need to leave the light on at the head of the bed. Have Cade give you his sunglasses to cut the glare further. I have to go back to the ER. My break is over. I'll check on you on my next break."

"Thanks, Grace."

"Hey, I want to see my favorite barista back at work. See you later, guys." Grace turned out the overhead light on the way out the door.

"I'm going for coffee," Matt said. "Be back in a few minutes with yours, Cade."

Sasha sighed. "That sounds good."

"Not a good idea right now. Besides, got a feeling the coffee in this place won't hold a candle to yours."

"You're probably right. I get a lot of business from hospital personnel." Wow. Cade could talk, after all. "I've been trying to strike up conversations with you for months. Why are you talking now?"

"I almost lost my chance with you."

She blinked. "Chance for what?"

"To ask you to dinner."

"Yes."

It was his turn to stare. "You don't want to think about it?"

"No."

A wry smile curved his lips. "Now who's being cryptic?"

"Listen, buster, I'd planned to call you this weekend to ask you to dinner if Bravo didn't deploy. I'm not letting you slip out of a date now."

Relief flooded his features. "Let's see how you feel Saturday before we make definite plans."

Saturday was two days away. Surely, she'd feel like eating by then.

Matt pushed open the door with his hip, holding a to-go coffee cup in each hand. "Black and strong enough to peel paint from the scent." He handed one to Cade. "I'll be outside the door. If you need anything, Sasha, tell Cade and I'll take care of it."

"An ice pack for her cheek," Cade said.

With a nod, the medic left again.

Sasha studied his face a moment. "Are you really going to stay all night?"

"Yes."

"You have work tomorrow, Cade."

"I've arranged for a substitute to cover my classes."

Something was definitely wrong. Before she could ask, Ethan Blackhawk knocked on the door and strode into the room with an ice pack in his hand. "Compliments of Matt." He handed the pack to Cade. "I need to ask both of you questions. Are you up for it, Sasha?"

"If you hurry. I took pain meds a few minutes ago."

Ethan grabbed the remaining empty chair in the room and sat down. He pulled out a notepad and pen. "Start at the beginning. What time did you go to the bank?"

When Sasha mentioned the bank robbers dropping the money bags in the alley before they took off with her in the car, Cade's hand jerked.

"They dumped the money?" He turned his gaze to Ethan.

"They did."

"What's the point of a bank robbery if you don't keep the cash?"

"That's what I want to know." The police chief returned his attention to Sasha. "What happened after they dropped the money?"

"The men shoved me in the backseat on the floor and they raced away. The one in the back with me hit me on the head with his gun. When I woke up, I was in the closet of the room where Cade found me. I called you, talked for maybe a couple minutes. The uninjured bank robber came back for me. He wanted me to help the injured man while he prowled around the house."

"Did you?" Ethan asked, his voice soft.

"I couldn't. I was so sick from the blow to the head, I threw up as soon as he jerked me to my feet in the closet. Made him angry enough that he dragged me into the bedroom and slugged me. That's the last thing I remember before I opened my eyes to see Cade."

"Anything strike you as odd?"

"Besides the whole thing being surreal?"

He chuckled.

"There was a bigger agenda than robbing the bank, and the men who took me weren't in charge."

CHAPTER FIVE

Cade frowned as Sasha went over her statement again with Ethan. Her impressions of the two men matched his own. The two clowns who robbed the bank weren't smart enough to have come up with this scheme on their own.

And to dump the cash in the alley behind the bank? What sense did that make? He pondered that for a few minutes as he half listened to Sasha and Ethan. This was a test run for something bigger.

His jaw clenched. Something involving Sasha or was she an innocent bystander caught up in someone else's dangerous game? Whatever the bottom line, Cade didn't like her being involved.

He removed the ice packs and laid them on the rolling table. Despite the ice packs, Sasha's cheek sported a good-sized bruise. At least the injury was to her cheek and not her jaw. The robber he shot was a big man with large hands. He could have easily broken her jaw when he punched her.

"Your turn to answer questions, Cade. Do you want to do this here or at the station?"

"I'm not leaving Sasha."

"Are you sure that's wise?"

Wise, no. Necessary? Absolutely. He couldn't hide the fact he'd killed the man who hurt her for long anyway. Would Sasha reject him when she found out? "Ask your questions, Ethan."

"Run it down for me."

Cade gave him the same rapid-fire report he would have given Trent or one of his commanders in the Army. "While Matt and I were in the hall outside the bedroom, the man I shot mentioned waiting for a call from Wes. I got the same sense as Sasha. The bank robbers weren't in charge."

An odd look crossed Sasha's face.

"What's wrong?"

She shook her head. "It's nothing."

Definitely something, Cade concluded. Maybe she didn't want to talk about it in front of Ethan.

"Continue," Ethan prompted.

He finished his report, afraid to look at the woman whose gaze Cade could feel locked on his face.

"Both robbers were shot?" Sasha's voice was soft.

Ethan nodded. "The first by one of my officers when they fled the bank, the second by Cade."

"They're both here. Is that why you and Matt are guarding me?" she asked Cade.

"The one shot at the bank is here," Ethan said.

Silence, then, "Where is the second one?"

"The morgue," Cade answered, his voice flat. He waited for her to recoil and cancel their date. To his surprise, Sasha did neither. Instead, she held out her hand to him.

Mystified, he laid his hand on her palm and she curled her fingers around his. He studied her face. She wasn't rejecting him?

"What happens now, Ethan?" Sasha's hand tightened on Cade's. "You aren't going to charge Cade with anything, are you?"

"We'll investigate, but from all indications the shooting was justified. Come by the station when you're released to sign your statement. You'll have to testify against the remaining bank robber, Sasha."

"I understand. I don't want him to have a chance to hurt someone else."

"I have what I need for now." Ethan stood. "By the way, my wife had a break in her cooking schedule and she's been baking muffins and scones all day. Paige Lang, Darcy Kincaid, and Serena have plans in place to keep your shop open until you return."

Sasha smiled, tears filling her eyes. "Tell them how much I appreciate their efforts. I have college students working part-time, but none of them can put in full days because of their class schedules."

"Do you have an extra key?"

"Paige has my extra key."

Ethan turned to Cade, nodded at him. "Thanks for your help tonight. I'll express that to St. Claire as well, but I wanted to remind you that your actions saved a hostage and possibly derailed a larger plot."

Cade shook his head. "Although we rescued Sasha, I don't think we derailed anything."

"Why do you say that?" Sasha asked.

"This was a test run. The bank robbers were expendable. Whoever was running this crew has a larger goal in mind."

"I agree," the police chief murmured. "We need to figure out their objective before someone else is hurt. If your team is deployed, I need to know. I'll talk to both of you tomorrow."

"Cade." Sasha patted the bed and scooted over to give him room to sit beside her.

Had she waited until Ethan left before booting him out of her life permanently? Mouth dry, dread curling in his gut, Cade sat facing her on the bed.

"Thank you for saving me. I don't know what would have happened to me if you and your teammates hadn't arrived when you did."

He didn't want to dwell too long on his worst fear, losing her to a bullet or a beating from one of those frustrated, angry bank robbers. "You're not repelled by what I did?"

"You killed him to protect me. I assume you're trained to dispatch a threat as efficiently as possible, much like the police. Cade, you saw a threat to me and you took care of it as you were taught to do. How can I be anything but grateful I'm still breathing and looking forward to my first date with you?"

The ball of ice in Cade's stomach melted and he recaptured her hand. "You would be open to more than one date?"

"Yes." She yawned. "Sorry," she mumbled behind her hand.

Cade chuckled and brushed a strand of hair away from her cheek. "Sleep, Sasha. It's the best thing for you."

"You won't leave?"

He trailed his fingers down her cheek in a gentle sweep over her silky skin. "The farthest I'll go is to the hall to talk to Matt and send him for more coffee if I need it. I'm not going anywhere."

She gave a slight nod and closed her eyes. Within two minutes, she was out.

Cade waited another fifteen to be sure she was deeply asleep before he released her hand and gathered the ice packs. As soon as he opened the door, Matt was on his feet.

"Is your girl okay?"

He liked the sound of that although he wasn't sure the woman in question would. "She's asleep. Thanks for the ice packs."

"She knows you're staying with her?"

"Yeah." Cade dropped his voice. "She knows about the bank robber I shot."

"How did she take it?"

He rubbed his jaw, not quite sure what to make of her reaction. "She thanked me for protecting her."

The medic clapped him on the shoulder. "I'm happy for you, Cade. You better hang on to that woman. If you're stupid enough to let Sasha slip through your fingers, I'm going after her myself."

Not a problem. He didn't plan on giving Matt or any other man in town the chance. He might not have said much to her in the months since Bravo had been permanently assigned to PSI, but that didn't mean he hadn't taken the opportunity to observe her every chance he got. Their friends, Marcus and Paige Lang, had made the process easier since they married and began inviting many of their friends over for dinner.

At first, he'd been horrified to think his secret was out, that he'd somehow given himself away especially when it became obvious Paige was playing matchmaker. Whenever Cade had been invited to their home, Sasha had always been part of the group also invited. Had to admit, having his friends and teammates along as a buffer made watching Sasha easier without forcing him to interact much.

"I'll take these back to the nurses' station if you keep watch out here."

While Matt was gone, Marcus and Paige Lang walked down the corridor, holding hands.

"Cade." Paige embraced him. "How is she?"

"She has a concussion from a blow to the head. She also took a fist to the face from one of the bank robbers. Doc Anderson is keeping her overnight to make sure there aren't complications. Barring that, she should be released tomorrow."

"I want to see her."

"You can look in on her, but she's sleeping. The nurse gave her meds for the headache and nausea a few minutes ago."

"We'll be glad to stay with her if you want to go home," Marcus offered.

"I'll leave the hospital when Sasha leaves."

"Can we bring you anything?" Paige asked. "Coffee, food?"

He started to refuse, but he hadn't eaten in almost ten hours. "I could use a meal." He reached for his wallet.

Marcus waved him off. "This one's on me. What do you want?"

"Anything is fine. Thanks, Marcus."

The pastor of Cornerstone Church clapped him on the shoulder and strode to the elevator.

"Thank you, Cade."

He turned his attention to Paige. "For what?"

"Saving my best friend."

"I did my job."

She inched closer. "You can't fool me, Cade Ramsey. I've seen the way you look at Sasha when she's not paying attention. This wasn't just a job to you. This was personal."

He couldn't deny it, and the truth would be obvious to everyone soon enough. "You're right."

Satisfaction filled her face. "I knew it. When are you going to tell her?"

Amusement washed over him. "I suppose I have. I asked her to have dinner with me."

Paige beamed at him. "Fantastic. When?"

"This weekend, if she's up to it."

"Will you need a crowd again?" she teased.

"I can handle this one myself."

"I turned in the ice packs." Matt walked to his side. "Good to see you, Paige."

"You, too. Were the members of Bravo team injured during Sasha's rescue?"

"Not a scratch. Where's Marcus?"

"Buying dinner for Cade. Do you want anything? I can text him to bring you something as well."

"I'll buy my own later."

They spent a few minutes talking about neutral topics while they waited for Marcus to return. Cade checked on Sasha every five minutes. So far, she hadn't moved an inch.

Ten minutes later, Marcus returned with two takeout meals from Delaney's, the diner in Otter Creek's town square and the only eating establishment open twenty-four hours a day. "Hope you both like meatloaf, mashed potatoes, and green beans. Delaney's comped your meals when they heard I was bringing them to you."

"Oh, man. I love their meatloaf. Thanks, Marcus. I'd planned to grab a sandwich in the cafeteria in a few minutes." Matt accepted one of the boxes and wrapped plastic utensils, then sat to start wolfing down food.

"Paige, why don't you go sit with Sasha. I'll find a vending machine to buy drinks for Matt and Cade." He kissed his wife and nudged her inside the room. "I assumed you didn't want Sasha to be alone," he said as he handed Cade the second dinner with the utensils.

"You're right. Thanks for being our food gofer."

Marcus inclined his head toward the box. "Start on that while I find drinks for you." He returned with two soft drinks and two bottles of water in his hands. "Wasn't sure what you preferred with the long night ahead of you."

"This is perfect." Matt popped the tab on one of the soft drinks and guzzled some of the carbonated liquid.

When they finished their meals, the preacher tossed the empty boxes in the nearby waiting room's trash can and returned. "The hall is empty. Tell me what happened tonight."

They gave him a shortened version of what they'd told the police.

Marcus was silent a moment. "Do you regret your actions, Cade?"

He started to bristle until he remembered that Marcus Lang was one of the counselors for Fortress and he routinely asked these types of questions of all operatives when they returned from a mission. "He didn't give me a choice. If I hadn't stopped him, he would have shot Sasha. I couldn't let him do that. So, no, I don't regret what I did and I won't lose any sleep over it."

A woman in a nurse's uniform walked toward them, a pleasant smile on her face. "How is my patient doing?"

"Resting," Matt answered.

"Oh, well, I won't be a minute. I need to check her vitals." She walked inside the room, paused when she noticed Paige. "Hello. Step outside a moment, please. I need to check my patient."

Cade frowned. Grace hadn't insisted they all leave. Where was the woman's hospital identification? It should have been pinned to her shirt or hanging around her neck. "Matt," he murmured.

One look at his face had the medic on his feet as Paige stepped into the hall. They rushed into the room in time to see the woman uncap a hypodermic needle.

CHAPTER SIX

Cade surged across the room and grabbed her wrist before the woman could plunge the needle into Sasha's vein. He confiscated the hypodermic and handed it to Matt. He'd apologize later if this woman was a legitimate nurse.

"What are you doing?" the woman screeched. "Let go of me."

"Where is your hospital identification?" Matt asked, his voice hard.

She glanced down at herself. "I guess I forgot it. Look, I need to give Ms. Ingram her meds. Doctor's orders."

"You'll wait here while I confirm that."

Panic flared in her eyes. "I have rounds to complete. I'll be in trouble if I'm late."

Another nurse walked into the room, this one pushing a cart. She pulled up short. "I'm Tracy, Ms. Ingram's nurse. What's going on? Who is this woman?"

"That's what we were going to ask you. This woman claims to have orders from Dr. Anderson to administer more meds to Sasha." Cade tightened his grip. "Do you know anything about this?"

The nurse with the cart scowled. "No, I don't." She pushed the cart to the side of the door. "I'll contact Dr. Anderson and security. Keep an eye on her."

"She's not going anywhere."

The woman fought to free herself, cursing Cade and Matt.

Sasha stirred. "Cade?" Her words were slurred.

"I'll take care of this one," Matt said, taking over restraining the woman.

Cade leaned down, brushed his lips over Sasha's forehead. "I'm here. Everything is fine."

"Okay." And she was out again.

"What was in the syringe?" Matt asked.

"I'm not saying another word." The woman renewed her efforts to free herself.

"Take her into the hall," Cade said. He didn't want the woman anywhere near Sasha. After his friend moved the still protesting woman to the hallway, he shot a glance at Marcus who nodded and followed Matt. Cade doubted the medic needed help, but he'd take no chances on the woman escaping.

He motioned for Paige to sit in the chair nearest Sasha while he pulled out his phone. A moment later, Ethan Blackhawk answered his phone.

"Blackhawk."

"It's Cade. I need you at the hospital."

"What happened?"

"Not positive, but I believe a woman just tried to kill Sasha."

"I'm at the station. I'll be there in ten minutes. Do I have a suspect to question?"

"Yes, sir."

"Excellent."

Cade slid his phone into his pocket.

"Do you really think that woman tried to hurt Sasha?" Paige asked.

He lifted one shoulder. "We'll know when the contents of the syringe are analyzed."

"What if you're wrong?"

"I'll apologize for scaring the lady, but I'm not sorry for protecting Sasha. I'd do it again in a heartbeat."

A light tap on the door. Marcus poked his head inside and motioned for Cade to step into the hallway. A burly security guard waited, hand on his weapon, his gaze shifting between Matt and his prisoner.

"Problem, Matt?"

"Officer Petty wants me to release the lady into his custody."

"No. Chief Blackhawk will be here in five minutes. He'll take charge of the woman."

Petty scowled. "We police our own grounds."

"Not when it comes to attempted murder."

The guard paled. "Murder?"

"He's lying," the woman spat out, hatred seething in her gaze. "I'll have your jobs, all of you."

Petty backed off a step, hand still on his weapon. "We'll wait for Blackhawk, then. I hope you boys know what you're doing. If the lady sues, you're going to be held responsible for this."

Cade scowled. He and Matt were Sasha's bodyguards. This woman was a threat to Sasha's safety. Cade was not handing her off to a two-bit hired guard.

Minutes later, the elevator chimed and the police chief strode down the hall with Rod Kelter, his brother-in-law and another of his detectives. "What have we got?"

Rod slipped a pair of handcuffs on the cursing woman.

"This woman went into Sasha's room, claiming she wanted to check her vitals. She didn't bring equipment to check anything. We caught her preparing to give Sasha a shot."

"Did the doctor order more medication?"

"I can answer that." Tracy walked up at that moment. "Dr. Anderson did not prescribe more medication. I don't know who this woman is, but she isn't authorized to administer any meds to Ms. Ingram."

"I assume one of you has the syringe?"

Matt handed it over with the cap covering the needle.

"Any idea what this is?"

"Afraid not."

Ethan turned his hard gaze on the woman who was now mute. "Who are you?"

She turned her sullen face away from him.

"Get her out of here, Rod."

"Yes, sir." He guided the woman toward the elevator. "We've got a nice cozy cell with your name on it, lady."

She found her tongue again as the silver doors slid open.

"Sasha all right?" Ethan asked.

"She's fine. Slept through most of it."

"I need to check on Ms. Ingram," the nurse said.

Cade glanced at Matt who followed her inside the room.

"Did the woman say anything to you, Cade?"

He repeated everything the woman had told them, which wasn't much.

"I'll run her prints and have the contents of the syringe analyzed. We'll know soon if the contents are lethal. Keep an eye on your girl, Cade. This can't be a coincidence." He left with the syringe.

"What is going on around here?" Marcus frowned. "First, a bank robbery with criminals who didn't want the money followed by an attempt to perhaps kill the rescued hostage."

"I don't know. I will get to the bottom of it." No one was going to hurt Sasha again on his watch. Cade entered Sasha's room as she answered the last of the nurse's questions and promptly drifted back to sleep.

"Good news," Tracy said. "Ms. Ingram is doing fine. I'll be back in a couple hours. If you need anything, push the call button or come find me."

"Thanks, Tracy."

"Sure." She pushed her cart out the door and continued on her floor rounds.

"What happened with our unwanted guest?" Matt asked Cade.

"Ethan and Rod took her back to the station. The police will test the contents of the syringe and let us know the results."

"It's late and Paige has a coffee shop to help run tomorrow in addition to her work at the community center." Marcus helped Paige to her feet. "Anything else we can do for you before we leave?"

"We're set." He shook his pastor's hand. "Thanks for the help, Marcus."

"Any time. Call or text if you need me for anything." After shaking Matt's hand, Marcus escorted his wife from the hospital room.

Matt turned to Cade, his expression grim. "We need to figure out what's going on and who's behind it before your girl is hurt or killed. I'll be outside the door."

Alone with Sasha once again, Cade settled into the chair vacated by Paige and threaded his fingers through Sasha's. He found a comfortable position and drifted into a light sleep.

He woke sometime later to Sasha thrashing in her sleep. Cade sat on the bed and laid his hand on her bruised cheek. "You're safe, Sasha." Gratified when she quieted, he rose to return to his seat but found his hand caught by her, Sasha's eyes open. "Hi," he murmured. "What do you need?"

"Would you...."

He raised her hand to his lips and pressed a gentle kiss to her knuckles. "Ask."

"Would you hold me for a few minutes?" She looked so unsure of herself Cade couldn't help the smile that curved his mouth.

"A request I'm happy to fulfill."

She scooted over to make room for him. Cade raised the head of the bed a bit more and slid his arm around Sasha. With a deep sigh, she settled against his side, her head resting on his heart, and went back to sleep.

Cade dozed again until Tracy returned to check Sasha. He started to rise, but the nurse motioned for him to stay in place.

Sasha answered the same questions again and glanced up at Cade after the nurse left. "What time is it?"

"Almost three."

"You should go home, Cade. I feel guilty keeping you here."

"Not a chance." He settled her against his chest again. "I'm too comfortable to move unless you need something."

"I'm thirsty," she admitted.

"Soft drink or water?"

"Something carbonated. I'm still nauseated."

He kissed her forehead again. "I'll be right back with your drink. Matt's at the door. No one will disturb you while I'm gone."

Matt turned when Cade walked into the hall. "Sasha all right?"

"Thirsty. Where's the vending machine?"

"In the waiting room at the end of the hall on your right."

"Need anything?"

"I wouldn't say no to more caffeine and a two-minute break."

"Go. I'll buy the drinks when you return."

Within five minutes, Cade was back in Sasha's room. He handed her a ginger ale. "Matt said this will help your stomach."

"Thanks." She drank several sips before handing him the can.

He set the drink aside and gathered her close again, stretching his legs out alongside hers. Despite the interruptions from Tracy, Cade had never felt such peace as he did while holding Sasha as she slept. Not sure what to make of that, he ran his hand up and down her back. The soothing rhythm lulled her to sleep again.

An hour later, his phone vibrated with an incoming text. He checked the screen and scowled. Ethan. The syringe their mysterious woman planned to use was filled with heroin. If she had injected the contents, Sasha would have died within minutes.

CHAPTER SEVEN

Sasha wondered if things would be awkward between her and Cade as she dressed to go home from the hospital. Man, she hoped not. He'd said more to her in the past twelve hours than he had since he moved to Otter Creek with the rest of Bravo team.

With her clothes in place, she bent to put on her tennis shoes and almost hit the floor, face first. Looked as though tying her shoes was a bad idea. Sasha eased herself to a sitting position. When the world finally settled and she was sure she wouldn't be sick, Sasha leaned back against the pillow and curled onto her side.

She must have dozed off because sometime later, she woke to roughened fingers stroking her cheek. Cade. "Sorry," she murmured. "Need help with my tennis shoes."

"Can't bend over, huh?"

"Not without dire consequences."

Cade slid the shoes on her feet and tied the laces. He helped Sasha sit up again, steadied her when she swayed. "Guess I'm not taking you skating tonight."

She narrowed her eyes. "That would be a definite no. I'm not coordinated enough on a good day to roller skate without getting another concussion."

"Too bad. There goes that date idea." His eyes twinkled.

"You can do better, cowboy."

He stilled.

What did she say that bothered him? "What's wrong?"

"Cowboy?"

He didn't like the nickname. Sasha studied his face a moment. "You look like a man who would be comfortable in a cowboy hat, sitting on the back of a horse, riding across the range."

Cade gave a huff of laughter. "My military nickname is Cowboy."

"Why did they call you that?"

"I'm originally from Oklahoma." He drew her to her feet. "Come on. Let's get you out of here."

She wanted to nudge him to talk. Now wasn't the time. "Sounds great. On the way home, we need to stop for food."

"You're hungry?"

The mention of her eating made Sasha flinch. "No. You have to be."

"I could eat."

An understatement, she was sure. Cade and his fellow team members were in top physical condition, a state which burned calories even while they slept. "I'm ready to leave. What about Delaney's?"

He shook his head. "Line is too long. Let's go to That's A Wrap. The scent of food isn't too heavy, and Darcy will have tea on hand to settle your stomach."

Since they arrived between the breakfast and lunch rush, Cade was able to park in front of the shop.

Sasha breathed a sigh of relief, grateful she wouldn't have to walk a long distance. Fatigue was making her legs shaky. Didn't make sense. She had slept for several hours while she suspected Cade hadn't slept much overnight.

Three customers sat at one table. They asked Sasha how she felt and expressed thanks to an embarrassed Cade for saving their favorite barista.

As they approached the counter, Darcy came from the kitchen. She hugged Sasha. "How are you?"

"I'm okay."

Darcy eased back, eyeing her critically. "You might be all right, but you look like you feel rough. I understand you have a concussion."

"Grapevine works fast around Otter Creek."

"Sit down. I have some tea that works wonders in settling upset stomachs. Rio keeps me supplied with this blend."

Darcy's husband was a medic with the Durango team and dropped into Perk a couple times a week when he was in town. "Thanks, Darcy."

Cade seated her at a table on the other side of the shop from the occupied table. "Didn't think you wanted to be quizzed about what happened yesterday."

"Not really."

"I'll be back in a minute." He returned to the counter and had a low-voiced conversation with Rio's wife. As he reached for his wallet, Darcy waved him off. When she turned to work on Sasha's tea, Cade pulled money from his wallet and dropped it into the tip jar beside the register.

He carried a loaded tray to their table a few minutes later and handed Sasha a covered to-go cup. "Chamomile mint tea." He placed a small plate with a plain toasted bagel in front of her. "This should settle on your stomach."

Sasha frowned. "That's A Wrap doesn't carry bagels. Where did Darcy find it?"

"Her assistant manager went to Delaney's to purchase one for you. Drink some tea first, then try a few bites of bagel."

"Are you sure you don't have medic training? You know a lot about treating a concussion."

He snorted. "I've had a few myself. Goes with the job."

She kept silent while she sipped her tea and gave Cade a chance to eat before she asked a question that had plagued her for months. "I know you work with Bravo team for Fortress." She leaned closer. "All of you have different jobs. What's yours?"

"EOD."

She blinked. "Explosive ordinance disposal?"

His eyebrows shot up. "That's right. How do you know that?"

Her cheeks burned. This wasn't a conversation she'd planned to have with this man. "I read a lot of romance and romantic suspense books. Most of them have military or law enforcement protagonists. I learned a few acronyms from the books."

He stared at her a moment. "You're not bothered by my specialty?"

"Why would I be? Because of what you do, Bravo team comes home alive from their missions." Obviously, he was good at it, or Cade wouldn't be sitting here eating breakfast and drinking coffee with her.

Cade dropped his voice further. "I also build bombs."

"You're good at your job and save people's lives with your skills."

"I also take them, Sassy. I won't apologize for it, either."

"Of course not. You fight terrorists at home and abroad."

The operative sat back, a stunned expression on his face. "You're okay with that part of my job?"

"Cade, I want you and your teammates to come home from every mission. You protect all of us every time you go and do the things we're too afraid to take on. Because of you, I'm safe. I won't condemn you for doing what's necessary to protect your principals and teammates, and to come home alive." To her.

He captured her hand and squeezed. "You're amazing, Sasha."

She smiled. "I know a good man when I see one. Tell me something fun about yourself." Time for a change in subject. The fearless warrior looked a little shell-shocked by their previous discussion.

Cade thought about her request for a moment, then said, "I collect comic books."

"What kind?"

"All kinds. I prefer DC and Marvel comics."

"Who doesn't? What smart person would pass up a story about Spiderman or the Justice League?"

"You read them?"

"When I was younger. Once I hit middle school, I started sneaking Mom's romances into my room to read after I finished my homework. She pretended not to notice. Fat chance of that, though. Mom knew everything that went on in the house." She stopped as a pain pierced her heart at the memories flooding her mind. "Well, almost everything."

"Mothers would have to have eyes in the back of their heads to know everything happening under their roofs. It's your turn. Tell me something fun about you."

"While you collect comic books, I collect snow globes."

"I'd love to see your collection."

"I'll give you the grand tour when you take me home. What about my car? I guess it's still parked at the bank."

"You won't feel like driving for a few days. Besides, I want to check it before I let you climb behind the wheel."

"Check for what?"

"Anything out of place."

"You know something about cars?"

"A fair amount."

She smiled. "Wish I'd known that a month ago when my starter kicked the bucket."

Cade pulled out his phone and sent her a text with his number. "Next time you have car trouble, call me."

"You're not always in town."

"If Bravo is gone, call Nate Armstrong. He's good with mechanical issues. Since he's with the Durango team, one of us will always be in town. Brent Maddox, the CEO of Fortress Security, never sends both teams out on missions at the same time. One of the teams has to be on site to train the bodyguards and work with new Fortress teams."

Sasha's gaze swept over the deli, empty since the other three customers had left. "Is it possible for you to tell me the type of training you do?"

He spent a few minutes going over some of the skills PSI taught and the reasoning behind them. "Would you like a tour sometime?"

"I've been wanting to see the place where you work since you drove into town. Maybe the tour can be part of a date."

"We can do that." Cade stood. "I'll have Darcy refresh your tea, then take you home."

She watched, bemused, as he requested more tea and a to-go box with a chicken salad wrap. Sasha wasn't used to someone taking care of her. It had been a long time since she'd live at home with her parents.

Cade returned to the table. "All set." He handed her the box and unlocked his SUV.

"Did one of your teammates bring your SUV to the hospital?"

"Trent worked it out while you were sleeping." He helped her into the vehicle. When he cranked the engine, his cell phone rang. Cade tapped his Bluetooth. "Ramsey."

"It's Zane. Got some information on your dead bank robber."

"You're on speaker with Sasha."

"Hello, Sasha. I'm Zane Murphy, a friend of Cade's. I work with Fortress in communications."

"Don't let him fool you," Cade said. "Z is the go-to guy when we need anything in communications and research. He's saved our hides on more missions than I can count."

"I'm glad to make your acquaintance, Zane. Thanks for keeping Cade and the others safe."

"You're comfortable with hearing the information I share with Cade? If not, he can call me when he's free."

"It's fine. Knowledge is power, right?"

"Always. Some knowledge hurts you to hear, though."

"Nothing graphic, please. My stomach is still queasy from the concussion."

"Understood. The bank robber's name is Mario Hart. He's a Marine vet, dishonorably discharged two years ago. He drifted for a couple months, then joined up with Black Dog."

Cade scowled. "Figures he'd end up with a group that like. Any idea what Hart was doing around these parts?"

"Not yet. I'm still looking into it. Adam Walker's team should be back in the country tomorrow night. I left a message on his phone to contact me as soon as he lands in Nashville. He might know something about Hart."

"Good idea. Once a Marine, always a Marine. If Adam doesn't have intel, he'll know who to contact."

"That's what I'm counting on.

"What about the woman Ethan has in custody?"

Woman? Sasha twisted to face Cade. What woman was he talking about?

"I'm running her picture and prints through our system. Nothing yet."

"Appreciate the help, Zane." He covered Sasha's hand with one of his own. "I have a feeling the fake bank robbery is just the opening gambit for a deadlier game."

"Agreed. If you need anything else, let me know. Anything involving Black Dog is bad news for all of us. Give Sasha my contact information and make sure I have hers."

"Copy that."

"Sasha, I'm sending a watch and some jewelry to Cade for you."

"Why?"

"They have trackers in them. Don't leave your home without wearing at least two of the items. Cell phone coverage can be spotty. If you're taken again, we won't have a problem finding you. Cade, I'll be in touch." And he was gone.

Sasha studied Cade's face, noticing the flush on his cheeks. "Should I be concerned about the jewelry?"

"No. It's a new safety precaution all the operatives are using for important people in their lives. Our job is dangerous, Sasha. We protect our friends and families, but a slip endangers those we care about. I don't want anything to happen to you because of me." He glanced at her. "You'll wear what Zane sends you?"

"Of course. Knowing my rescue depended on cell phone coverage makes me cringe. What if I'd been in a dead zone?"

He squeezed her hand. "Thank you. I'll breathe easier knowing I can find you if you're in danger again."

"How likely is that? I've lived almost thirty years without rubbing elbows with the criminal class. Wouldn't the likelihood of being involved in another dangerous situation be minimal?"

"Until we have answers to what's going on, I wouldn't count on that."

He parked in the driveway of her condo and hurried around the hood to help her from the SUV.

Glad to be home, Sasha led the way to her front door. She stopped, dismay replacing the joy of a moment earlier.

"What's wrong?"

"I don't have my purse or keys."

"The police probably have it. We'll call the station once we're inside."

She eyed the bay window she loved, hoping Cade wouldn't have to break the glass. "Which window are we breaking?"

"None of them. Wait here." He returned to his SUV and opened the hatch back. A moment later, he crouched in front of her door with two thin metal instruments in his hand.

"What are those?"

"Lock picks."

She leaned against the door frame, fascinated with his hand movements. Before long, she heard a soft metallic click and Cade opened her door.

He listened a moment, frowned. "Why didn't your alarm go off?"

"Because I don't have one."

"You need an alarm system, Sassy."

"I had to prioritize the money. The shop's alarm system came first. I'm still saving for the one here."

He cupped her cheek with his palm. "Your safety is my priority. I'll talk to Maddox about a system for you. He'll work out an arrangement you can afford."

A man strode up the walkway. "Take your hands off my sister, Ramsey."

CHAPTER EIGHT

Between one heartbeat and the next, Cade spun to face the threat bearing down on them and moved to put himself in front of Sasha. Dean Ingram was Sasha's brother? His fists clenched. Perfect. Spelled trouble for him and Sasha both if he pursued a relationship with her, and he most definitely was. He was crazy about her. Learning what she'd been through with the bank robbery and abduction, and watching her deal with the aftermath heightened his admiration for her. Too bad her brother was such a louse.

"Move away from Sasha, Ramsey." Dean glared at him. "If you don't move, I'll be happy to move you."

"Dean, what are you doing here?" Sasha braced her hand against Cade's back.

A frown, this time for her. "Is that any way to greet your long-lost brother?"

"I haven't seen you in twelve years and the absence was your choice. Why show up now?"

Cade adjusted his stance slightly to better take Sasha's weight. He doubted she realized how much she was leaning against him. "Sasha, let's go inside." She needed to be off her feet and out of sight from a secondary potential threat, and he doubted she wanted her brother to know how weak she was.

"You can leave now, Ramsey. I can take care of my own sister without your interference."

Cade ignored Dean as he wrapped his arm around Sasha's waist, taking as much of her weight as possible without giving her brother ammunition, and urged her into the house. He walked her to the sofa as her brother slammed the front door.

He took the to-go box from her hand. "I'll put this in the refrigerator for you." Cade tapped the tea gently. "Sip on this." Used to healthy color in her cheeks, he didn't like the pallor of her skin. Although reluctant to leave her alone with Dean, Sasha needed an ice pack to help with the headache and nausea.

Cade flicked Dean a warning glance and went to the kitchen. After storing the remainder of her bagel and the chicken wrap in the refrigerator, he rummaged in her freezer for an ice pack. Not finding one, he searched again and came up with a bag of frozen peas. That would work. He had several bags in his freezer for bumps and bruises from training and missions.

Cade returned with the makeshift ice pack in hand, sat beside Sasha, and laid the bag against the back of her neck.

She leaned against his side, her uninjured cheek against his shoulder. "How did you know?" she murmured.

"Your skin is pale."

"What happened to your face?" Dean growled. "If Ramsey belted you, I'll kill him, and put us all out of our misery."

She scowled at him. "Stop it. He would never hurt me. Cade is a protector and has too much honor to lay a hand on me in anger."

Sasha's brother snorted, derision in his gaze. "You don't know the real Ramsey or you're too stupid to see the truth."

"Knock it off." What was wrong with him? Cade had never known Dean to be rude to a woman. If anything, he had always been the ultimate ladies' man. Smooth, polished, and charming. Cade found that out the hard way. "I would never hurt a woman, especially one I care about. Answer Sasha's question. What are you doing here?"

"Oh, that's rich." The other man leaned against the door, arms folded on his chest, his booted feet crossed at the ankles. "Guess you haven't told your new girlfriend about your old one. You remember her, don't you? The woman who ran in terror from you."

Yeah, straight into Dean Ingram's arms and bed while Cade had been deployed with his Ranger unit.

"Dean, this isn't about Cade." Sasha lifted her head from Cade's shoulder. "Why are you in Otter Creek?"

"I was in the neighborhood. Heard you got yourself into trouble and decided to check on you." A dark frown settled on his lips. "Didn't know I'd find you cozied up to Ramsey."

He tilted his head. "But I'll bet he knew all about you before he even said a word to you. He works for the all-knowing Fortress Security. Nothing is a secret to their operatives. You really are a fool, Sash. Ramsey is using you. He doesn't care about you. He wants revenge."

"You expect me to believe that you happened to be in the neighborhood?" Sasha shook her head. "No way, bro. Try again."

Cade slid his arm around her shoulders, repositioning the bag of peas. Would she believe her brother or Cade? Would she reject him when she heard the story? Man, he hoped not.

"Believe what you want. At least tell me if you're okay before I leave. I don't want to be around Ramsey any more than I have to."

"I have a concussion from a bank robber hitting me over the head with the butt of his gun and slugging me in the face. Other than that, I'm fine thanks to Cade and his teammates."

"Do yourself a favor, little sis. Don't believe anything Ramsey tells you." With a final glare at Cade, Dean wrenched open the door and walked out without a backward glance.

Cade waited for the inevitable questions, dreading her reaction. Instead, she leaned her head against his shoulder once more.

"I'm sorry."

"For what? You didn't do anything wrong."

"For being related to a man filled with hate. Dean wasn't like that growing up. I don't know what happened to make him change."

"War can bring out the worst."

"Not you."

"You aren't going to ask me about your brother's accusations?"

"Tell me when you're ready."

Hope burned inside. "I would never hurt a woman, Sasha."

"I know."

She trusted him with nothing to go on but what she'd observed since he arrived in Otter Creek? He pressed his lips to her cheek. "Thank you for your trust."

Sasha smiled. "When will I receive a real kiss?"

"When your headache is gone."

A sigh. "Can't happen soon enough for me."

Cade chuckled, his tension evaporating like mist. "Me, too. Let me make sure the rest of the house is secure." He dropped a light kiss on her mouth and stood.

He returned to the kitchen to begin his security sweep, checking windows and exterior doors, peering into every place someone might hide. Nothing. Uneasiness gnawed at him.

When Cade retraced his steps to the living room, he found Sasha curled up on the sofa, a pillow beneath her head. He unfolded an afghan and draped the cover over her body, then tossed the peas back in the freezer.

Reluctant to leave her alone and defenseless with nonexistent security, he sat in the recliner, raised the footrest, and settled in for a nap of his own. He'd spent most of the hours in the hospital awake and alert for more trouble. Sometime later, he woke to the scent of something wonderful.

Cade opened his eyes and noted the empty sofa. If Sasha was cooking, maybe she felt better. He followed the scent of food to the kitchen and leaned one shoulder against the door frame.

Sasha stirred something in a large pot, then opened the oven to peek inside. The scent of baking bread filled the air, making Cade's stomach rumble. She twisted, smiled. "Are you hungry?"

"Starving. You didn't have to cook. I'd planned to pick up a meal for us at Delaney's."

"I feel better and I like to cook. Sit at the breakfast bar and keep me company. Dinner will be ready in a few minutes."

"How can I help?"

"Tell me another interesting fact about you."

"I'm not a fan of watching golf."

Sasha laughed. "I thought all men liked golf."

"I like to play a round. I don't like watching someone else play. I liked your snow globe collection. Got a look at it while I was checking your doors and windows. Your turn now. Tell me something else interesting about you."

"I love to go to baseball games."

He grinned. "What a coincidence. So do I. Does it matter if it's a professional team?"

"No. However, I insist on a decent concession stand. My secret vice at a ball game is a hot dog or hamburger and a soft drink."

"Same here. Hamburgers, hot dogs, nachos. It's a date. Know any teams around here?"

"Actually, the high school and community college have good ones. The games are community events. Everyone in town shows up for them to cheer on the home team."

"I'll be sure to find out their schedules in the spring."

"What would you like to drink?"

"Water is fine."

She pulled two bottles of water from the refrigerator and set them on the breakfast bar. Within a couple minutes, Sasha set two steaming bowls of soup and a basket of rolls on the bar. "Chicken and wild rice soup. I can make you a sandwich, too."

"This is great. Thanks." He took a bite of the soup, closed his eyes. "Sasha, this is fantastic."

"Glad you like it."

"I'm serious. If you didn't run a coffee shop, you could open a restaurant."

She froze. "You think so?"

"Oh, yeah. Think about it. Otter Creek needs another restaurant."

"I'll keep the idea in mind."

After the meal, he carried the empty bowls to the dishwasher, wrapped the remaining two rolls, and tossed the empty water bottles into the garbage. "Do you feel well enough to watch a movie on television?" Cade didn't want to leave her. He still wasn't comfortable with her security situation although he didn't figure he'd have much luck convincing Sasha to let him stay overnight on the couch. He intended to try and convince her, though.

"Sure. I have cable and a bunch of DVDs to choose from."

"Only one rule."

"Let me guess. No chick flicks?"

He winked at her. "You got it in one shot."

"I'm sure we can come up with a compromise. How about an action film with a romance subplot?"

"I can live with that." They scrolled through several choices and made a selection. When Sasha sat beside him, Cade snagged the afghan again and draped it over her legs, then wrapped his arm around her shoulders. "Have you seen this movie before?"

Sasha shook her head. "I've been meaning to watch it, but I haven't had time. I'm usually planning menus for Perk and doing the books. I really hate messing with the accounts."

"I understand. Accounting isn't something I would enjoy, either."

They were silent as the movie started. Twenty minutes in, Sasha was asleep again. This time, however, he had the pleasure of holding her. He'd already seen the movie, but the film was one he enjoyed. When the end credits rolled, the woman in his arms was still out cold.

Cade decided to let her sleep since it was still early. Maybe his presence helped her feel secure enough to rest without fear. He hoped that was the case. Holding a beautiful woman for hours at a time was certainly no hardship on his part.

By the time the credits rolled on the second movie, Sasha was beginning to stir.

"Sasha."

She tilted her head back and opened her eyes, blinked. "I missed the movie, huh?"

"Plus another one."

"I've been sleeping for four hours?" She groaned. "I'll never go to sleep tonight. Naps always mess with my body clock, and I've had two today."

"Your body is healing from trauma. It's normal."

"Experience?"

Cade cupped the side of her neck. "My job is dangerous. Every member of Bravo team was injured on our last mission."

Sasha sat up, concern filling her eyes. "Where were you injured and how bad?"

"Knife wound to my side. The injury is healing well."

"Show me."

Wondering how Sasha would react when she saw the line of stitches, Cade released her and stripped off his shirt.

She didn't say anything for a moment, trailing her finger tips over his bare skin.

Cade sucked in a breath, his reaction to her touch immediate and intense. Where two minutes ago he'd thought the temperature comfortable, now he was burning up.

"Oh, Cade, this must have hurt."

His lips curved. "Not at the time." He'd been too busy keeping the guerrilla from slashing his throat to worry about his side. Compared to wounds he suffered in the past, this was a scratch.

"Is this Matt's work?" she asked, indicating the stitches.

He nodded.

Sasha pressed a kiss over his heart. "I'm glad he was there to help you and the others. You said all of you were injured. Who patched up Matt?"

"I did. He would have done it himself, but he couldn't reach the wound." He stepped back and shrugged into his shirt, then wrapped his arms around her. "I'm worried about your safety overnight."

Her brow furrowed. "Why? The bank robbers aren't a threat any longer thanks to you and your teammates. I'm safe now."

"I'm not convinced you are. Something happened in the hospital while you were asleep, an incident I'm almost sure is connected to the fake robbery."

CHAPTER NINE

Uneasiness roiled in Sasha's stomach. "Does this incident relate to the woman you mentioned to Zane?" Whatever happened must have occurred while she was knocked out from the pain meds.

"A woman dressed in scrubs came to your hospital room early this morning, claiming to be a nurse. She insisted on checking your vitals. When she kicked Paige Lang from your room, Matt and I realized the woman didn't have a hospital ID. We walked in just as she was about to inject you with something. I stopped her and called Ethan."

"What happened?"

"He took her to the station to question her and had the contents of the syringe tested. The woman was seconds away from injecting enough heroin in your vein to kill you."

Sasha felt the blood drain from her face. Good grief. Why would anyone want to kill her? "Maybe she chose the wrong room."

"She knew your name, Sasha. This woman zeroed in on you for a reason, and I won't give up until I know the reason behind her plan."

She'd survived a bank robbery that wasn't a robbery and a kidnapping only to have some strange woman try to murder her. Someone needed to wake her from this nightmare. "Thank you for saving my life a second time. How can I ever repay you?"

"Let me sleep on your sofa tonight."

"You're worried about me."

"If you agree, I'll have Matt, Liam, or Simon come stay, too, so the town busybodies won't have anything to gossip about." He pressed a gentle kiss to her mouth. "Say yes, Sassy. Otherwise, I'll have to keep watch from my SUV in your driveway and walk the perimeter overnight."

If he planned to keep watch all night, he might as well be comfortable. "Call a teammate and stay inside. I have a guest room available."

Cade tightened his hold on her. "Thank you."

"Will you sleep tonight?"

"Some. Don't worry about us. We're used to pulling alternate shifts when we're guarding a principal. We'll be fine."

"I'll make coffee while you find a teammate to assist you tonight." She considered what food she had to offer the operatives. Sasha suspected they would need to eat. She hoped they were bored enough to need something to do while she slept. They didn't need to worry about the extra calorie consumption, not with the pace at which Bravo team trained.

Sasha opened her cabinet and chose a stout Columbian blend. The coffee ought to help the men stay awake. She prepped her coffee maker for the full twelve cups and pushed the start button.

Next, she needed snacks for the men. Sasha found cinnamon rolls in the freezer that she'd baked last week and laid several on a plate to thaw in the microwave. While she waited, Sasha whipped up a batch of icing. When the rolls were hot, she spread the icing over the tops.

"What smells good enough to eat in here besides you?" Matt lumbered into the kitchen, a smile on his face.

On his heels was a frowning Cade. "Knock it off, Matt."

Cade's teammate laughed. "I'm yanking your chain, Cowboy. You know I wouldn't poach." He turned back to Sasha. "Seriously, what smells so good?"

"Cinnamon rolls."

Matt groaned. "Oh, man. Cade, I just might fight you for this woman. She's beautiful and she cooks."

A muscular arm circled her waist as Sasha finished icing the last cinnamon roll. She smiled at Cade over her shoulder and set her bowl in the sink. "Do you add anything to your coffee, Matt?"

"Nope. Can't carry sugar and creamer on missions. Bravo team members drink coffee straight."

She set two mugs on the counter, then rummaged for a bag of chips she placed beside a bowl of bananas and apples. "I have chicken and wild rice soup in the refrigerator. You have the rolls, chips, and fruit. Water and tea are in the refrigerator, too. More coffee is in the cabinet along with the filters. Get whatever you need while you're keeping watch."

Sasha circled the breakfast bar and hugged Matt. "Thank you for helping Cade protect me tonight."

"No problem, Sasha. Are you calling it a night?"

"I shouldn't. I've done nothing except sleep since Cade brought me home from the hospital." She sighed. "Although it's hard for me to believe, I don't think I'll have a hard time falling asleep."

"How is your head?"

"Headache is more manageable now."

"Good. Let me know if that changes."

She patted his arm. "Nice to have a medic in the house. The bathroom is the first door on the right in the hallway. Washcloths and towels are in the cabinet in the bathroom."

"Come on." Cade held out his hand to her. "I'll walk you to your room. I want to make sure everything is secure before you turn in."

"Okay. Goodnight, Matt."

"Sleep well, Sasha. Cade, I'm going to walk around the outside. I'll be back in a few minutes."

When she and Cade reached her bedroom door, he said, "Wait here." A moment later, he returned. "It's clear. Leave your curtains closed and your light off. Let's not pinpoint your location in case someone is watching."

"You'll tell me if something happens?"

"Absolutely. If you hear anything that makes you uneasy, tell me. One simple rule for you to follow. If there's a problem overnight, do exactly what Matt or I tell you to do. No questions until you're safe and the danger is past."

"I promise."

After a kiss far briefer than she wanted, Cade nudged Sasha inside the room and closed the door.

Sasha leaned against the door for a few seconds. Wow. A Cade Ramsey peck was potent. She'd probably pass out after a real kiss. Sasha completed her bedtime routine by the dim glow of night lights. She started to put on her pajamas, then thought better of it. Although she didn't think a problem would develop overnight, she'd rather not have to run in her nightwear and slippers.

A comfortable track suit and her socks seemed like the best alternative. Sasha placed her tennis shoes near the bed for easy access and prayed the precautions were a wasted effort.

Instead of taking the chance of getting tangled up in her sheet and comforter, she dragged the quilt up from the foot of the bed and spread it over her. Despite the naps, she fell asleep fast.

Sasha woke in the early morning hours, coughing. She opened her eyes, blinking against the darkness. Why were her eyes stinging? Another round of coughing racked her body.

She threw off the quilt and sat up. The coughing intensified. What was wrong with her? Was she coming down with a cold or the flu?

Someone pounded on the door, hard. "Sasha?"

"Cade," she choked out, then fell into another coughing fit.

The door opened, then, "Matt," Cade shouted. "Fire." He rushed inside Sasha's bedroom.

She had the presence of mind to snatch her shoes from the floor and grab her cell phone from the charger on the nightstand before Cade scooped her into his arms and raced down the hall.

Matt waited for them by the back door, gun in hand. "I called 911. The fire department should be here soon. We have to get her out of here."

Sasha waggled her shoes. "I can run." Her voice came out hoarse.

Cade set her on a chair. "Hurry."

Hands shaking, she tied on her tennis shoes. As soon as she finished, Matt opened the door far enough to slip into the backyard. When Sasha tried to follow, Cade stopped her.

"Wait."

Seconds later, the medic returned. "It's clear immediately around the house. I felt eyes on me, though."

"Copy that. Head for the stand of trees to the left. We'll circle around to the end of the block and work our way back." He palmed his weapon and wrapped his free arm around Sasha's shoulders. "Run as fast as you can, Sasha. Ready?"

She nodded. Sasha kept her eyes on the trees Cade had mentioned. The three of them were mere feet from safety when shots pierced the sounds of the roaring fire.

CHAPTER TEN

Cade propelled Sasha forward and dropped back to place his body between her and the shooter. Matt pivoted and fired behind them. The three of them raced for the safety of the trees.

When Sasha slowed just inside the tree line, Cade urged her deeper into cover, worried the shooter might keep firing at them. While his teammate trailed behind, Cade wrapped his hand around Sasha's and urged her to pick up the pace.

Ten minutes later, they broke from the tree line on the far side of the wooded area and worked their way back to the street where Sasha lived. Two police cars and a fire engine were on the scene, firefighters battling to save her home.

Three houses away, Cade nudged Sasha toward a detached garage on a poorly lit part of her neighbor's lot. "Matt, stay with Sasha." He jogged up the street, heading for the police chief who stood in a neighbor's yard, scowling.

"Ethan."

"Sasha?"

"Up the street and safe. Matt's with her."

The subtle tension in Ethan's frame eased. "Sit rep."

"I checked the perimeter about forty minutes ago. I heard Sasha coughing fifteen minutes later. When I went to check, her room was filled with smoke. Matt and I took her out the back door toward the tree line, and someone fired shots at us."

"Injuries?"

He shook his head.

"I already know the answer, but I have to ask. Anyone else in the house?"

Another head shake.

"Where was the shooter?"

Cade pointed to the house next to Sasha's. "West rear corner. Homeowner has a large bush that's perfect for concealment."

"I need to talk to Sasha."

"I'm not bringing her into the open."

"Understood." He turned. "Rod, I'll be back. Tell the fire chief I confirmed the house is clear of occupants."

"Yes, sir."

Ethan followed Cade down the street where Matt and Sasha waited. "Are you okay, Sasha?"

"I'm fine, thanks to Cade and Matt." She wrapped her arms around her middle. "I'm afraid my house isn't, though."

"That's what insurance is for. The arson investigator will be out here when the sun rises."

Cade drew Sasha into his arms, offering support and comfort. There was no doubt in his mind the fire had been set by the shooter to smoke Sasha out of the house, making her an easier target.

"Tell me what happened," Ethan said. "When did you go to bed?"

As Sasha answered his questions, her body started to shake so hard her teeth chattered.

The police chief tossed his keys to Matt. "I have a blanket in the hatchback." When the medic loped off, Ethan took his place in blocking Sasha and Cade from the prying eyes of neighbors or the shooter if he or she stuck around. Doubtful. Too much activity around the area to go unnoticed for long. A neighbor was sure to look out a window and see a stranger lurking in the shadows.

Matt returned, blanket in hand. Cade loosened his arms enough for his teammate to wrap the covering around her, then tucked Sasha against his chest again. "Finish your questions, Ethan. I need to take Sasha somewhere safe to decompress."

He didn't know what form decompression would take. Men and women he'd worked with in the military and Fortress all reacted to combat situations in different ways. Sasha's reaction might be volatile considering she'd been attacked twice in as many days, and she wasn't used to dealing with anything more dangerous than the rare irate customer who didn't like the coffee or a pastry.

"Doesn't seem to be a safe place for me," she said.

"Your house may be damaged, but you don't have new injuries," Ethan pointed out. "Your bodyguards did their job well."

She burrowed deeper into Cade's arms. "I'm not disputing their abilities. I don't know what would have happened if Cade and Matt weren't with me."

Cade could picture the most likely scenario too easily. Sasha would have operated by rote and left the house by the front door. She'd have taken a bullet as soon as she stepped foot on the porch. The shooter had tried to shoot to her as they ran for the trees, but didn't have a good line of sight. That was the reason they had escaped the yard without a bullet in the back.

"The person who wants me dead is persistent. What if he'd shot Cade or Matt?"

"It's a hazard of the job." The police chief folded his arms across his chest. "One you'll come to terms with if you and Cade have a chance of making your relationship work." He turned to Matt. "Get a look at the shooter?"

"Not enough to matter. A male, dressed in black, about six feet, maybe 225 pounds. He wore a skull cap so I can't tell you the color of his hair. He's Caucasian, though. He's also trained. The angle was crap and he still almost nailed us. A bullet missed Cade by inches."

"Rifle, then."

"Too far for a handgun to be accurate," Matt confirmed.

"Show me where the shooter stood, then take Sasha away from here. You should have enough room to drive by the fire truck."

As Matt walked with Ethan, Cade threaded the fingers of one hand through Sasha's hair and cupped the back of her head. "How are you holding up?"

"I'm not falling apart. I'll take that as a win. What will I do, Cade? I don't know why someone is fixated on me. How will I survive if I don't know who to watch for?"

"You won't do anything alone. We will find out who's doing this together and stop them."

"Maybe you should rethink dating a woman with a bull's-eye on her back."

He kissed her, the caress full of heat though brief. "Not a chance. I finally figured out how to talk to you. I'm not backing away now. Besides, I have a target on my back every day."

Sasha raised her head to stare at him. "Are you serious?"

"Fortress makes enemies. Although we do our best to keep our identities a secret, there's always a chance of a security breach." Not much of one, he admitted to himself. Zane kept a close watch on Fortress's cybersecurity and over its operatives. If he'd detected a problem, Z would have let him know. Still, he'd have his friend double check, especially now that he knew about Dean Ingram's connection to Sasha.

Would his former friend do anything that to harm his sister? Not based on his past knowledge of Dean. Now, however, Cade couldn't say for sure. Dean had always been tough. These days, he surrounded himself with an impenetrable obsidian shield. This Dean might be capable of things the old one would never do.

"Ethan's right."

She smiled. "He's right about many things. Which one are you referring to?"

"Not many women can handle the hazards of an operative's job."

"Ah. Keep in mind while you were working up the courage to say more than one sentence at a time to me, I made friends with the wives of Fortress operatives. I was part of the team keeping them occupied while their husbands deployed. I also read everything I could find to help me understand the difficulties of being a military wife."

"Both good things, Sassy. It's not the same as caring for a man who walks into a hail of bullets when others run the other way. You won't know when I'll be sent on a mission or when I'll return. I won't be able to tell you what I'm doing or where. I may come home injured. The absences are hard on the operatives. They're worse on those left behind, waiting and wondering. You don't know what you're letting yourself in for, Sasha."

"I'm strong, and I'll grow stronger. I'll find ways to cope with the uncertainty. I have a business to run, and if you have your way, a new one to plan. I want to be with you."

"Are you sure?" Hope kindled in his heart. He'd laid out the stark reality of his life, and she hadn't run. Cade believed Sasha could handle the stress of his work. She had to believe he was worth the effort of making a relationship work.

"Trust me."

Before he could respond, Matt and Ethan returned.

"I think the firefighters have almost knocked down the blaze, Sasha," Ethan said. "The site will be too hot to look at the damage, and the crew will stay for a while to douse hotspots. Go with Cade and Matt. Let the arson investigator look around tomorrow. I'll be in touch as soon as I know it's safe for you inspect your house. Cade, send me a text with the information about Sasha's location. In the meantime, rest while you can." His expression darkened. "This is only the beginning."

CHAPTER ELEVEN

Sasha scrunched the pillow and rolled to her side. No position seemed comfortable. How long had she been trying to sleep? She squinted at the clock on the nightstand, and groaned. Two hours moving from one position to another, trying to find a spot to lull her back to dreamland with no luck.

Frustrated, Sasha threw off the covers and swung her legs to the side of the bed. This was hopeless. She might as well make herself useful. She hoped Cade's kitchen was fully stocked. When she was stressed or worried, she cooked. Sasha figured someone trying to kill her counted as a serious source of stress and worry, hence the driving need to cook. At least Cade and Matt would eat well.

Dressing in jeans and a sweatshirt borrowed from Grace, Sasha tied on her tennis shoes and made her way to the kitchen. A dim light glowed in the living room. The operative on night watch was sure to investigate when she began making noise in here.

She opened cabinets and drawers, then scanned the contents of the refrigerator and freezer. Her eyebrows soared when she spotted the familiar storage containers

Serena Blackhawk used to freeze meals for her Home Runs, Inc., customers. The police chief's wife owned a personal chef business. Made sense for Cade to hire Serena to cook for him. Cooking for one person was tough, if Cade cooked at all. He had never mentioned doing much in a kitchen. A smile curved her mouth. Then again, he hadn't said much at all to her before the night he and Bravo team rescued her.

Sasha considered the ingredients she'd found in the kitchen and weighed her options. Scones, she decided, along with a breakfast casserole and fruit. A hearty meal for men who trained for hours every day. Cade and Matt had to be at work by six. They should have enough time to finish their breakfast and commute to work without a problem.

Sasha pulled out the ingredients for scones and went to work. Within five minutes, Cade walked into the room.

"You okay?" he asked, voice soft.

"Can't sleep, so I thought I'd make breakfast for you and Matt."

"You don't have to cook." His hands settled on her waist and squeezed gently. "Matt can give you something to help you sleep."

And be totally out of it if something else happened? No, thanks. Being unable to defend herself or help Cade and Matt was unacceptable and the stuff of more nightmares. "I'll be fine. Remember, I slept most of yesterday. Thank you for letting me stay in your home, Cade."

Another squeeze, then he kissed the top of her head. "I'm glad to have you here. How can I help with breakfast?"

They worked together to prepare the meal, then sat at the four top and sipped coffee while they waited for the scones and breakfast casserole to bake.

"I wonder how long the arson investigation will take," Sasha said as she refilled their mugs with the steaming brew.

"Ethan thinks we should have some answers this afternoon."

She had been afraid the process would take longer. "What will I be allowed to do today while you and Matt are at work?" She envisioned a quiet day watching daytime television and cringed. Not happening. That left scouring Cade's bookshelves for something to read. Safe bet he wasn't a romance reader.

What did he read? She didn't remember seeing any bookshelves when they had arrived earlier in the morning. If Cade told her she couldn't leave the house, Sasha might have to call Del Cahill, the owner of Otter Creek Books, to deliver books by her favorite authors.

Cade's lips curved. "You think I'm going to leave you alone today?"

"You have to train. I don't want you or Matt to miss work." She couldn't protect Cade and his teammates better than to encourage them to train. She refused to be the reason they skipped training and opened themselves to injury.

"We won't skip work. You're going with us."

Sasha set her mug down with a dull thud. "I'm going to PSI?"

"You said you wanted a tour, and I can't think of a safer place for you than in the middle of one hundred bodyguard trainees and Fortress operatives. When I can't be by your side, at least one of the others will be."

"Will I be able to watch you train?"

"Sure. We have an infirmary, too. You can take a nap if you grow tired. We also have a fully stocked kitchen. While Nate Armstrong is out of the country on a mission with his team, one of the trainees is filling in as chef. I'm sure Molly would be happy to have help if you want to lend her a hand."

"I'll be glad to pitch in." Nothing made her happier than feeding people. Perhaps Cade was right about opening a restaurant. She'd have to come up with enough money and create another business plan. Definitely not a quick proposition and not something she'd be pursuing in the next year or two. She doubted the bank or Small Business Administration would be enthusiastic about backing another business venture for her this soon. Though her track record was impressive, she'd only been in business for a year.

"You gave a party and forgot to invite me?" Matt walked to the counter, grabbed an empty mug, and poured coffee for himself.

"No party," Sasha said. "I couldn't sleep so I made breakfast."

His eyes brightened. "Yeah? I'm starving."

She grinned. "Can't say I'm surprised to hear that. Sit down while I check the casserole." A moment later, she pulled the casserole from the oven and set it beside the plate of cooling scones.

Cade rose. "Sit down, Sasha. You cooked. I'll fill the plates and bring one to you."

"I don't need much."

Matt's eyes narrowed. "First, you can't sleep, and now you don't want much food. You feel all right, Sasha?"

"I'm fine. I just don't eat nearly as much as you and Cade. You're much more physically active than I am."

When they had almost finished the meal, Cade's cell phone chirped with a text. He checked the screen. "It's Trent, wanting to know if we're coming in today."

"Are we?" Matt finished the last of his coffee.

"Sasha's been wanting to see PSI and watch Trent run us through our paces. I thought we'd take her with us."

"It will be fun," Sasha said.

The medic grimaced. "For you, maybe. Not so much for the rest of us. Trent's training regimen is tough."

"It works, though," Cade pointed out. "We're in top physical form."

"True," Matt admitted.

"Cade said all of you were injured on your last mission. You're recovering well?"

"Hey, I'm the medic here. Focus on your own recovery."

"In other words, he's fine," Cade said. He shot off a text to Trent, then both men helped store the food in the refrigerator and cleaned up the kitchen.

Within minutes, Sasha rode in Cade's SUV while Matt followed behind them in his own. "I really like your vehicle. Why do you and the others from PSI all drive the same kind?"

"Corporate discount if Fortress buys in bulk. A black SUV also blends in better if we have an operation on US soil." He slid her a look. "Do you think you'd mind driving one like this?"

"I'd love it, but I can't afford to trade my car in right now. I assume this one has upgrades."

He chuckled. "Several. The glass is bullet resistant and the vehicle has armor plating and heavy-duty suspension. If we have any mechanical problems, we take the SUVs to Bear. He's magic with machines."

"Bear?"

"That's what he goes by. Fortress employees have the option of ordering the upgraded SUVs for their families and close friends. We protect those we care about, Sasha. In fact, we probably go overboard with the protection, but that's how we're able to focus on our jobs. If things progress between us like I think they will, I'll want you to have to extra protection."

Sasha's heart skipped a beat, then surged ahead at a mad pace. "What do you mean by progress?"

He slid her another look. "You know exactly what I mean. The heat between us is off the charts, and I haven't really kissed you yet. That's only the smallest part of this relationship. I believe we have something special, and I want the chance to find out where this will go. Will you take a chance on me, despite what your brother insinuated?"

"I'm not inclined to take Dean's advice on anything. I make my own choices, Cade, and I choose to go on this journey with you. I can say with certainty the journey won't be dull."

He lifted her hand to his mouth and kissed her knuckles. "You won't regret it, I promise." Cade swung up to the gated entrance to PSI and swiped his card across the scanner. The metal gate opened, and he drove around to the back of the main building.

Sasha wrinkled her nose. The building wasn't attractive. It was a single-story structure without landscaping. Outside the SUV, she glanced around at the shadowed area behind the parking lot.

Sasha frowned. If she didn't know better, she'd swear that was a town.

Cade noticed where she was staring. "That's Crime Town, our urban warfare training facility. When the sun comes up, you'll be able to see better." He pointed to the left of the town. "The obstacle course. To the right is a training field surrounded by a track where Trent runs us into the ground at every opportunity."

"Care to go for double the miles today, Ramsey?" a deep voice said.

"No, thanks." Cade patted his stomach as he grinned at his team leader. "I just finished a meal Sasha prepared."

"You shouldn't do that, Sasha." Trent smiled. "He'll come to expect such treatment all the time. Don't want the Army grunt going soft on me."

"Breakfast was a little heavier than what I make for the coffee shop, but I enjoyed the work."

"Is your coffee shop open today?"

"Serena, Paige, and Darcy are keeping it running. I want to go back tomorrow, though. They have their own lives and responsibilities without the added burden of keeping my business open."

"Let's see how you feel tonight before we make that call and tell the ladies they're off duty," Cade murmured.

"What's the schedule for today, Trent?" Matt asked as he walked up.

"We're covering classes today since Durango is out. After lunch, we'll start our own training session with PT." He smirked. "You might want to go light on lunch, boys."

Cade glanced at Sasha. "And you said watching us train would be fun. I hope you like to see grown men sweat because that's what's on the agenda this afternoon."

"As long as you're one of the men, you bet." She slipped her hand into his and walked with him into the building. Cade gave her a quick tour before guiding her to the cafeteria where breakfast was in full swing. The dining facility was filled with men and women dressed much the same as Cade, Matt, and Trent. Most of them looked half asleep.

Curious about the coffee, she filled a mug for herself from the dispenser and sipped. Oh, man. No wonder the troops appeared ready for a nap. The coffee was weak. While Cade and his teammates stopped by each table to talk to the trainees, Sasha headed for the kitchen.

She found a dark-haired woman wearing a baseball hat with the PSI logo on the front up to her elbows in hot, sudsy water at the industrial-size sink, a scowl on her face. "Molly?"

The woman turned. A smile curved her lips. "You're the coffee queen from Perk. What are you doing here?"

"Cade Ramsey brought me to work with him today. We think someone set my house on fire overnight. Cade appointed himself my bodyguard and didn't want me to be alone in case of more trouble. Looks like you could use some help."

"I wouldn't turn down an extra pair of hands. The trainees and staff eat like they've been on a desert island with no food for a week. I don't know how Nate feeds these starving wolves all the time. He makes it look so easy."

"That's the mark of a true professional." Sasha lifted her coffee mug. "I'd like to refresh the coffee in the dispenser."

Molly flinched. "That bad, huh?"

"Not bad, weak."

The other woman sighed. "I told Nate I'm terrible at making coffee. I don't drink it."

"Show me where he keeps the supplies and I'll teach you a foolproof method for making the magic elixir."

Within minutes, Sasha and Molly had dumped the weak coffee and replaced it with a fresh batch. "Let's see how they like this." Sasha handed a sample to Cade.

He sighed. "Perfect. Thank you."

"Pass the word to your trainees and staff about the new coffee, and maybe you'll have more lively students to teach."

"No problem." He put two fingers in his mouth and gave an ear-splitting whistle. "Coffee's fresh. Sasha, the owner of Perk, made this batch." He laughed as the occupants of the room rushed for the coffee dispensers. "I think you just made a lot of friends."

She grinned. "I taught Molly how to replicate this. She'll have it down pat for lunch, I promise. When is your first class?"

"In thirty minutes in the gym. I'm teaching the CQC class."

"CQC?" One acronym she hadn't run across yet.

"Close quarters combat."

"I'll give Molly a hand in the kitchen until it's time for your class. I'd like to watch if it's all right with you."

"Sure. The gym is through those double doors." Cade pointed to the right side of the room. "Come in when you're ready. I'll be in there until lunch."

A few minutes after Cade's class session began, Sasha slipped in the door and sat on a chair positioned against the wall. She watched him run the class through a series of exercises, each more complicated than the last.

Cade split them into teams of four and drilled them on taking down multiple opponents, then had them practice on each other. Once he was satisfied they were competent in those techniques, he told them to form a circle and took them on, one at a time. When the trainees made mistakes, he showed them the right way to stop him.

He was patient and found something to compliment each student on. Quite simply, Cade Ramsey was an amazing teacher. Sasha didn't know anything about combat techniques, but even she could see a difference in the trainees' skills by the end of their class. Yeah, she was definitely biased and didn't care.

Sasha stayed with Cade for another hour, then slipped back into the kitchen to help a frazzled Molly deal with lunch preparations. At least Nate had taken pity on his understudy and scheduled a meal of hamburgers and chips. For two hours, Sasha and Molly flipped burgers and refilled the coffee and tea dispensers.

Near the end of the meal, Cade received a call on his cell. He glanced at the screen and rose to take the call outside the dining hall. While Sasha helped Molly clean up, she kept an eye out for him.

When Cade returned, the expression on his face was grim. He walked toward her. "Molly, can you spare Sasha for a couple minutes?"

"Take her. She's more than done her part to help out today. Thanks for pitching in, Sasha."

"Glad I could help."

Cade wrapped his hand around hers and led Sasha from the cafeteria and down the corridor to an empty office. He closed them into the room and drew her into his arms.

Oh, man. Whatever he'd heard couldn't be good. "What's wrong?"

"Ethan called."

"And?"

"The fire at your house was arson."

CHAPTER TWELVE

"Arson." Sasha's voice sounded faint. "I'd hoped Ethan was wrong."

Fat chance of that. An Army Ranger with a sterling reputation in the Special Forces community, the police chief didn't miss much from what Cade had heard and observed himself. "We'll find out who did this, Sasha. You have my word on that." Didn't matter what he had to do to find the firebug. Unlike Ethan, Cade didn't have to stick close to a set of rules and this was personal. Very personal.

Her arms tightened around his waist. "Wonder how long my insurance company will take to process the claim since there's a crime involved?"

"If they drag out the process, Ethan might be able to nudge them along. You didn't set the fire. You shouldn't be penalized."

"If I'm lucky, they'll see it your way. In the meantime, I need a place to live temporarily. I have a feeling you won't let me live in a house that can't be secured."

"Stay in my home until Rio is back in town. One of my teammates will stay with us to keep the grapevine speculation down." Durango's medic lived in a huge

Victorian house with his wife. Rio's cousin worked for Elliott Construction. Mason might be able to nudge his boss into taking on Sasha's home repairs. With the construction boom in Dunlap County, the waiting list for their services was long. "We'll talk to Rio and Darcy about you staying with them. They have plenty of room. It's not unusual for injured teammates or Mason to stay at the house."

"I don't want to impose."

"We'll ask. If it's not convenient for them, we'll come up with another plan." He cupped her jaw. "I don't want you to stay by yourself until the person focused on you is behind bars. You aren't safe. Don't ask me to go along with that, Sassy. I can't do it. I won't risk your life."

"I don't want to bring danger to Darcy's doorstep. She's my friend, Cade. I can't do that to her."

"Rio has the best security system Fortress offers. He adores his wife. Anyone invading their home won't leave alive." Cade needed Sasha to accept the arrangement. Rio and Darcy would offer her sanctuary. The house was large enough that Cade could stay and protect both women when Rio was deployed. The medic would be more than willing to watch over his favorite coffee maker while Cade was on a mission. In his mind, this was the perfect arrangement until Sasha's home was repaired.

"We'll ask," Sasha agreed. "Maybe Darcy will let me help prepare meals."

An excellent suggestion to help sweeten the pot although extra incentive was unnecessary. Cade cupped her face between his palms and pressed his lips to hers, the touch as light as a soap bubble. This wasn't the time or place to indulge in the kiss he wanted. His need to really kiss her drove Cade crazy, but the indulgence would have to wait.

She kissed his jaw, teasing affection in the touch.

How could an innocent caress fire him up in two seconds flat? Sasha might have reservations about how far their relationship could go. Cade didn't.

"My headache is almost gone," she murmured.

He chuckled, tempted to take what they both wanted. Not the time or place, he reminded himself. Anyone could walk in on them, and Trent would have his hide if he was late to their training session because he couldn't keep his head in the game. If he kissed the woman in his arms, Cade wouldn't stop for a while. He was already addicted to her touches. He had no doubt a real kiss would be even more habit forming. "Don't tempt me. Bravo's training session starts in five minutes."

"That's enough time."

He shook his head. "Not even close. I don't want our first kiss to be rushed or in an open-access office."

"Are you romancing me?"

"I'm courting you, Sasha. You deserve the best from me. Let me show you how special you are."

She sighed. "How have you stayed single this long, Cade Ramsey?"

"Easy. I don't date much, not since...."

Sasha pressed her fingers over his mouth to stop his next words. "If there's no time for a kiss, we don't have time for an explanation, especially not two minutes before a training session." She smiled. "Besides, I want to watch you work with Bravo team. I missed the rescue since I was unconscious. I want to see what your team can do."

Cade stepped back and held out his hand. "Come on. I don't want Trent to add more training time because I'm late." He squeezed her hand as he led her from the office to the training area.

Trent turned as they approached. "I was about to send a search party for you, Sasha."

"What about Cade?"

A wicked smile curved Trent's mouth. "He was fifteen seconds from having another two miles added to his run."

Liam whistled. "Close call, Cowboy."

"Worth it." He'd gladly run an extra two miles to hold Sasha Ingram in his arms.

"Quit bragging," Simon griped. "Except for Trent and you, the rest of us are currently dateless."

"It's because Cade is such a smooth talker," Matt said.

He scowled as his teammates burst into good-hearted laughter. "Let's go to work. I have plans later."

"You staying to watch, Sasha?" Trent asked.

"If I won't be in the way."

"I could use your help."

Cade's eyebrows shot up. Trent never needed help torturing Bravo team.

"What do you want me to do?" Sasha asked.

Trent handed her a stopwatch. "We need to run through the obstacle course in less than six minutes. We'll keep doing it until we meet the goal." He gave Sasha a clipboard. "Record the time for each person on here." Trent's gaze over his team. "Five miles for warmup."

Cade squeezed Sasha's shoulder. "There's a bench at the side of the track where you can sit while we run. After that, we'll shift to the obstacle course." He dropped a quick kiss on her lips and hurried to catch up with his teammates as Trent signaled him to move.

"Good thing you kissed her now." Matt elbowed him as they ran. "Beautiful Sasha won't want anything to do with you after Trent's finished with us, at least not until you shower."

"You won't be as fresh as a daisy, either, buddy."

"How are we handling Sasha's security tonight?"

"Depends. Do you want me to tap Simon or Liam for tonight?"

"And miss her magic coffee? No way."

"Thanks, Matt." He would have been happy to have any of his teammates watch his back and Sasha's. Matt, however, was his best friend, and he trusted the medic more than he trusted his own family.

"Yep. Come on. Let's show these trainees how it's done." He tilted his chin at the growing audience of students watching on the sidelines.

They picked up their speed and pushed the team's pace. After they'd finished the run, Trent led Bravo to the obstacle course.

His team leader's skill and quickness amazed Cade. Trent was well over six feet tall and 250 pounds of pure muscle, and yet he moved faster than Liam, the shortest and lightest member of Bravo.

As Cade sailed over the climbing wall and sprinted toward the finish line, he noticed their audience now included most of the PSI staff as well, including the Search and Rescue trainers with their dogs.

Sasha scribbled his time on the clipboard, then recorded the time for the rest of his teammates as they sprinted over the finish line.

Trent bent over at the waist, huffing as much as the rest of them. "How did we do, Sasha?"

"Incredible."

He grinned. "Time?"

"All of you were under the allotted time."

Applause broke out from the sidelines. Trent held up his fist, and the noise petered out. "Six minutes is your benchmark. To do what we did, you must be in top physical shape. It's time to stop whining about PT. If you haven't run today, hit the track. Five miles." He signaled two other instructors to monitor the trainees who left to run, then turned to his team. "Crime Town. We need a hostage and terrorists to defeat."

"Use Gerard's and Kelso's teams," Cade said. "Let them hunt us while we search for the hostage."

"We need a hostage." Trent turned to Sasha. "Want to be a willing hostage this time?"

"What do I do?"

Trent signaled Gerard and Kelso to approach. The two men jogged across the open expanse.

"Yes, sir?" Gerard gaze skimmed over Sasha before he faced Trent.

Cade moved to Sasha's side, not liking the gleam he'd seen in the trainee's eyes. Yeah, Cade was acting like a jealous jerk. He trusted Sasha. Tony Gerard was another matter.

"Bravo needs to run a drill in Crime Town. We'd like your team and Kelso's to be terrorists with a hostage."

Kelso frowned. "Two to one? That doesn't seem fair."

"The odds aren't in our favor in the field," Cade said.

"Who's the hostage?" Gerard asked.

"Sasha has agreed to play hostage for us. Kelso, escort the hostage to the building and room of your choice in Crime Town. Your job is to stop us from rescuing the fair maiden." Trent smiled. "If you can."

The operative snorted. "No problem."

Behind Kelso, Cade's teammates scowled. Both team leaders were arrogant, a trait that would bite them if they weren't careful. And that was the reason Cade suggested them for this exercise. Durango's leader had talked with Gerard and Kelso two weeks ago about this problem, apparently without success.

"Make sure you switch the bullets," Trent said.

"Bullets?" Sasha pivoted to Cade, worry in her gaze. "I thought this was an exercise."

"We use rubber bullets for this training. Still hurts if we're hit, but we'll be in full gear." This wasn't the time to tell Sasha some of their injuries occurred during training. Training hard meant a better chance to walk away from a mission. "You sure you want to do this? One of the trainees could be the hostage."

"I'll be fine. This time, I know it's not real."

"You have your phone?"

She nodded.

"If there's a problem or you're uneasy for any reason, call me." He kissed her, then stepped back.

"Let's play hide-and-seek with Bravo, Sasha." Kelso cupped her elbow and led her into Crime Town followed by the two teams.

"Suit up," Trent ordered when the trainees were out of sight. Ten minutes later, he said, "Kelso and Gerard are ready, and the hostage is secured. Fifteen minutes to complete the exercise. If we go beyond that time limit, we do it again."

Cade frowned. "If Sasha's up to it."

Trent inclined his head. "If she's not, I'll draft another hostage. Cade, Matt, go right. Liam and Simon, go left. I'll take the center. Don't let the trainees show us up."

Bravo team moved into position. At Trent's signal, the five men surged into Crime Town.

CHAPTER THIRTEEN

Sasha sat on the floor in the corner of a plywood building. Kelso had escorted her to the third-floor room and pointed at the corner. With one last instruction to stay put and keep quiet, he left.

Unfortunately, he'd been replaced by Gerard. What was it about the blond-haired, blue-eyed trainee that gave her the creeps? Sasha slipped a hand in her pocket and wrapped cold fingers around the cell phone, her lifeline to Cade. Had he suspected a problem might develop when he confirmed she had her phone? Maybe he anticipated Sasha's memories surfacing from her own hostage situation. She had to admit, the similarity was eerie.

Gerard stood near the window opening across the room. He alternated between watching for Bravo team and staring at her. How long before Cade and his teammates located her? Not long, she suspected. Trent pushed his team members to their limits. As long as the training kept them safe.

"Are you dating Ramsey?"

Sasha's gaze jumped to Gerard's. "Yes."

"Why?"

Odd question. "Why not?"

"You could do better."

Not in her estimation. "You don't like him?"

"Nope."

"He's a good, honorable man. I'm happy to be with him."

A smirk. "You deserve a real man, not a jerk like Ramsey."

"A man like you?"

"You're not my type."

Good thing. Didn't make him less creepy. A loud curse drifted up from below. Gerard stiffened and edged closer to the opening in the plywood wall. Sasha scrunched deeper into the corner and rested her forehead against her raised knees. Only then did she allow a small smile to curve her lips. She had a good idea what the cursing meant. From the darkening expression on Gerard's face, so did he.

"Get up."

She raised her head. "Excuse me?"

"You heard me. On your feet."

Was this part of the exercise? She didn't want the trainee touching her, even if it was to better train Bravo. Sasha was about the refuse when he grabbed her wrist and yanked her to her feet. Between one heartbeat and the next, he pressed his real gun hopefully loaded with fake bullets to the side of her head and jerked her back against his chest.

"Let go of me."

"Shut up, Sasha. You volunteered to help your boyfriend. I guarantee he's the one coming into the room to save you. Let's give him some real practice. If he cares about you as much as you think, he'll be willing to die for you."

Had this idiot changed his bullets to the rubber kind? She wouldn't put it past this trainee to use the real thing.

Would Cade's gear protect him if Gerard was arrogant enough to try to hurt him?

Sasha swallowed hard. If Gerard was using real bullets, that meant she had a fully loaded weapon pressed to her head. Again.

Although Sasha didn't hear anything, the trainee must have because he tightened his grip on her and moved her closer to another window opening. Was she allowed to fight back? She opened her mouth to again demand that release her.

Gerard clamped a hand over her mouth and pressed hard enough to hurt. Panic flared in her gut. What was he doing? Trent hadn't mentioned anything about this. Cade wouldn't have agreed to let her participate if he'd known.

She fought to free herself. Gerard's response was to press the gun tighter to the side of her head. The gun dug into the bruise left by the bank robber. Sasha moved her head, hoping to ease the pressure. Gerard's hold on her made it impossible.

Tears trickled down her cheeks as the pain multiplied by the second. Once this was over, she would have a massive headache. Great. Just when the original headache was almost gone. She wanted that kiss Cade promised her. A shadow moving in the hallway told her Cade and the others were seconds away from storming the room.

Cade dove into the room along with Matt. They both rolled to their feet, weapons in hand. A second later, the gun was gone from Sasha's head, and the weapon discharged. The trainee flung Sasha aside as Cade hissed and charged. Although Gerard swung a fist at Cade's head, Cade inclined his head enough for the punch to miss, then took Gerard to the floor. Seconds later, the trainee was immobilized.

Matt knelt beside Sasha. "Are you hurt?" Rage filled his voice although his touch was gentle as he helped her sit up.

"Head hurts again," she whispered.

"Matt," Trent said.

The medic turned toward his team leader who pointed at his best friend. He scowled. "Cade, how bad?"

Sasha pushed away from Matt and peered around his broad shoulder. She gasped when she saw blood streaming down his arm. "Cade."

"I'm all right, Sasha." He torqued Gerard's arm, making the trainee howl with pain and rage. "Gerard won't be in another minute."

Trent crossed the room with Simon at his side. "Let him go, Cade. We'll take it from here." The two reached down plucked the cursing trainee from the floor. They marched him from the room.

Cade crouched beside Sasha and gathered her against his side with the uninjured arm. "Did he hurt you?"

"Not really."

He lifted her chin with the edge of his fist. "Those tears on your face say otherwise. What happened?"

"He pressed the gun into the bruised side of my head. He couldn't have known about the previous injury."

Cade frowned and studied her face. "You're pale. Headache is back?"

"It will pass." Hopefully before she embarrassed herself by vomiting.

"I'll give her something for pain, Cade," Matt said. "We'll take Sasha to the infirmary. I need to look at your arm."

"After you check Sasha," Cade insisted as he rose.

Stubborn man. She wasn't the one bleeding all over the floor. Sasha gripped the hand Cade extended her and stood. "Come on." The quicker Matt declared she had aggravated the bruise, the sooner the medic would take care of Cade. "I need an ice pack."

Liam met them in the hallway. "You okay?" He scowled when he caught sight of Cade's arm. "Never mind.

I can see for myself you're not. Guess Gerard didn't bother to change his ammunition."

"Lucky we suited up before invading Crime Town," Matt said. "If he'd tagged you somewhere more vital, you'd be on the way to the hospital."

That comment earned a scowl from Cade.

Sasha pressed closer to his side, afraid he would go after the disgraced trainee again. "What happens to Gerard now?" Would PSI keep him in the program? She didn't wish him harm, but the thought of him protecting a vulnerable person didn't sit well with Sasha. He hadn't concerned himself with Cade's safety earlier.

"Trent will recommend Maddox kick Gerard from the training program. We can't trust him on missions if he won't follow orders. He was given explicit instructions for this exercise that he blatantly ignored. If he was on a mission and decided to do what he wanted instead of staying with the plan, a teammate could die."

"This isn't the first time he's screwed up," Liam said. "Gerard makes a habit of disregarding instructions. If our lives depend on him, we won't survive."

Two minutes later, they walked out of Crime Town and into the main building. Matt led the way to the infirmary and patted the examination table. "Sit here, Sasha. I'll check you, then take care of Cade."

After a cursory look at the side of her head, Matt snagged an ice pack from the freezer for her, then unlocked the medicine cabinet and shook a capsule into the palm of her hand. He handed her a bottle of water. "Take the pain medicine and sit for a bit."

He turned to Cade. "Your turn."

Cade grimaced as he removed his vest and two shirts.

Sasha sucked in a breath when she saw the injury to Cade's arm. A deep furrow marred the perfection of his muscle, an ugly wound needing stitches.

Matt whistled. "Glad you're quick. Not sure where he was aiming, but my guess is he tried for a chest shot."

"He missed."

"Yep. Climb up there beside your girl and hold her hand."

"That's not a hardship, but why?" Sasha asked.

"He's afraid of needles. Don't want him running out of here, screaming like a kid. Messes with Bravo's image when he does that."

Cade snorted.

Sasha doubted the truth of those words. Matt must be worried she'd pass out. "Can't have your reputation ruined." She scooted closer to Cade, swallowed her pill with a drink of water, then set the bottle aside and pressed the ice pack to her head. "Will Cade need stitches?"

"Several." Matt washed his hands and grabbed a kit from a cabinet. "Are you squeamish, Sasha?"

"Not over my own injuries. The sight of blood bothers me if it's someone I care about."

Cade kissed her temple.

"Lay your head on Cade's shoulder while I work on his arm. He can use the comfort."

"Why do I have the impression you're giving these instructions for my benefit, not his?"

"Smart woman." Cade wrapped his uninjured arm around her and drew Sasha close.

Knowing he was safe and Gerard was no longer a threat allowed the tension in her body to dissipate. She had it bad for Cade Ramsey. Would he bolt if he knew she was falling for him, hard?

Matt filled a needle with a clear liquid, then capped it and set it aside. "I need to clean the wound to see what I'm up against."

A moment later, the scent of alcohol stung Sasha's nose.

"I'm sorry, Sasha," Cade murmured.

"You didn't do anything wrong."

"I shouldn't have allowed you to play hostage after your own ordeal. More important, Gerard had no reason to put his hands on you. I should have mentioned the bank robbery and warned the trainees to keep their distance."

"Your instructions wouldn't have mattered."

"What happened after you entered Crime Town?"

"Kelso took me to the room where you found me. He pointed to the corner, told me to sit there quietly, and left. Gerard came and spent his time watching for Bravo and staring at me."

"Did he say anything to you?"

"Asked if we were dating and told me I could do better."

"He's right."

"A little stick," Matt said as he uncapped the syringe.

"How can you say that?" Sasha glared at Cade. "It's not true. I waited for months to have this chance with you. I'm not walking away because of a little bump in the road."

The medic grinned. "Go, Sasha."

"Matt." Cade frowned at his teammate.

"Don't sell yourself short, Cowboy." He disposed of the empty syringe before sitting on a rolling stool. "Your lady isn't running no matter what you tell her."

Sasha flashed a smile at the medic. "Listen to your best friend, Cade. He's right."

"We need to talk before you commit yourself to sticking with me."

"It's too late to make me run." She could handle his job and his past. "You already know about Dean. What could be worse than that?"

Matt's eyebrows soared. "Dean who?"

"Ingram. He's Sasha's brother."

He rubbed the back of his neck. "Oh, man. No wonder you've been uptight."

"He's in town."

"Why?"

Sasha shifted the ice pack to another aching spot on her head. "Dean claimed to hear I'd gotten myself into trouble and, since he was in the area, decided to check on me."

"I take it you two aren't close."

"I haven't seen him in twelve years."

"Wish I could say the same," Cade muttered.

Matt tugged on a pair of gloves and checked Cade's arm. "Feel anything?"

"Pressure."

"Perfect. Sasha, keep your eyes on your boyfriend while I stitch his arm."

"Cade said you take care of Bravo when you're on missions. Do you render medical aid when you're not deployed?"

"Depends on the injury. If Gerard's bullet had hit Cade, you'd be at the hospital, waiting for the surgeon's report. With injuries like this, my teammates prefer I repair the damage. We avoid hospitals unless it's absolutely necessary." While he worked, Matt talked about an incident on one of Bravo's missions involving a goat that had taken a liking to Cade.

By the end of the story, Sasha's sides were hurting from laughing. "Did that really happen, or were you distracting me?"

"Both. Did it work?" He ripped off his gloves and walked to the medicine cabinet. He returned with two packets of pills for Cade. He waggled one pack. "Antibiotics. You know the drill. Two a day until they're gone. Don't skip any doses. The other pack is mild pain pills."

"Thanks."

Matt took the ice pack from Sasha. "How does your head feel now?"

"Better."

"Tell me if that changes." He tossed the ice pack in the freezer, then placed a bandage over Cade's stitches. "Waterproof. Go clean up. I'll stay with Sasha."

The medic waited until Cade was gone before rounding on Sasha. "Tell me the rest of the encounter with Gerard before Cade returns. I know something else happened. Did he touch you other than what we saw when we entered the room?"

She shook her head. "He moved me closer to the window opening and clamped a hand over my mouth to keep me from making noise."

He frowned. "Did you cut your lip?"

"No, why?"

"It's puffy. Now I know Cade was in a lot of pain or he would have noticed and hunted down Gerard." Matt wrapped a small ice pack in a towel and handed it to her. "If we're lucky, the swelling will go down by the time Cade returns. What else happened, Sasha?"

"He knew Cade would be the first one through the door. Gerard said if Cade cared about me, he'd be willing to die for me." Remembering the venom in the trainee's voice made her stomach churn. "He planned to shoot Cade, didn't he?"

"The incident wasn't an accident." Matt pulled out his cell phone and sent a text. Seconds later, his phone chimed with a response. Satisfaction gleamed in his eyes. "He won't be a problem. Trent was debating giving Gerard one more chance although he leaned toward booting him from the program. Knowing he deliberately tried to shoot Cade sealed his fate. Gerard will be escorted off the campus in ten minutes. Trent and Simon will go with him to his dorm room while he packs his gear."

"I shouldn't have said anything."

"Would you want him protecting Cade when we're in hostile territory?"

Sasha shuddered. "No."

"Trent will debrief you for his report. There's also a good chance Brent Maddox will talk to you."

Cade returned, hair still glistening with dampness. He wore another pair of black fatigues and a long-sleeved black t-shirt along with his combat boots. The man looked good enough to bite.

Sasha sighed. She was a goner.

Matt tossed the medical detritus in the trash and headed for the door. He stopped, glanced over his shoulder at Sasha. "Tell Cade the rest. He needs to know. I'll be back in a few minutes."

"Sasha?" Cade sat beside her and curled his hand around hers.

"I didn't tell you everything what happened with Gerard."

He listened without interrupting until she finished. "Matt relayed the information to Trent?"

She nodded.

"Gerard should be gone by now." He frowned. "His remark doesn't make sense. We risk our lives every time we're on a mission, whether it's overseas or on a protection detail in the US. No question I would take a bullet for you."

Sasha pressed her lips to his in a brief caress. "I don't want to talk about that."

Cade's cell phone chimed. He stared at her for a moment longer, then checked the screen. Frowning, he called Zane. "Z, you're on speaker with Sasha."

"I have information on the fake nurse who tried to kill Sasha."

CHAPTER FOURTEEN

"Who is she?" Cade's hand tightened around the cell phone. Perhaps they would obtain answers about the woman who planned to kill his girlfriend. His gaze slid to Sasha. If she agreed to be called that after he told her about the debacle with her brother and Emily.

"Her name is Celeste Hart."

He stiffened. No. "Hart? As in Mario Hart, the bank robber I shot?"

"Mario was her brother."

Hart would have shot Sasha at point-blank range if Cade had waited another second to fire. "Was this simple revenge?" If so, why didn't she come after him rather than Sasha? His girlfriend wasn't responsible for Hart's death. Hart's poor choices and Cade's Sig were to blame for his death.

"I don't know. She and her brother were involved with a mercenary group. I haven't been able to nail down the name yet, but I'll keep digging."

"Thanks, Zane. You'll probably receive an update soon from Maddox. We had a problem with one of the trainees involving Sasha."

"Talk to me."

Cade summarized the incident. "I need you to keep tabs on him. If you see indications he's hanging around Otter Creek or planning payback for being fired, I need to know."

"Copy that. You all right, Sasha?"

"I'll be fine as soon as Cade feeds me dinner."

Zane chuckled. "Order the most expensive thing on the menu. He can afford to spoil you after the day you've had."

"I might do that. Thanks for the suggestion."

Cade scowled. "Keep it up, Z, and I'll send you the bill."

His friend's laughter rumbled from the phone's speaker. "When are you coming to Nashville again?"

"Next month. Why?"

"Bring Sasha with you. I'd love to meet her in person."

He winked at the woman beside him. "I'll try to convince her to take a road trip with me." He got a blinding smile. Guess that was a definite yes, provided she was still with him. Not a guarantee after she knew everything.

"I'll let you know when I learn something more about the Harts."

Cade slid his phone into his pocket. "You spent more than enough time in the kitchen today. What restaurant sounds good to you?"

"The steakhouse."

A woman after his own heart. "Good choice. Matt will appreciate it, too. He loves that place."

"What place?" Matt walked into the infirmary, his Go bag and mike bag in hand.

"The steakhouse for dinner tonight."

The medic grinned. "Just what I was thinking about. Food. Sounds great to me." He turned to Cade. "Unless three's a crowd tonight. I can go somewhere else if you two want to be alone."

Didn't bother Cade if his friend ate dinner with them. However, if Sasha considered this dinner a date, she might not want a third person. "Sasha?"

"Of course you'll come, Matt." She slid off the exam table. "Both of you will be more relaxed with someone you trust watching your back."

They may not have spent a great deal time together the past few months, but Sasha knew him better than the woman he'd planned to marry ever did. Although he never thought he'd come to this point, Cade believed he'd dodged a bullet when Emily betrayed him with his former best friend. Sasha knew Bravo was an important part of his life and didn't seem to have a problem being around his teammates.

Guess that also said something about his taste in friends before he'd hooked up with Fortress five years ago. He'd raised his standard of quality when it came to his friends and the woman he planned to spend a lot of time with.

He clapped Matt on the shoulder. "Sasha and I have plenty of time for romantic dinners and dates. Should we check in with Trent before we leave?"

"I saw him in the hall. He said he'd stop by your place about nine on his way home from the hospital. He's taking dinner to Grace."

Matt followed them to the SUVs. "I'll be on your six."

When they arrived at the steakhouse, the hostess took them to the corner table. Nice. This table was the preferred place for Fortress operatives. Occupants seated with their backs to the walls could see the room's occupants, entrances, and exits at a glance. Cade seated Sasha and sat beside her.

His mouth watered thinking about the ribeye with a baked potato and salad. He'd wanted to bring Sasha here for dinner if he gathered enough courage to ask her out. Now he'd find another good restaurant, maybe one in Cherry Hill or Summerton where he wouldn't have to worry as much about watching his back.

After the waitress took their orders, Matt's attention shifted to a table across the dining room. He frowned.

Cade went on alert. Trouble? He saw the pretty candle shop owner sitting at a table by herself. She seemed upset. "You want to ask Delilah to join us?" he asked. "Looks like she could use company."

Matt turned to Sasha. "Do you mind?"

She shook her head. "Go talk to her."

The medic was on his feet before Sasha finished the last of her sentence. "Thanks." He wove his way through tables and restaurant patrons, and sat next to Delilah for a moment. She looked surprised, but nodded and got to her feet.

"Oh, good. He convinced her to join us."

Cade stood as Matt and Delilah approached. "It's good to see you, Delilah."

She smiled. "Thanks. Sasha, I was horrified when I heard about the bank robbery. Are you okay?" Matt seated her before reclaiming his own chair.

"Headaches from a concussion. Otherwise, I'm fine. Matt and Cade have been taking good care of me."

The other woman darted a quick glance at the medic, her cheeks flaming. "I'm not surprised."

The waitress returned with their glasses of iced tea. "What can I bring you, Delilah?"

When she gave her order, Matt scowled. "A side salad isn't enough. You need protein." He looked at the waitress. "Add four-ounces of grilled chicken to her order."

"Matt, I'm not sure I can eat that much," she murmured.

"Take it home, then. You have to take care of yourself."

Cade and Sasha exchanged puzzled glances. Matt knew more about Delilah than he'd let on. In fact, he was positive his best friend was sweet on the candle shop owner. Why hadn't he said anything? Bravo knew Cade was crazy about Sasha and had teased him mercilessly. Maybe that was the reason Matt had remained silent. The medic should know Cade was a vault when it came to secrets. He knew how to keep his mouth shut.

Delilah's lips curved. "You're right. Add grilled chicken, Trish."

"I'll bring your order with the rest."

By unspoken consent, Cade, Matt, and Sasha kept the topics of conversation light. By the time their meals were consumed, Delilah's eyes were sparkling with laughter and a genuine smile curved her mouth.

Although curious, Cade refrained from asking questions about what upset her. From Matt's protective attitude and gentle touches, he was well aware of Delilah's trouble. If his friend needed help, all he had to do was ask. He'd offer aid to the medic and leave things alone until he was needed.

After dinner, Matt walked with Delilah to the door. "I'm following her home," he said to Cade.

"That's not necessary," she protested. "You have better things to do."

"Give it up." Sasha clasped her hand briefly. "Matt and Cade have an overprotective nature. Think about it this way. Matt will rest better knowing you're safe."

Matt winked at Delilah. "Take pity on me. I'm too old to go without sleep."

That comment brought laughter from the other three. If Delilah only knew how many nights of sleep Cade and Matt had missed over the years.

"Can't have that. I don't want you to miss your beauty sleep."

"It's hopeless," Cade said.

"Don't listen to him." Matt shoulder checked him as they left the restaurant. He escorted Delilah to her car, then climbed into his SUV and followed her from the parking lot.

"I sense a romance blooming." Sasha grinned. "This will be fun to watch."

"If you say so." Threading their fingers together, he walked with her to his SUV. "I'm more interested in our romance than Matt's."

"Are we having a romance?"

The teasing note in her voice warmed him inside. "Oh, yeah. We definitely are." Cade helped her into the cab of the SUV. "You don't have any idea how much I want to kiss you right now."

"Please don't tell me you're waiting two or three days. I can't stand the buildup much longer."

He flashed a grin at her. "Me, either. Not here, Sassy. You won't be safe."

"Why not?"

"I won't be able to pay attention to my surroundings. I don't want to focus on anything except you." Cade shut the door, circled the hood, and slid behind the wheel.

Although he longed to speed to his house, anticipating that kiss he'd dreamed about for months, he forced himself to obey all traffic laws. If one of the Otter Creek police officers pulled him over for unsafe driving, Cade would be delayed even longer. Besides, he wouldn't endanger Sasha or an innocent civilian because of his own carelessness.

Finally, Cade turned into his driveway and drove to the back. He positioned his SUV to ensure Sasha only had a few feet between her and safety. Aching for that kiss or not, nothing took priority over protecting Sasha. "Wait until I'm sure it's safe for you to leave the vehicle. If you see something that makes you uneasy, honk the horn. I won't be far."

"Be careful."

"Always." Cade trailed his fingers over her cheek and made himself back off. Sasha wasn't safe enough for him to lower his guard yet. Soon, he promised himself. Sasha would be in his arms and his entire focus.

Sig in hand, he left the vehicle and surveyed his property. Nothing out of place and no signs of a disturbance. Cade walked the perimeter, checking for any trace of an intruder in or near his house.

Satisfied Sasha was safe, he returned to the SUV, slung his Go bag over his shoulder, and escorted her to the back door. Once inside the house, Cade locked up and set the alarm. He'd given Matt his spare key and the code before they left PSI. He wasn't sure how soon the medic would make an appearance. He doubted his friend would push too hard with Delilah yet.

Cade set the Go bag on the floor and gently pushed Sasha back against the wall.

"Don't you want to turn on the lights?"

"I'm a little busy at the moment." He lowered his head and captured her lips. Everything in him focused on the woman in his arms. His heart rate spiked. Wow. Sasha shredded his hard-earned patience and control with one touch.

When she flinched, Cade eased away, concern knotting his gut. "What's wrong?" Would she reject him after all?

"Sore spot on my lip."

His gaze dropped and he noticed her swollen lower lip. "I'm sorry. I didn't mean to hurt you." Knowing he had made him feel sick.

Sasha laid her hand against his jaw. "It wasn't you."

Cade froze. "Who was it? Wait. Gerard hurt you, didn't he? Your lip was fine before you entered Crime Town."

"I don't think he realized what he was doing."

Not a chance. Fortress operatives were too well trained in restraining prisoners. No, this was a deliberate assault on Sasha, one meant to punch at Cade. "He knew."

He released Sasha and would have stepped away except she wrapped her arms around his neck.

"No way, buster. You aren't escaping until you give me what I want, what we both want."

"I don't want to cause you pain." The thought of waiting another few days for a kiss almost brought him to his knees.

"You're skillful enough to work around the injury." Sasha eliminated the distance between them and initiated this kiss herself.

What was a man to do? Cade used great care as he sank into the soft, gentle kisses. Minutes or hours later, he brushed her bottom lip with his tongue, asking permission to deepen the caress. When she opened her mouth for him, he indulged in the kiss he'd been longing for since the first moment he met Sasha Ingram.

The combination of her sweetness and explosive chemistry ignited a firestorm in his body. At that moment, the memory of other kisses he'd exchanged with other women vanished. The only touch that mattered was Sasha's. Cade knew he would remember this moment for the rest of his life as his world shifted and realigned, his brain imprinting her responses.

He didn't know how long they kissed in the dimly lit kitchen when he became aware of the front door opening and his alarm being disabled. Cade broke the kiss, then stole two more before turning to stand in front of Sasha, wrenching his focus away from the silk of her mouth and the soft curves of her body. The intruder was probably Matt. Still, he wanted his girlfriend safe in case he was wrong.

A moment later, Matt walked in. He stopped. "Everything okay?"

"You didn't tell me Gerard hurt Sasha."

"We iced her lip while you were showering at PSI."

Sasha gently patted Cade on the back of the shoulder. "I haven't noticed the soreness in the past few minutes. Someone distracted me with great skill."

Remembering those minutes, he smiled. "Glad you appreciated my efforts." Cade moved away from Sasha to prep his coffeemaker. If Trent stayed long enough, he'd want coffee. "How was Delilah when you left?"

Matt shifted his weight.

Hmm. Looked as though Sasha was right. A romance was blooming, at least on Matt's side.

"Better."

"Why was she upset?" Sasha asked.

"I can't say. I won't violate her trust."

"Can we help?"

Matt shook his head. "Be there for her. That's all anyone can do at the moment."

"Tell us if we can help."

A nod. "Do you plan to work tomorrow, Sasha?"

"I have a business to run."

The medic turned to Cade, eyebrow raised.

His friend didn't know women if he thought Cade would tell Sasha no. As long as one of Bravo team was with her, he wouldn't insist she stay in a place better secured although his instincts insisted he do just that. "It's her decision."

"You're staying with her?"

Sasha frowned. "You can't babysit me, Cade. What could happen in broad daylight?"

Both operatives stared at her. She'd been taken hostage in a fake bank robbery in broad daylight. "A lot," Cade murmured.

She gave a huff of laughter. "You're right. I'm living proof. Will Trent be upset if you're with me instead of helping at PSI and training with your team?"

"He'll want you safe. I taught four classes today. I pulled my weight. Someone else will step up tomorrow."

The doorbell rang.

"That's Trent." Matt pivoted and retraced his steps to the living room.

The two men returned a minute later.

"Tell me you have coffee." Trent sat in a chair at the table. "The stuff masquerading as coffee in the hospital is brown swill."

Cade pushed the start button. "Coffee will be ready in five minutes."

"How is Grace?" Sasha asked.

"Worried about you. Tell me what happened with Gerard."

Sasha told him everything that happened in Crime Town. "What will Gerard do now?"

"He'll be looking for another job without a recommendation from Fortress. We won't endorse a loose cannon."

Distress filled her eyes. "I don't want to be responsible for his unemployment."

"He's made a series of bad decisions during his training at PSI. Since his choices improved the past two weeks, we thought he'd matured. We missed something."

"Or he's good at hiding his true nature," Matt said.

Cade drew Sasha into his arms. "Character can't be hidden for long. What did Maddox say?"

Trent grimaced. "He tore a strip off my hide for keeping Gerard in the program as long as I did. He completed the separation papers and faxed them to me before I kicked Gerard out of PSI."

"How did he take it?"

"Vowed revenge, particularly against you. Watch your back, Cade."

CHAPTER FIFTEEN

Fury filled Sasha at Trent's words of warning. "Cade didn't do anything to him." Talk about a sore loser. Worse, the man's sense of entitlement and arrogance made him more dangerous than she realized. If he blamed Cade, how soon would he turn that anger and blame on Sasha? Cade had been protecting her when he went after the trainee.

"Gerard doesn't see it that way. According to him, Cade sabotaged him at every turn since he stepped foot on the PSI campus."

"That's ridiculous. Did he offer proof?"

"Cade recommended Gerard's training be extended another six months."

She turned to Cade, positive he had good reasons for the recommendation. "Why?"

"His skills weren't up to par. He preferred to work alone instead of with his team. He failed two of his classes because he refused to follow instructions." He sighed. "Maddox is right. We should have canned him several weeks ago, but his teammates lobbied to keep him in the program. They agreed to stay in the training program with him if I gave him another opportunity to prove he could make the cut. Trent, we need to talk to his teammates." Cade dropped a quick kiss on Sasha's lips, then released her to pour his team leader a mug of coffee.

Trent glanced at his watch. "I'm meeting with them in an hour."

"Bravo should be at your back," Sasha said. She didn't know Trent's background, but suspected he was more than capable of defending himself. Still, he needed people he trusted when meeting with four potentially angry, dangerous men.

The corners of his lips curved. "Worried about me?"

"You bet I am. You fired Gerard because he was an arrogant jerk and would have endangered himself and his teammates on missions. Don't be guilty of being arrogant yourself. Take backup."

Bravo's team leader chuckled. "Cade, hang onto Sasha. She's a keeper who reminds me of Grace."

Cade's gaze locked with Sasha's. "I agree."

Her eyes widened. Did he mean it? She prayed he spoke the absolute truth because she wanted to keep him, too. Cade Ramsey was the total package for her, one she was finding more and more irresistible.

"Conference room at PSI?" Matt asked.

"I can handle Gerard's team," Trent insisted.

Cade's eyes narrowed. "With us at your back. Bravo spent as much time training them as Durango. We'll deal with it together."

"What about your girlfriend?"

Cade sat next to her at the table. "She's coming with us. I won't leave her here alone, especially now."

Trent nodded. "I'll have Simon and Liam meet us in the conference room in fifteen minutes. We need to toss around ideas for Gerard's replacement. I'd like to make a recommendation to them when we meet." He finished the last of his coffee and took the empty mug to the dishwasher. "I'll wait for you in the living room."

On this trip to PSI, Matt rode with Cade and Sasha. "What are the odds we'll have a confrontation with the rest of Gerard's team?" he asked.

"Minimal." Cade glanced in the rearview mirror at the medic. "Of the five men, only Gerard gave us problems. He'll try to stir up trouble, but I don't think he'll succeed. They worked hard to achieve as much as they have in the last few months."

"They volunteered to stay in the program with him. That has to mean something."

"Loyalty. Doesn't mean they're best buds."

As Cade parked beside Trent in PSI's parking lot, two more black SUVs rolled up. Liam and Simon climbed from their vehicles and waited on the sidewalk for the rest of them to emerge.

"Hate to drag you back to PSI," Trent said. "I thought talking to Gerard's team tonight might cool tempers before discontent spreads to the rest of the trainees."

A snort from Liam. "If there are hot tempers. Gerard wasn't a favorite of most of the trainees."

"Maybe not. However, his team trained together from their first day at PSI," Simon said. "We've watched them in the field. They bonded over the last few months."

Matt shrugged. "Only one way to find out."

Liam turned to Sasha. "You okay after that debacle in Crime Town?"

"I'm fine."

When he looked skeptical, she smiled. "It's sweet of you to worry."

That comment made him flinch and the rest of Bravo laugh. Guess the tough soldier didn't like to be called sweet. He was all soldier on the outside. Inside, though, he was a good man who cared about people. Otherwise, he wouldn't have asked about her wellbeing.

The members of Bravo and Sasha followed Trent into the main building. Trent turned on lights as they walked toward the conference room. Once inside, Cade sat Sasha in a chair beside his. Matt took up position on her other side. Still on bodyguard duty.

Cade raised her hand to his lips and kissed her knuckles. "If trouble erupts, leave the room. Don't wait for me to tell you to run, just take off. Go to the kitchen and wait for me."

That's when she noticed Cade had chosen a chair for her with quick access to the door. If the confrontation with Gerard's teammates turned violent, Cade and Matt would place their bodies between her and the other men, giving her a chance to run for safety.

Her heart squeezed. He'd thought this through on the way to PSI, she realized, and had chosen the safest place for her. "I will, I promise."

"We need to talk about a replacement for Gerard on his team." Trent found a marker and walked to the white board. "Ideas?"

The five men tossed names out, then eliminated all but one in their discussion of each candidate.

"Will they take the suggestion?" Simon asked. "They might want to choose their own replacement."

"We can suggest." Trent replaced the cap on the marker and erased all the names. "It will be up to them to decide if they accept her or not."

A low rumble of voices and footsteps heralded the arrival of Gerard's teammates. Cade wrapped his hand around Sasha's. Through their connection, she felt his tension.

Matt shifted his chair, placing his body between hers and the approaching men. Simon and Liam leaned against the wall at her back. Trent stood at the head of the table.

As soon as the trainees filed into the room, Trent motioned for them to take seats on the other side of the table. "I'm sure you're aware we released Gerard from PSI and Fortress this afternoon."

"Why?" The man who asked the question sat with his hands folded on the table, his attention fixed on Trent.

"He didn't tell you?"

"We want to hear your side."

Careful words. Sasha studied each of the remaining men. They didn't seem poised to break into violence. Then again, Bravo's speed astonished her during their training sessions this afternoon, including the confrontation with Gerard in Crime Town.

Trent ran through a list of problems Bravo and Durango had noted during Gerard's time at PSI. "The incident today in Crime Town was the final straw. When you're on a mission, you can't afford to have someone refuse to follow instructions. Your lives depend on your teammates doing their jobs and following the plan." His lips curled. "Until you can't follow the plan. Things always go wrong which is why we make contingency plans. You couldn't trust him in the field. I wouldn't have allowed him to work joint ops with my team and neither would Durango."

Another member of Gerard's team spoke up. "Gerard said he got the boot because of Ramsey."

"Do you disagree with our assessment of Gerard's skills and abilities?"

"No, sir. However, a trainee who doesn't get a fair shake won't improve enough to make the cut no matter what he does."

"I got in your face several times over the past few months," Cade reminded the trainee. "Did you consider me unfair?"

"No, sir. I deserved it." He glanced at his teammates. "We all did."

"The purpose was instructive," the first man said. "You corrected bad habits or reactions, and pointed out why the behavior needed to change."

"You and the other instructors are trying to keep us and our principals alive," a third man added. "Gerard's been improving."

"You and your teammates kept him in line," Liam said. "That's not the same thing."

"As soon as Gerard was on that training op without one of you to make him toe the line, he did what he wanted." Simon placed his hands, palms down, on the table and leaned closer, his expression stony. "Worse, he hurt Cade's girlfriend, an innocent who volunteered to help us train. There's no excuse for what he did. He had no reason to touch Sasha, but he did it anyway to poke at Cade."

The trainees stared at Sasha. Her cheeks heated.

"What if you had been on a mission?" Cade asked. "The situations we encounter are fluid, the emotions volatile. He deliberately put his hands on my woman, hurting her in the process. She was already injured from the bank incident. He held a loaded gun to her head."

The fourth man sneered. "Come on, Ramsey. The gun was loaded with rubber bullets."

Cade yanked up his sleeve to show them the bandage on his arm. "Fifteen stitches in my arm says otherwise. You might have loaded rubber bullets in your weapons. Gerard didn't."

"I don't believe you. Why would he be that irresponsible?"

"That's the question, isn't it?" Trent folded his arms across his chest. "We have no reason to lie to you." He looked at each of the four men. "You have some decisions to make."

"What kind?" the first man asked.

"Do you plan to stay at PSI and continue your training?"

"You're aren't terminating our team?" Hope gleamed in his eyes.

"The problem is Gerard, not your whole team. The rest of you are clear to continue training."

"What if we don't want to stay?" the fourth man asked.

"We'll walk to the office and prepare the release papers immediately. Two of us will walk you to your room and you will have ten minutes to gather your gear and leave the premises."

"Gary, don't do it, man." The first man eyed his teammate. "Gerard isn't worth throwing away a great opportunity."

A head shake. "He's my friend. Where I come from, that means something." He shoved away from table and stood. "I'm out. Good luck to the rest of you. You'll need it."

Trent turned to Liam. "Do the paperwork and escort him to his dorm room."

"I don't need an escort," the man protested.

"Policy." Simon flanked Liam. "Let's go."

The other three teammates exchanged glances, then turned to face Trent.

"What's the verdict?" Bravo's leader asked.

"We're staying," the first man said.

"Excellent. I have a suggestion for one of the replacements on your team. The choice is ultimately up to you."

"Who do you suggest?" the second man asked.

"Molly Fisher. Her personality and skills should complement your own."

Again, the men glanced at each other. "We'll work with her, see if she works out," the third man said.

Trent nodded. "We'll find another trainee to fill Gary's place. In the meantime, do yourselves a favor and stay away from Gerard."

The three men left the conference room without incident. Sasha breathed a sigh of relief. She'd been afraid

Gary might go after Cade although the action would have been foolish.

"What do you think?" Matt asked his team leader.

"The core of their team is a good one. I hope Molly works out. Be thinking about a replacement for Gary. I'll see you at six tomorrow morning, Matt. Cade, take good care of your girl tomorrow."

"I plan on it."

"Sasha, don't push yourself too hard. Your college students can cover a few hours without you. We start training after lunch tomorrow, Cade."

"Yes, sir."

A cell phone signaled an incoming text. All three of them checked their phones.

"Mine." Cade tapped his screen. "It's Zane."

"Call him. Let's find out what he wants." Trent dropped into the chair beside Sasha.

Cade placed the call.

"Murphy."

"It's Cade. You're on speaker with Trent, Matt, and Sasha."

"I have information on the Harts."

"What did you discover, Z?" Trent asked.

"I told Cade they have ties to a mercenary group. Took me a while to ferret out the name."

"Who are they associated with?" Cade wrapped his hand around Sasha's.

She glanced at him, then Trent. Both of them looked tense.

"Black Dog."

CHAPTER SIXTEEN

Cade closed his eyes for a moment. Oh, man. Not what he wanted to hear. Concern for Sasha's safety exploded in his gut. "Are you sure, Zane?"

"Unfortunately."

Sasha twisted to face him. "You know about this Black Dog group?"

"They're a new startup with a bad reputation in the black ops field."

"How new?"

"Two years," Zane said. "They're cheap, have zero ethics, and love taking on dirty jobs the rest of us won't touch. They're all about the money."

"They also have no regard for life." Matt leaned back in his chair and stretched his legs out in front of him. "Killing innocents doesn't bother them. Their operatives enjoy hurting people. Being able to kill on a mission is a bonus for them. They'll do anything to accomplish the mission, and they won't quit until the job's done."

"Why is Black Dog in Otter Creek?" Trent went to the mini-refrigerator, grabbed four bottles of water, and passed them out. "It's no secret in the black ops community that this is the Fortress training base. What's their end game?"

"Wait." Sasha frowned. "I understand the Harts are part of Black Dog which means the mercenary group might be thumbing its nose at Fortress. What I don't understand is why Mario Hart and his buddy faked robbing the bank."

"Good question," Zane said. "I'll see what I can find out about the group online and through discreet, private sources. Trent, you want to update the boss, or should I?"

"I'll call him in a few minutes."

"Copy that. Let me know if I can do anything else to help."

"When is Durango scheduled to return?"

"They just boarded the jet. They should be back in Otter Creek before noon tomorrow."

"Outstanding." Trent brightened. "Perfect timing."

"I have to go. Claire's waiting for me to bring the SUV around. Hauling her photography equipment long distances is more difficult for her now."

"How is she?" Matt asked.

"She and the baby are great. The doc says we have four weeks to go. We can't wait to hold our child."

"I'm happy for you, man. Can't wait to see the pictures."

"Thanks. Later."

Cade's heart squeezed. He wanted the same thing Claire and Zane had. A marriage to the love of his life and a family. Did Sasha want the same thing? A question he would ask as their relationship progressed. Could he see himself with Sasha for a lifetime? Oh, yeah. "Zane and Claire weren't sure they would be able to have children," he told Sasha. "This baby is a huge blessing."

"Z is combat modified," Matt said. "He's confined to a wheelchair. Claire never seemed to see the chair, though. She only saw Zane. They are devoted to each other."

Sasha's eyes glazed with tears. "That's wonderful. I'm happy for them."

Oh, man. No tears. He couldn't take her tears, even happy ones. Cade stood and helped Sasha to her feet. "Come on. If you're working tomorrow, we need to let the other ladies know. After that, you need to rest. You didn't have a chance to sleep today."

"That's my cue to leave, too," Matt said. "See you in the morning, Trent."

He and Matt were on high alert during the drive to Cade's home. Despite the precautions and many detours, they arrived without incident.

Matt climbed from the SUV as soon as Cade shut off the engine. "I'll check the perimeter."

Cade glanced at Sasha and found her sound asleep. He decided to let her rest while Matt searched for signs of an intruder. Minutes later, the medic signaled the house was clear, then he waited at the back door, weapon in hand as he scanned the area.

Cade opened Sasha's door. He unlatched her seatbelt and cupped her cheek. "Sasha."

She sighed, opened heavy-lidded eyes, and nuzzled his hand. "I didn't mean to fall asleep."

"You needed the rest. Matt's waiting for us." He helped her from the vehicle and walked with her to the house. Once she was safely inside, he said, "Do you need anything? I think Serena leaves a stash of tea here for days when she cooks. I'm sure she wouldn't mind if I make you a cup."

"I'd love some tea. I'll call Serena and the others and let them know they're off duty tomorrow."

Although Sasha might think she was ready for a full day tomorrow, her body had been through trauma twice in three days. A twelve-hour day may tax her too much. "Do you have an extra college student to help with the shop tomorrow afternoon?"

She thought a moment. "I might have someone I can ask to lend a hand. Why?"

"Give your body a chance to heal. If you don't need the extra help, send one of your employees home. Make your calls while I fix your tea. Matt, go rest. I'll take the first watch."

"Wake me if there's a problem."

Cade filled a mug with water, dumped a packet of chamomile mint tea in the water, and placed it in the microwave. When the heating cycle ended, he grabbed a spoon and saucer, and carried everything into the living room.

Sasha set down her phone. "Thanks, Cade."

He sat beside her and picked up the remote. "Movie?"

"A cozy mystery."

His eyebrows rose. "What's that?"

"Murder mystery where the violence happens off screen."

While she sipped her tea, Cade scrolled through the offerings and settled on a movie he thought fit her description. "Did you secure extra help for tomorrow afternoon?"

She nodded. "Will you sleep tonight?"

Cade slipped his arm around her shoulders and squeezed. "Matt will take over the watch at midnight. I'll be fine. The military taught us to operate at peak capacity with three or four hours of sleep."

"Wish I could say the same for me. Tomorrow will be rough."

"Why?"

Sasha leaned her head on his shoulder. "I have to go to the shop at three to prepare the muffins and scones, and start the coffee."

He frowned. "You do that every morning?"

No Regrets

"Who else is there? I love the early mornings. The scent of baked goods and coffee makes me happy. Perk is quiet and I watch Otter Creek wake up every day."

"I hope I don't crowd you tomorrow."

"Why would you?"

"I want to help. I'm not a baker, but I can haul stuff around and dump things in the mixer with the best of them."

"What will you charge me for your services?"

"Ten kisses."

She smiled. "You're hired. I'm looking forward to paying your bill."

Cade chuckled. "Finish your tea, then it's off to bed with you."

Despite Sasha's halfhearted protests to stay with him a while longer after she finished her tea, Cade plucked the empty mug from her hand and walked Sasha to her room.

He stepped inside, closed the door halfway, and embraced her. Cade covered Sasha's mouth with his and indulged in the sweet heat. Mindful of the time, he forced himself to release her and step back a minute later.

Touching his forehead to hers, he said, "I need to go. Now. My control is hanging by a thread. What time do we leave?"

"A few minutes before three."

He brushed her lips with his. "I'll be close if you need me."

When Cade returned to the living room, he turned off the television and booted up his laptop. A message in his inbox from Brent Maddox had him grabbing his phone and placing a call.

"Maddox."

"It's Cade. Hope I'm not calling too late." Although his boss had requested the call as soon as Cade read his message, he was well aware the CEO of Fortress had a wife and daughter. The last thing he wanted to do was disturb them.

"My daughter has been asleep for two hours, and Rowan is making cookies for Alexa's class at school."

"I bet your house smells good."

"I'll need to run an extra mile or two tomorrow. Trent called. Black Dog, huh?"

"Looks like. Have you heard anything about them recently?" No one knew all the sources Maddox tapped, but he seemed to know things no one else did.

"Not enough. I put a few feelers out earlier in the month. So far, I have nothing concrete. The general feeling is Black Dog is preparing to make a move. No one knows what kind, how soon, or the target."

"Have to consider someone set his sights on Fortress."

"Maybe. They'd be foolish to take a run at us. We also have to consider Hart and his partner had a separate, personal agenda. Robbing the bank and dumping the cash doesn't make sense unless they had a different agenda."

Cade considered that a moment. "Something concerning Sasha?"

"That's what you need to find out. My gut says this has nothing to do with her and everything to do with us."

He leaned his head back against the sofa. "That's not the worst problem. Word spreads like wildfire around Otter Creek. Everyone in town knows Sasha and I are dating."

Cade's timing couldn't have been worse. By starting a relationship with her, he'd made Sasha a target.

CHAPTER SEVENTEEN

Sasha fumbled in the darkness for her phone to shut off the infernal alarm. Why had she decided an annoying buzzer was the perfect sound to wake up to each morning? She threw off the covers and made the bed to shut down the temptation to crawl back in, a serious consideration today.

If she didn't go to the shop, Perk would remain closed and her bank account would suffer. The bills didn't stop because she'd slept only three hours and had the mother of all headaches.

She needed caffeine. A big vat of it. Perhaps a cappuccino would blunt the edge of the headache and clear cobwebs from her brain.

Sasha gathered the clothes she'd laid out the night before and trudged into the bathroom. Fifteen minutes later, she emerged from the steam feeling a little more awake.

After tying her tennis shoes, she grabbed her phone and went to the kitchen. Sasha pulled up short when she saw the tall, muscular man she'd dreamed about during the night. "Hey."

Cade turned, a smile warming his expression. "Good morning. Ready to make Otter Creek's day?"

"Can't wait." Not quite true, but by the time morning morphed into afternoon, it would be. She loved Perk and her customers. They made getting up early every day worth the effort. "How long did you sleep?"

"Two hours."

Her heart sank. "Cade."

He leaned over and kissed her. "I'm fine. I'll catch a nap later if there's time."

There wouldn't be, not if his schedule for the past few days was the norm. "You could stay here. The police drop in the shop all the time." She doubted he'd agree to her suggestion, but she felt guilty for shortchanging his rest.

"Not a chance, Sassy. After wishing for opportunities to be with you, I wouldn't give up this time for anything." He handed her a travel mug. "Thought you might need this."

Curious, she sipped. "Oh, man. This is great." She detected a hint of caramel and cream to smooth out the edge of the Sumatra coffee. Perfect. "Thank you."

He shrugged. "Just taking care of my girlfriend."

Sasha's cheeks burned. "Does that mean I can claim you, too?"

Another kiss from Cade, this one full of blistering heat. "I haven't dated any woman since the first time I saw you, Sasha. I've been yours for months."

When her eyes stung, she flapped a hand in front of her face. "We have to go. I don't want to start my day off with tears, even happy ones."

Cade laughed. "Whatever you say, Sassy." He snagged another travel mug from the counter, slung his black bag over his shoulder, and headed for the back door. He deactivated the alarm. "Stay here while I take my bag to the SUV. I'll come back for you."

Although impatient to leave, Sasha wasn't stupid. She knew her boyfriend was scanning the area while he stored his bag in the hatchback. Cade took his time walking to the vehicle. When he closed the hatchback again, he walked around his SUV with a small black gadget in his hand. Once he'd made a complete circuit, he dropped to the ground and shone a light on the undercarriage. What was he doing?

Cade appeared satisfied with what he found and returned to the back door for her. "We're clear. Straight to the vehicle." After he reset the alarm, the operative wrapped his arm around Sasha's shoulder, hustled her across the few feet of open space, and helped her inside.

As they drove from his home, Sasha asked, "What were you doing with the black gadget in your hand?"

"Checking for tracking devices or some other electronic signal."

"And when you dropped to the ground?"

"Looking for a bomb."

Sasha twisted to stare at him. "If you had found one, would you have disarmed it?"

"It's what I do, Sasha." He flicked a glance at her. "I'm well trained."

If he was a sloppy bomb tech, they wouldn't be having this conversation, she reminded herself. "What happened while I was asleep?"

"Nothing."

Protection or truth? Truth, she decided. Nothing active had happened or he would have woken her. "What did you learn?"

A wry smile curved his mouth. "You're perceptive. I talked to my boss, Brent Maddox, after you went to bed."

"What did he say?" Whatever it was had upset Cade.

"He's heard rumors about Black Dog preparing to make a move. No one knows what or where. He doesn't know if BD's presence in Otter Creek is a sign Fortress is their objective or if the Harts went rogue and the mercenary organization has nothing to do with what happened."

"That's not what upset you."

He captured her hand and pressed his lips to her knuckles. "I'm afraid I brought you to the attention of ruthless operatives, Sasha."

"How?"

"I'm part of Fortress, and one of two teams tasked with training Fortress recruits. If Black Dog is here to test the waters, they'll do their homework and find out who is important to all of us. This group won't hesitate to make use of that information."

She remained silent for a beat. "Do you believe that's why Hart took me from the bank?"

"They weren't interested in taking the money. I'll understand if you want to put our relationship on hold until we figure out their agenda."

"Whether it's Black Dog or another group, I'm not walking away from you, Cade."

He squeezed her hand. "I'll protect you with my life, Sasha. You have my word."

"I never doubted that." If she had, running straight at Gerard while the trainee had a loaded weapon and an ax to grind would have confirmed it beyond question.

When they parked behind Perk, excitement bubbled in her blood. Sasha was determined to make today a great day despite the questions surrounding the Harts and Black Dog.

Sasha unlocked the shop door and shut off the alarm. When Cade signaled for her to remain in place while he checked out the coffee shop, she didn't protest. The operative was extra vigilant. Facing danger to himself was normal. Knowing she might be in danger increased his protectiveness. She had to appreciate his desire to protect her from further harm.

A moment later, Cade returned. "It's clear."

"Great. Let's get busy."

They worked side by side for the next three hours. Cade turned out to be handy in the kitchen. Once the baking was completed and the display cases filled, they shifted to preparing coffee. Soon the shop filled with scents that made her mouth water and her stomach growl.

Across the square, lights were on in That's A Wrap and customers were filling seats in Delaney's. Sasha glanced at the clock. Fifteen minutes to spare. "Are you hungry?"

"Starving."

"I saved two blueberry scones and two raspberry cheesecake muffins for us. When one of the policemen stop in, you can go across the square to Darcy's place for something more substantial."

"Sounds great. What kind of coffee do you want with your breakfast?"

"Columbian with three shots of espresso."

"Coming up." He eyed her. "Grab a bottle of water for yourself. Dehydration will make the headache worse."

Sasha laughed. "I thought I hid it well."

"You did. Most people wouldn't notice."

"But you did."

Cade shrugged one shoulder. "I notice everything about you." He turned away to refill their travel mugs.

Sasha went to the cooler where she'd set aside the scones and muffins. If she wasn't already falling in love with the man, Cade's last statement would have nudged her that direction. How could she resist him when he said things like that? She plated the food and carried the dishes to the front.

He sat at the far end of the counter with his back to the kitchen, the main room and door in plain view, his laptop on the counter. He took a bite of the blueberry scone she placed in front of him and moaned. "Sasha, this is terrific."

She smiled. "You'd know how they tasted if you had stayed in the shop longer than it took to fill your travel mug. I always hoped you would stay for a few minutes. I had plans to grab your interest with my baking."

"My mistake, one I won't be repeating." He tapped her plate. "You have ten minutes before the shop opens. Eat while you can."

When they finished the quick meal, Sasha dashed into the kitchen to deposit the plates in the dishwasher. Another glance at the clock. Time to open for business.

The mad rush of morning customers made time pass in a blur. One of her workers had a class that canceled and dropped in to lend a hand. As the hours passed, Cade kept an eye on the customers and people walking past the shop on the sidewalk. When she needed more supplies from the kitchen, he brought in trays of scones and muffins and refilled the cases. A couple times when the line stood six people deep, Cade bagged to-go orders of pastries and helped pour coffee if the order wasn't a complicated one. Between the three of them, they easily handled the larger than normal traffic through the shop.

Once Perk was in the lull between breakfast and lunch and the shop was empty, Sasha sat on the stool next to Cade. "If you ever decide to hang up your weapons and look for other work, I'll hire you in an instant."

He laughed. "Good to know I have job options. I'm glad I could help."

"You were a lifesaver." Sasha rolled her shoulders, her muscles aching. "I'll miss having you here when you're gone for work."

"Hurting?" he murmured.

"Shoulders and head."

"Did you drink the water?"

"Half."

"Finish the rest while I work on your shoulders." His hands kneaded her muscles.

She moaned. His hands were magic. Maybe she'd survive the day's labor now. "You can stop sometime next year."

"How are you holding up, Sassy?"

"I'm more tired than I thought I would be." Galled her to admit it.

"Understandable. Another day or two and you will be back on your game."

Renee, her part-timer, set a bottle of water beside Cade's computer. "Sasha, Jason is coming in before noon. I can handle things here if you want to go home."

She wished. Unfortunately, her house was still off limits. According to the fire marshal, her bedroom had been heavily damaged in the fire. That meant she needed to dig into her savings account and buy more clothes. Would Cade be willing to take her to one of the malls in Knoxville? That was the fastest way to replenish her clothing choices. Maybe after he finished with his training this afternoon.

"I'll stay until Jason arrives." She didn't want to leave the college student alone in the shop in case one of the Black Dog crew decided to cause trouble. The mercenary group had no way of knowing if Sasha was in the shop. She couldn't take that chance with Renee's safety.

The chimes over the door rang and Ethan Blackhawk walked inside. He had a handbag under his arm.

"Welcome to Perk, Ethan." Sasha smiled at him. "Would you like the Columbian today? It's a bold roast that will make your taste buds wake up and sing."

"Sold. The largest cup you have." He laid the handbag on the coffee bar. "I found your purse in the living room the night of the fire and grabbed it. Haven't had a chance to drop it by before now."

Relief swept through her. Thank goodness she didn't have to go through the hassle of canceling her cards and securing another driver's license. "Thank you. You saved me a boatload of time and trouble." She studied his face a moment. "Rough day?"

"And night. Lucas is teething. I was up half the night walking the floor with him. It's one thing for him to cry when he's tired or mad. It's different when he's hurting. Hurts me almost as much as it does him."

"Poor guy." She started to rise, but Cade laid a hand on her arm.

"I'll take care of it." He walked behind the counter and grabbed the extra-large cups Sasha used most of the time for the Fortress operatives and law enforcement personnel who stopped in. The hospital staff generally chose a smaller size.

"Anything new on the fire?" Sasha asked.

"We found a gas can near the tree line in the back. Did you leave one out?"

"I don't have lawn equipment. I hire someone to take care of that for me."

"Prints?" Cade asked as he handed the police chief his coffee.

"None." Ethan nodded his thanks and sipped. "I won't torture your eardrums by singing, but this is great, Sasha. How are you feeling?"

"Tired with a nagging headache."

"I'm glad you're recovering." His gaze shifted to Renee.

Sasha took the hint. "Renee, check our supplies. I'd like to make chocolate chip muffins and strawberry scones tomorrow. See if I have all the ingredients or if we need to do a supply run."

"Yes, ma'am."

As soon as the swinging door closed behind the college student, Ethan said, "I heard there was a problem yesterday at PSI. What happened?"

Cade gave him the highlights without going into great detail.

Ethan scowled. "Any idea what Black Dog wants?"

"Not yet. Zane and Maddox are looking into it."

"I want to know the minute you hear anything. In the meantime, I'll alert my officers to be watching for strangers in town."

Sasha hopped off the stool and opened one of the display cases. She bagged two of the raspberry cheesecake muffins and handed them to Ethan. "In case you don't have time to stop for lunch."

"That's the case most days." He reached for his wallet.

"On the house, Ethan."

He smiled. "Thanks." He withdrew money from his wallet and dropped it into the tip jar. "I'll be expecting word from you soon, Cade. I don't want my town caught in the crossfire."

"Understood."

With that, the chief left.

After a quick glance to make sure Renee was still in the kitchen, Sasha said, "Do you think Black Dog will try something in Otter Creek?"

"I don't know. We can't be complacent. Innocent people could be hurt."

"What will you do?"

His eyes held grim determination. "Prepare for the worst."

CHAPTER EIGHTEEN

Just before noon, Sasha's other part-time worker, Jason, walked in the shop with another girl close on his heels and headed straight for Sasha.

"Hi, Sasha." The girl hurried around the counter to embrace Cade's girlfriend. "I've missed you. How is business?"

Sasha returned the hug. "Marley, it's great to see you again. The shop is busy. You sure you want to work for the motel? I could use more help. Renee and Jason are graduating in a few months and will be seeking full-time work in their fields."

"The motel job isn't working out like I thought it would. Turns out I hate working overnight."

"Don't you have more time to study?"

"I spend my time trying to stay awake and I'm tired all the time."

"You have a job at Perk if you want one." She turned to Jason and Renee. "Remind Marley how things run in case she decides to rejoin us. If you need me, call or text. I'll be with Cade at PSI until the shop closes."

The three students stared at Cade. "Is he your boyfriend?" Renee asked.

Sasha nodded.

Satisfaction filled Cade. He'd waited a long time to hear Sasha say those words.

"Wow," the girl whispered, her eyes wide.

"Double wow," Marley said.

Cade eyed Jason. "You plan to one-up the ladies?"

He snorted. "Not me. It's fine as long as you take care of Sasha. If you don't, you and I will be having a talk."

Sasha's eyes widened. "Jason!"

Cade nodded at the college student, understanding the need to protect one you cared about. "If I louse up and hurt her, you get a free punch. Okay?"

"Deal."

The kid would never have the opportunity to take advantage of his offer. Cade wouldn't hurt Sasha, ever. He handed Sasha her purse, grabbed his laptop, and escorted her to the SUV. "Hungry?"

"I'll take anything as long as it's not too heavy."

"I'm not sure what Nate planned for lunch today. Burger Heaven has a great grilled chicken sandwich. Does that sound appealing?"

Sasha nodded. "Since my bedroom is toast, including my closet, would you mind going with me to Knoxville? I won't take long, but I need clothes. I can't continue borrowing from Grace."

"No problem. Think about what you might want for dinner. We'll count this as our first date." The first of many. He had a lot of time to make up.

Cade glanced at the dashboard clock. To make his training session on time, he'd have to use the drive-through. Minutes later, he escorted Sasha into the dining hall where they sat with his teammates.

"Everything okay at Perk?" Trent asked.

Sasha nodded as she unwrapped her sandwich.

"The shop still open?" Liam asked.

"Two part-time helpers are closing for me."

"Should we send a trainee in to keep an eye on things?" Simon asked Trent. "I don't like the idea of the students being there alone."

"It's good on-the-job practice," Cade agreed. He planned to broach the subject with his team leader after lunch. He wasn't worried about their safety during the lunch rush in town. Too much foot traffic in the square and people dropping in for their afternoon coffee. Around three, though, foot traffic in the shop slowed down.

Trent scanned the trainees at various tables across the large room. He strode to the far corner and talked to a man and woman seated together. After a moment, both nodded, disposed of their trash, and left.

Bravo's leader returned. "Done. Didn't take much persuading. Kat and Abe love Perk. I promised them free coffee as long as they were on duty. Hope that was okay, Sasha."

"Of course." She pulled out her phone and sent a text. "I let Jason know the trainees would be in the shop for a training exercise. He'll provide them with coffee and pastries on the house."

"I'll cover the cost."

"Kat and Abe are doing me a favor by protecting my employees and property. I'm happy to provide fuel to keep them awake."

Matt sighed. "They'll have to run two more miles tomorrow to work off the extra calorie intake."

Cade chuckled. "Sounds like you wish you had Perk duty."

"Absolutely. I love that place."

The noise level in the dining hall picked up as trainees and staff called greetings to the five men dressed in the standard Fortress uniform who walked in. Durango had returned. "I'm surprised to see them on campus. I thought they would spend time with their wives." Especially Josh and Alex. Their wives were expecting babies any time. For the next two months, if Maddox needed to send one of the PSI teams on a mission, he'd send Bravo. Cade needed to warn Sasha he might be gone more than normal in the next few weeks.

Trent shook the hand of Durango's leader. "How did the mission go?" he asked Josh Cahill.

"Like clockwork." He shrugged. "Can't explain it."

Sasha turned to Cade, her expression puzzled.

"Something always goes wrong on missions. We make plans and several contingency plans."

"And then we operate on the fly," Matt said.

Liam scowled. "Their intel must have been better than ours."

"Doubt it. Luck of the draw," Josh said. "I heard we had a problem with one of the trainees."

"Two." Trent pivoted to face Bravo. "Indoor gun range. I'll update Josh and meet you there."

When his teammates stood, Cade said, "How is your headache, Sasha?"

"Much better. Is it all right if I go to the gun range with you?"

He looked at Trent, eyebrow raised. When he received permission, Cade stood and held out his hand to Sasha. "Ever fired a weapon before?"

"No, but I'd like to learn."

Not what he'd expected to hear from her. Emily had been afraid of his weapons and refused to touch one or him if he was wearing one. That had been a problem since he wore weapons everywhere.

"You use them for your work," she continued. "I want to learn how to handle weapons. I don't want to be afraid of the tools you use to keep yourself and your teammates safe."

Unable to stop himself, he leaned down and kissed her. "I'll be glad to teach you." Finding a woman like her was a blessing, one he wouldn't take for granted.

When Cade raised his head, he noticed the members of Durango staring at him and Sasha, wide grins curving their mouths.

"About time," Rio said. "Marcus and Paige were ready to declare you hopeless."

Cade scowled. "I didn't need a matchmaker. I knew what I wanted. I was working up the courage to approach her."

Alex, Durango's sniper, clapped Cade on the shoulder. "Good job." He looked at Sasha. "If he hurts you, tell me."

Cold chills ran up his spine as he protested. "I'll never hurt Sasha." No one wanted to be in Alex Morgan's sights when he was angry. The sniper would tear into him if Cade screwed up with Sasha. Alex had a soft spot for women and children.

Sasha nestled her hand into Cade's and smiled at Alex. "If he does, you can have him after I'm finished with him."

The trainees and staff remaining in the dining hall erupted into whistles, catcalls, and applause at her words, earning a scowl from him. He gathered their trash and led her toward the door. "I need to find the appropriate weapon for you before we start."

"Something small and pink?" she teased.

Cade flinched. "I doubt we have anything fitting that description." At least, he hoped not.

Ten minutes later, they walked into the building housing PSI's indoor gun range. He selected two sets of ear protectors and safety goggles, then went to the vault and pulled out three weapons he thought might fit her hand.

Cade checked the chamber of each to be sure they were empty, found magazines for each, and shoved them into his pocket. He nudged her toward one of the empty rooms. "A few pointers before we shoot targets."

He taught Sasha handgun safety and how to hold her weapon in a two-handed grip, correcting her stance until she moved into it naturally. "Excellent. Go into your stance and aim at the wall. Draw in a deep breath, let it out halfway, and squeeze the trigger."

She followed his instructions.

"Again." He had her repeat the procedure until she was comfortable. "Perfect. Ready to try it in the range?"

"I don't want to hurt anyone."

"You won't. Each shooter is separated by barriers. The weapons will kick each time you fire. Don't fight it. Relax and absorb it. Even with the ear protectors, the range will be noisy."

He led her to an empty corral. With the eye and ear protection in place, he motioned for her to shove the magazine into the Sig he'd selected for her. When Sasha was ready, she fired at the target he'd set at twenty feet. He corrected her aim and nodded for her to fire again. After she emptied the magazine, he brought the paper close to see how she fared. Not bad for a first try. Half the shots hit the paper. With a little more practice, Sasha would be a good shot.

When he switched Sasha to a Berretta, her accuracy improved. Nice. After finishing the three magazines he'd brought, Cade reloaded them, sent the target farther away, and completed his own practice with each of the weapons he'd selected for her.

She scowled when she saw almost every shot hit the heart or head. He grinned and dropped a quick kiss on her lips, then showed her how to clean the weapons and load the magazines.

Once they were outside, she threw her arms around his neck. "That was fun. I'd love to do that again when we have time."

Cade settled his hands on her waist. "Sure. Would you like a weapon of your own?"

"Do I need one?"

"You will if you decide to have one at the shop or your home."

"What would I need to do?"

"Take a gun safety class and apply for your carry permit. We teach the safety class at PSI at the end of the month."

"Sign me up. We'll see how it goes from there."

Cade tightened his hold. "You don't know how much that means to me."

"I don't want you to worry about my safety while you're deployed."

"I may deploy more than normal the next two months. With Josh and Alex's wives about to have their first babies, Bravo is taking their missions plus our own. Maddox wants to give them time with their families."

"Will I hear from you while you're gone?"

"Depends on what's happening. I'll try to call."

"It's okay, Cade. Focus on keeping yourself and your teammates safe."

He kissed her. "You are a treasure, Sasha."

"Hope you think so on days when I'm tired and grumpy."

Trent walked up to them. "Gym next. How did Sasha do?"

"With training, she could be a sharpshooter. I need a Beretta for her."

"Talk to Josh. A friend of his owns a gun store and will cut you a good deal."

The rest of the afternoon, Bravo ran through a series of close-quarter-combat drills with trainees as attackers, hit the obstacle course, and ran their miles.

Once he'd cleaned up, Cade found Sasha in the kitchen helping Nate with dinner preparations. "You ready?" he asked.

"As soon as I chop the celery and carrots." Two minutes later, she scraped diced vegetables into a waiting bowl.

"Thanks, Sasha." Durango's EOD expert gave her a one-armed hug. "Enjoy your date."

In Knoxville, Cade took Sasha to an Italian restaurant for dinner and drove to the mall she selected. Sasha was a power shopper. She knew exactly what she wanted and went for it. Thirty minutes after entering her favorite store, they left with three bags of clothes.

At the exit, Cade handed her the bags. "I need my hands free." He wrapped one arm around her shoulders, his weapon easily accessible.

They had almost reached his SUV when a vehicle revved its engine. He turned. A dark-colored pickup raced toward them.

CHAPTER NINETEEN

One minute Sasha was walking with her boyfriend, looking forward to a quiet ride to Otter Creek. The next her back was against the vehicle, her body covered by Cade. His gun was in his hand, the barrel aimed at the truck racing away from them.

Cade fired one shot. Although windows shattered, the driver didn't stop. He careened from the aisle, turned toward the main thoroughfare, and sped away.

"Are you okay?" he asked.

She nodded. "They tried to kill us, didn't they?"

His head whipped toward her. "You saw them?"

"The driver. I didn't see the passenger well."

"Could you describe the driver to a sketch artist?"

"I'll try. Do you have one on staff at PSI?"

"No, but I know someone who can help us find one." He stepped back. "We need to go in case they take another run at us." Once she was settled, he placed the bags behind her seat.

She fastened her safety belt after several failed attempts. Sasha's shaking hands annoyed her.

Cade circled the vehicle with his plastic gadget in hand. A minute later, he drove away from the mall. She expected Cade to head for the interstate. He didn't.

"Where are we going?"

"Taking a few detours. I don't want them to follow us or try to run the SUV off the road."

"Would you take the risk if you were alone?"

"What do you think?"

That's what she thought. If he'd been by himself, he would have drawn them into a trap of his own and perhaps stopped the madness tonight. "I have another question."

"Shoot."

"When we were at the gun range, you told me never to fire a weapon unless I knew where the bullet would stop."

"You want to know why I fired at the truck." He gave a short nod. "Good observation. The truck was heading toward a high, dense berm of dirt. No civilians were in the area and no other vehicles were in the line of fire. I aimed for the center of the back window in case there was a passenger. With both front and back windows blown out, the truck will be more noticeable."

Wow. All Sasha had noticed was the truck and driver. Cade assessed the situation in a split second and acted. "Why didn't we call the police to report the incident?"

"They would have taken me in for questioning. With my background in the military and now Fortress, I would have drawn a lot of suspicion. I don't want to be separated from you for any reason. We'll report the incident to Ethan to have it on record, but we can't offer much information yet."

"Yet?"

Cade activated his Bluetooth and placed a call.

A moment later, Zane's voice filled the cabin of the SUV. "Murphy."

"It's Cade. You're on speaker with Sasha. We ran into trouble at a mall in Knoxville. Hack the traffic and security cameras in the area. A truck almost mowed us down in the parking lot. I want to know who was in the vehicle and the license plate."

"Name of the mall?"

Cade gave him the information and answered other questions about the make and model of the truck. Sasha was amazed at the amount of information Cade had gathered in less than a minute.

"Did either of you see the driver or passenger?"

"I saw the driver," Sasha said. "I'm not sure I could identify him."

"Let me see if I can find a shot of the driver or passenger. If not, we'll locate a sketch artist."

"How long, Z?" Cade asked. "This is the third attempt on Sasha's life in four days."

"Two or three hours. I'll contact you as soon as I have something."

A soft voice spoke in the background.

"Claire sends her best," Zane said.

"Give her a hug for me. Talk to you soon."

Sasha sighed. "This is crazy. I run a coffee shop in a small town. I don't hang out with the wrong people or put myself in dangerous situations. This shouldn't be happening to me."

"We'll figure it out and stop it."

"Since we're driving in circles, can we stop at a coffee shop? I'm craving hot chocolate." She was desperate for a comfort drink.

"We're turning squares to spot a tail." Cade found a coffee shop with a drive-through and ordered her drink plus coffee for himself and two bottles of water.

While they waited for the order, he asked for her cell phone. To her surprise, he popped the phone from the case and took out her battery. His expression darkened as he fished something small from her phone case and flicked the item from the SUV.

He activated his Bluetooth again. "Zane, I need a secure cell phone for Sasha. How fast can I get one?"

"The Shadow unit is leaving Nashville in a few minutes. I'll divert the plane to Knoxville. Expect the jet in 90 minutes. Same number as her current one. I'll handle the details of switching her carrier."

Cade grinned. "You had the phone ready."

"Guilty. Later."

Sasha eyed Cade over the rim of her chocolate as she sipped. "Why am I receiving a new phone now?"

"Hart or his buddy placed a tracking device in your phone. I got rid of it. Should give us some breathing room."

When he returned to the main road, Cade headed in the opposite direction. Sasha thought they were continuing the squares until she saw the interstate sign. "Are we going to the airport?"

He nodded. "No sign of a tail." His lips curved. "If Black Dog is behind this latest incident, they know we'll drive to Otter Creek eventually."

"I hope they wait to engage us until I finish the hot chocolate. It's fabulous."

Cade laughed. "The coffee isn't half bad, but it's not yours."

Pleasure filled her at his words. "Am I turning you into a coffee snob?"

"You're helping me develop discerning taste in coffee."

"I like that. I'm glad we're going home soon. The early morning is catching up with me." She twisted to face him. "You didn't have a chance to nap today."

"Noticed that, did you?"

"Hard to miss. Are your days usually this busy?"

He glanced at her. "I'll always have time for you."

They parked near the airfield for private jets and Cade turned to Sasha. "We have a few minutes before the Fortress jet lands. You must have questions. Ask. I'll answer if I can."

She considered her choices. One topic topped the list of questions. "Tell me about the woman you planned to marry."

Cade's hand fisted on his knee. "It's not a pretty story."

"She hurt you."

He inclined his head in silent agreement. "I don't know where to start."

"At the beginning. When and where did you meet?"

"I met Emily Whitfield at a fundraiser for combat-modified veterans eight years ago. She was the event coordinator and ran into me, literally. Emily was hurrying to another part of the ballroom and plowed into me. We talked. I asked her to dinner the next night."

He grimaced. "We dated for three months. I thought I was in love with her and asked her to marry me. She accepted. My unit deployed a week later. We were gone for six months. When I returned, something had changed between me and Emily. I didn't know what was wrong. I asked if she was having second thoughts about marrying me. Emily said everything was fine, that I was having trouble adjusting to being stateside again."

Sasha scowled. "I hope you denied that."

Humor lit his eyes. "You don't believe I had a problem?"

"Oh, come on. You're deployed often with Bravo, sometimes for weeks at a time, but you never have problems adjusting to Otter Creek."

A huff of laughter escaped him. "Yeah, I denied it. She blew off my protest. I knew something was wrong, but couldn't figure out what. Two months later, I was sent out of the country for a short-term assignment and returned after six weeks."

When his knuckles turned white, Sasha laid her hand over his, sorry now she'd asked about Emily. This wasn't a case of two people in love drifting apart. "What happened, Cade?"

"After reporting to my commander, I drove to Emily's house. Her front door was ajar. I went inside, afraid someone had broken into her place. While checking the house, I walked down the hall toward her bedroom. I expected Emily to be at work. I had planned to wait for her on the porch."

He drew in a deep breath. "She was home and in bed with another man."

Oh, no. "What did you do?"

"Backed away and waited in the living room. I wanted to know who she was seeing behind my back and to break off the engagement. I could have waited until later, but she would have denied the whole thing and I needed answers."

His gaze locked with hers. "She was sleeping with my best friend. I'd been transferred into a different unit a year earlier. That's why he was home when I deployed with my Ranger unit."

Sasha's grip on his hand tightened as ice water flowed through her veins. She knew without asking the identity of the man Emily betrayed Cade with. He needed to tell her, though, and to see her reaction. "Who was he?"

"Your brother."

Knowing the probable identity of Emily's lover didn't stop her jerk. "I'm sorry he hurt you, Cade."

"Emily lied to Dean, Sasha."

"About what?"

He looked haunted for a moment. "She was lonely while I was gone. I understand that."

"I don't." She frowned. "If she loved you, she would have connected with other military wives who understood what she was going through, not turned to Dean for comfort. That doesn't absolve Dean of responsibility. He knew she was engaged to you, and still he betrayed you."

"You haven't been involved with a military man. The absences are hard on the families."

"If our dating relationship doesn't work, I won't betray you. I'll tell you face-to-face when you return."

"And if we're married?"

Sasha's heart leaped at the thought. A dream come true. "No betrayal, ever. Marriage vows are for life. If I fall in love with you, I would never hurt you like Emily did. We work together to resolve issues. I would treat you like the gift you are until one of us draws our last breath."

Cade stared at her. "Do you have any idea how much those words mean to me?"

She squeezed his hand. There was more to the story. "Tell me the rest."

"Emily told your brother I had PTSD, that I was hitting her and verbally abusive. She convinced Dean she was afraid of me."

Sasha's mouth gaped. "Are you serious?"

"When I confronted them in Emily's living room, he threatened to kill me if I touched her again. I denied everything, but Dean didn't believe me. When it became obvious I was wasting my breath trying to convince him, I told Emily to keep the ring. I would never marry her, even if she came clean about the lies and wanted to resume our relationship."

"Why didn't you ask for the ring?"

"I wouldn't place that ring on another woman's finger." He shrugged. "Sounds stupid, but she dishonored the ring. I won't dishonor another woman by placing it on her finger. I could have traded the ring for something different later, but I didn't want to see it again."

"How could you avoid Emily and Dean? You lived on the same base."

"The military moved my Ranger unit to another base soon after I broke the engagement." He trailed the backs of his fingers over her cheek. "Now you know the whole sordid story, you understand why your brother jumped to the wrong conclusions."

"How long were you and Dean friends?"

"Seven years. We went through boot camp together and were assigned to the same unit until I became a Ranger. Dean applied, but didn't make the cut for Ranger school."

"What happened to Emily?"

"Last I heard, she and Dean were married."

Shock reverberated through Sasha. "He married her? Why didn't he tell us?" Her head dropped against the headrest. "Oh, man. That means I have to be nice to this woman when I meet her."

"I don't know if they're still together. I didn't keep up with them after my unit changed locations. Three years later, I mustered out and joined Fortress." He sat up, his attention focused on the plane taxiing down the runway. "That's the Fortress jet."

He came around to open her door. "I'll introduce you to the Shadow unit."

"What's with the name?"

"The team is assigned some of the toughest cases Fortress handles. They spend a lot of time in the shadows, hence the name."

"Can you tell me what kind of cases?"

"Human trafficking, especially those involving children. They also specialize in rescuing kidnapping victims."

"They can't work those difficult cases all the time."

Cade slipped his arm around her waist as they walked toward the concourse. "Maddox controls how many trafficking cases they take on. He intersperses them with bodyguard duty and other types of cases, even the occasional canine protection. He doesn't want to burn them out."

She couldn't have heard that right. "Canine protection?"

"Many people treat their pets as members of the family. Most of the time, dognapping is less risky than kidnapping."

They waited for the jet to stop. Within five minutes, a broad-shouldered man about Liam's height walked down the stairs to the concourse.

Cade placed his hand on Sasha's lower back and guided her forward. "Good to see you, Nico. Sorry your team had to detour."

"Our mission is a protection detail this time. We'll arrive in plenty of time." He tipped his head toward Sasha. "Introduce me to your friend."

"Sasha Ingram, this is Nico Rivera, leader of the Shadow unit."

Nico smiled and handed Sasha the phone. "I'm glad to finally meet you. Ramsey won't shut up about you when he's in town. I was beginning to think you were a figment of his imagination."

Sasha grinned. "Next time we see each other, you'll have to tell me what he's saying about me."

"Deal. It's all good, though. My team would love to meet you, Sasha. Do you mind?"

"I'd like that." She and Cade followed Nico up the stairs and into the cabin of the Lear jet. Three men and one woman glanced up.

"Look at that." The speaker shook his head. "She is real."

"Unless she's a ringer," the woman said, sending the others into peals of laughter.

"Yeah, yeah. Laugh it up," Cade grumbled. "Sasha Ingram, meet Trace Young, Joe Gray, Ben Martin, and Shadow unit's medic, Sam Coleman. This is my girlfriend, Sasha."

Stunned silence greeted his pronouncement. Nico whistled. "You moved fast, Cade."

"Fast?" He scowled. "I've been wanting to date Sasha for months. Her kidnapping and rescue gave me the opportunity I needed to convince her to take a chance on me."

The Shadow unit turned as one to look at Sasha. "What happened?" Sam asked. Her eyes registered concern.

Cade gave the operatives a short version. By the end of the explanation, his friends were frowning.

"Black Dog, huh?" Joe rubbed his jaw. "Never thought I'd see them make a move on Fortress."

"We don't know if they are."

"They haven't bothered us before now. If this latest incident is tied to BD, I'd say we have another security firm attempting a hostile takeover."

"We'll return within the week," Nico said. "If things haven't resolved before then, we'll be glad to help."

"Do you think this will be over that fast?" Sasha asked Cade.

"The way things are playing out, you can count on it."

CHAPTER TWENTY

Cade glanced at his traveling companion. An invisible band squeezed his heart at the sight of Sasha slumped against the door. She had fallen asleep as soon as they left Knoxville.

He turned on his signal, took the exit for Highway 18, and guided them toward Otter Creek. As he drove. Cade contemplated the events of the past few days. He couldn't figure out why Sasha was at risk. Had he neglected to ask her the right questions? Not likely. Between him, Matt, Ethan, and Nick, Cade didn't see how one of them hadn't stumbled on the right question.

His hands tightened on the steering wheel. Sasha was right. She didn't engage in risky behavior. She shouldn't have been in danger. That left him with one possible conclusion. His gut knotted. He was the cause of her problems.

He needed to ask Zane if the bots he'd set up to troll for hits on the names of operatives had detected recent activity. It was also possible someone in his family told the wrong person where he was living now. They knew not to give out that information, but people made mistakes.

Since Durango was in town, Cade would teach fewer classes. His schedule tomorrow included another CQC session. This time he'd give pointers on defense against multiple opponents.

The lightened teaching load would leave him free to help Sasha in the morning. If Trent planned another afternoon training session, Cade would have to find someone to stay with his girlfriend if she worked the full day. One problem at a time. First, he had to get them home, then see how the rest played out.

Sasha moaned. Her brow wrinkled as though she was in pain.

Cade divided his attention between her and the black ribbon in front of them, concerned she might be battling another headache. She didn't complain about the aches and pains, but Gerard aggravated the original injury. Had he hurt her worse than she admitted?

"No," Sasha murmured. "Don't hurt him."

Another glance told him she was still asleep. When tears trickled down her cheeks, Cade couldn't handle it anymore. He cupped her wet cheek. "Sasha, wake up."

She sighed and opened her eyes. "Are we home?"

"In twenty minutes. Were you having a bad dream?"

Sasha froze. "How did you know?"

Cade pulled his hand away and held it up for her to see the moisture against his palm. "You were crying in your sleep. What were you dreaming about?"

"Doesn't matter. It wasn't real."

"Sasha."

"Did I say anything?"

"You were begging for someone not to be hurt. Tell me." She hesitated so long, Cade wondered if she would answer.

"I dreamed a man captured us and he threatened to kill you. I'm glad it wasn't real."

"One day it might be, though. My job isn't a safe one. Sometimes people we care about become pawns for those who want revenge against the operatives."

"Doesn't Fortress protect your identities?"

"They have multiple layers of protection in place. Nothing is foolproof. Zane has bots set up to scour the Internet for mention of our names, including our aliases. Most of the time, the problem is the families. One slip sets a cascade in motion. Z works fast to seal breaches in security and he's constantly developing new and better cybersecurity, but information can leak to the wrong people."

"Did Emily have difficult with your job secrecy?"

Had to admire his girlfriend's mind. She was sharp. "She hated it. Emily complained she couldn't talk to her friends for fear she would slip and say something she shouldn't."

Sasha broke the seal on her bottle of water. "There are creative ways to avoid sharing information without making your friends suspicious. I've heard Durango's wives do it. No one questions their answers."

"Can you handle the half-truths you'll be forced to tell if you're with me?"

"I'm with you by choice. To protect you, I'll learn to be an expert at giving vague answers and deflecting questions to a safer topic. I'm assuming these security breaches aren't frequent or Zane wouldn't have a job at Fortress. If we're in a situation like I dreamed, what should I do?"

"I'll handle it."

"No. We'll handle it together. You make plans all the time for missions. I want a plan to follow."

"I'm trained to deal with that scenario. You aren't."

"I refuse to panic and melt into a puddle of tears."

"You've already proved that's not your default response to stress."

"Teach me what to do, Cade. I don't want to be a liability to you or your teammates. When Hart took me hostage, I felt helpless because I didn't know what to do. You teach trainees defensive moves. Teach me."

"You're serious?"

"I've never been more serious in my life."

Relief swept over him in a slow wave. She wasn't running. Sasha Ingram had serious grit. "I'll be glad to teach you a few moves to protect yourself."

"And we'll make a plan?"

He nodded. "Durango's wives also train with their husbands."

"I didn't know that." She sounded fascinated.

"Ivy Morgan was the first one to train with her husband, Alex. The rest of the women decided they should do something similar. Of course, Nate's wife, Stella, is a cop. She works with the other wives when Durango is out of town."

"Maybe I can train with them when you're deployed."

"Sounds like a great idea. I'll talk to Alex tomorrow. He's the one who sets up their training schedule."

"They can't be training much with Ivy and Josh's wife, Del, almost ready to have their babies."

"Those two aren't. The other three women are." He'd seen them in the gym at PSI several times over the past few weeks. Del and Ivy worked on breaking handholds while the others tussled on the mats with their spouses, learning how to escape attackers.

"Sounds like I'll have fun training with them. Do you know when you deploy again?"

"Sometime in the next two weeks." Cade needed to figure out who was after Sasha before then. He didn't want to leave town with her still in danger.

"I need defense lessons before you go."

"I'll find out when the other women are scheduled for another training session and let you know." Cade took the exit ramp into the outskirts of Otter Creek. He passed two vehicles on his way into town. As they drove through the town square, he glanced into the windows of Perk and noticed a light moving in the interior of the shop.

He frowned and turned into the alley behind the store.

"Why are we here?"

"I saw something odd through the window at Perk. I want to check it before we go to the house." He parked at the end of the alley, not wanting the SUV to be easily visible in case whoever was in the shop looked out the back door. "Hand me your keys and tell me your alarm code."

She did both and opened her door. "I'm going with you." She held up her hand. "I would feel more vulnerable out here alone."

He wanted to point out again that the vehicle was reinforced. Someone would have to do a lot of damage to reach her. On the other hand, he understood her sentiments. This was her business and she was fiercely protective of it. "Stay behind me. Do exactly what I tell you. Wait for me to come to you."

Cade rounded the hood and helped Sasha to the pavement. He closed the door with a soft snick. Clasping her hand, he led her down the alley toward her back door. He didn't need her keys. The door was ajar.

He let out a slow breath. Not good. At least one tango was inside the coffee shop, maybe more. Why break in? Money?

Sasha's grip tightened around his hand.

He turned and put a finger to his lips. Cade pulled his weapon, nudging Sasha directly behind him. Back pressed against the wall, he eased the door open. A soft rustling came from inside the main room of the store.

He peered into the kitchen. Empty. Cade pressed his lips to Sasha's ear. "Move as quiet as you can. I want to catch this clown." When he received a nod, he walked through the doorway with Sasha on his heels.

At the entrance to the dining room, he signaled Sasha to crouch by the wall. If the intruder was armed, he didn't want a stray bullet to hit her.

Cade spotted the intruder behind the counter. The man stood, shrugged into his backpack, and walked toward the front door. Cade holstered his weapon and, with silent steps, sprinted across the distance separating them.

At the last second, the intruder turned. His eyes widened and he ran for the large glass window.

Cade leaped on the man's back before he broke the glass and escaped. After a short scuffle, the stranger was subdued and cursed Cade. A pair of zip ties secured him. "Turn on the lights, Sassy."

A moment later, light flooded the coffee shop. Sasha gasped. "Cade."

He twisted to look in the direction she pointed. His blood ran cold. At opposite sides of the shop, digital clocks counted down the minutes until two bombs exploded.

CHAPTER TWENTY-ONE

The man who broke into Sasha's shop laughed. "You're too late. You'll never defuse my handiwork in time. This place will be gone in thirty minutes along with everything else on this side of the square. Run while you can."

Cade had to get his girlfriend out of here. "Sasha, unlock the front door and run to the police station. I need officers to cordon off the square and someone to take this clown off my hands. Have the desk sergeant call Ethan."

She caught the keys he tossed her, unlocked the door, and ran.

"Take me out of here." The thug at his feet thrashed. "I don't want to die in here."

Cade double-checked the zip ties. The man wouldn't free himself before the cops arrived. "You picked the wrong line of work."

"Hey, I just set them. I don't stick around and watch the results."

Cade studied the first bomb. This was going to be a bear to defuse. Worse, there were two of them. He needed more time or another pair of hands.

Running footsteps had him spinning toward the front door, weapon in hand. Nick Santana slipped inside the shop. "Sasha said you needed help. What's going on, Cade?" He stopped, stared at the bombs. "Oh, man."

"There's enough Semtex here to blow up the whole square."

Nick glared at the bomber who had gone pale. "Are you out of your mind?"

"That's not right," the man protested. "Only this side of the block is in danger."

Cade snorted as he pulled out his cell phone. "You don't have a clue what you're doing, sport. Take him out of here, Nick, and make sure Sasha doesn't come back before it's clear. Evacuate people from Delaney's." The rest of the businesses should be vacant this time of night.

"Copy that." Nick yanked the bomber from the floor. "Let's go." As he marched the man out the door, he read the bomber his rights.

Cade called the one man he knew could help him save the town.

"Armstrong."

"It's Cade. I need help, fast."

"Where?"

"Perk. Some yahoo set up two bombs in there with enough Semtex to take out the center of town."

"Crap. How much time?"

"Twenty-five minutes and counting."

"Two minutes." Nate ended the call.

Cade studied the bombs. He considered various options to dismantle them and tossed aside all but one. The bombs couldn't be moved before they were defused. Any movement would detonate them.

He ran to his SUV and grabbed the bag containing his tools. By the time he stepped into the main room of Perk, Nate was running full tilt across the square with his bag slung over one shoulder.

The operative entered the shop, his gaze tracking to the bombs on both side of the counter. He studied them a few seconds, then whistled. "We'll have to defuse them at the same time."

"That's why I called you. I didn't have time to coach a newbie."

Nate slid his bag off his shoulder and knelt in front of the bomb on the left. "Lucky Durango was in town."

"Yeah." But was it luck? Cade's gut said otherwise. But what was the purpose? Whoever ordered this attack on Sasha's place had a reason. Was this Black Dog's handiwork? If the terror campaign was aimed at Cade, why bring Durango into the mix?

He knelt in front of the bomb on the right and began to trace wires. Cade and Nate worked in silence a few minutes.

"Third black wire from the back?" Nate asked.

"Yeah."

"On three." The other EOD man counted down.

Cade cut the wire. No detonation and the clock continued to run. "First wire at the front."

"Copy. On three."

Another snip. Clock counted down the remaining time. Sweat stung his eyes. Cade wiped his forehead with his sleeve. They were running out of time. "Last black wire against the timer."

"Wait." Nate leaned in close to the bomb, his attention riveted on something. "That wire is connected to a dead man's switch. It's hidden so well I almost missed it." A pause. "The wire next to that one is connected to the timer."

Cade scooted around to the side and peered at the assembled spaghetti of wires. He visually traced the wire in question. "Roger that."

Nate counted down.

Snip.

Both operatives breathed a sigh of relief when the timer froze at the ten-second mark. So close. "Thanks, Nate."

"Who has it in for Sasha?"

"I don't know."

Nate studied his expression a moment. "You're worried this is connected to you, not her."

Cade shoved a hand through his hair. "Nothing else makes sense. I planned to ask Z if any threats had surfaced."

"Anything connected to you would trigger a red flag right now."

Still, he had to be sure.

"What about Black Dog? Do they have a problem with you?"

He shrugged. "No more than with the rest of Fortress."

Nate frowned. "Weird."

Cade worked the Semtex free and disengaged the electronics to be sure the device was safe to transport. He glanced at Nate in time to see his friend lay the Semtex aside and start work on the electronics.

A moment later, Nate finished the dismantling process. "Ethan will want the pieces for evidence. Need me for anything else?"

Cade shook his head. "Go home and sleep."

"Not much chance of that. I have to be at PSI by 5:00 to have breakfast ready in time for the trainees." Nate stood and shouldered his bag. "I think I'll stop by Delaney's for a takeout breakfast for Stella. She'll eat in the morning before work if she has food easy to heat." He squeezed Cade's shoulder as he passed.

Ethan walked into the coffee shop. "Talk to me."

Cade gave the police chief a rundown of how he and Sasha discovered the intruder and Cade's call to Nate for help. "The pieces are ready for transport. House this stuff in a vault. Once the trial is over, get rid of the Semtex. It's not a safe to keep long-term."

"Any idea where the Semtex came from?"

"I'd start with construction and demolition companies in the area, then widen your search."

"Would I be able to trace the explosive from its ingredients?"

Cade shook his head. "If a company is missing some of their supply, they should have reported the theft." He glanced at the clock on the wall. "Will Sasha be able to open on time?"

"Perk is a crime scene. Tell her to plan for tomorrow." Ethan shook Cade's hand. "Thanks. You saved a lot of lives and business. It's our turn to work now. Sasha's waiting for you in front of the police station. Nick's with her."

Cade shrugged into his Go bag and strode from the shop. He found Sasha where Ethan said she would be. As he walked across the square, her face lit up. She broke free from Nick and ran into his arms.

"Cade." Sasha kissed him, long and deep.

When she finally released him, he said, "Nate and I defused the bombs."

"I'm happy you're safe. I could rebuild if necessary, but I couldn't replace you."

"Good job, Cade." Nick clapped him on the back. "I'll grab my crime scene kit and go to work. Where's Ethan?"

"Stayed on site. You need something to transport the bomb components. I wouldn't hand the job to a nervous rookie."

"Ethan and I will handle it ourselves."

Cade turned to Sasha after the detective left. "Ready to go home now?"

Home. Great word that brought to mind a crackling fire on a cold winter day, hot coffee or chocolate, and Sasha in his arms. His heart skipped a beat. Not possible. He couldn't have fallen in love with her.

"Will I be able to open for business in the morning?"

He shook his head. "Ethan said to plan for tomorrow."

"Does that mean we can sleep in?"

"If you call 5:00 a.m. sleeping in."

"I'll take it."

He draped his arm over her shoulders and headed for his SUV. "You realize our relationship is no longer a secret, right?"

"What do you mean? We've already been on a date at the steakhouse."

"With Matt. People in the square saw us kissing. The news is sure to fire up Otter Creek's grapevine."

She snuggled closer to his side. "The single women in town knowing you're taken is a great idea." Sasha fell silent a moment. "Were the bombs meant for me or you?"

Yep, his girlfriend was sharp. "I can't say for sure."

"But?" she said, her tone wry.

"It's probably meant for me."

"Because you're EOD."

"The threat was aimed at my skill set. If I made a mistake or ran out of time, killing me would have been a bonus for the person who commissioned the bomber. Did you recognize him? Was he one of the men in the truck at the mall?"

"Those men had dark hair and swarthy skin. This one has Nordic coloring."

He stopped her at the alley. "Stay here while I check the SUV." Doubtful if someone planted a bomb on his vehicle while he was inside Perk. Still, he wouldn't take a chance with Sasha's safety or his own. If something happened to him, she was more vulnerable.

From a safe distance, he unlocked his vehicle, then opened the hatchback and dumped his Go bag inside. Cade checked his ride for trackers or a bomb. Clean.

Cade tucked Sasha inside the SUV. A moment later, he headed for home. The lights were on in the living room and a flickering blue light indicated the medic was still awake and waiting for them.

"About time you kids got home. You missed curfew." The medic's eyes glinted with amusement.

"Ran into a problem at Perk."

Matt straightened from the wall. "What happened?"

"Found a tango on site setting up two bombs."

"Well, you're still in one piece. You must have defused them successfully."

"With help from Nate. The bombs were set to go off unless they were defused at the same time."

"How much time was on the clock?"

"By the time I subdued the bomber, I had 28 minutes to work."

"A lifetime for you." Matt looked at Sasha. "You okay?"

"Other than needing to sit down, I'm great. My boyfriend is safe, my shop is still in one piece, and the bomber is in jail. A win all the way around."

"Do you need anything before you go to sleep?" Cade asked.

She shook her head. "I think a hot bath will rid me of the chill in my bones." Sasha pressed a kiss to Cade's lips. "I'll see you at 5:00. Good night, Matt."

"Sleep well, Sasha."

Cade watched her until she disappeared down the hall and closed herself into the bedroom. "Whoever ordered those bombs in Perk knows what I do, Matt."

"Made that pretty obvious. Sasha looks like she's holding up well."

"She won't be if I can't find a way to stop this. I don't want to lose her."

CHAPTER TWENTY-TWO

Sasha leaned her forehead against the shower wall a few minutes after five the next morning. Between the late hour going to bed and the nightmares while she slept, she felt as though she hadn't rested at all.

Sasha made quick work of the rest of her shower and stepped onto a plush blue bath mat. Once dressed, she peered at her reflection in the mirror and frowned. Wow, she looked rough. Circles under her eyes and a purple bruise where the bank robber's fist connected with her face.

She did what she could to hide the damage from the past few days. Sasha dressed, tied on her tennis shoes, and went to find Cade.

Once again, he was in the kitchen preparing to-go cups of coffee. Matt leaned against the counter, sipping from a mug in his hand.

Sasha walked into the kitchen and both men focused on her. "Good morning. Can I help?"

"Are you hungry?" Cade asked.

"I'll find something at PSI. I want to help Nate with breakfast."

"He'll appreciate it since I interrupted his night." Cade kissed Sasha and handed her one of the three to-go cups he'd prepared. "We're ready to roll."

Matt rinsed his empty coffee cup and placed it in the dishwasher. "I'll lock up and set the alarm."

Sasha grabbed her purse and waited for Cade to check his SUV. Once he was satisfied, he returned to the door for her.

"Same deal, Sassy. Straight to the SUV." He pulled her tight against his body and moved the toward the vehicle at a fast clip, scanning the area as they walked.

As soon as Matt was in his SUV, they drove to PSI. To his credit, Cade didn't try to break the silence, giving Sasha a chance to drink the coffee. By the time they parked in the lot behind PSI's main building, the brain fog had begun to dissipate.

While Matt greeted several trainees in the dining hall, Cade walked with Sasha into the kitchen.

Nate glanced up, smiled. "Morning. What are you doing in here, Sasha?"

"Need help?"

"Biscuits are ready to come out of the oven."

"I'll leave you to it," Cade said. He brushed his lips over hers. "Stay with Nate, his teammates, or one of mine. No one else."

"I'll be fine." She laid her hand over his jaw for a moment and placed a soft kiss on his mouth.

"I'll be close if you need me." With a pointed look at Nate, who nodded, he left.

Sasha found a safe place for her bag, grabbed oven mitts, and got to work. She and Nate fell into a fast rhythm, and kept the food trays full for the trainees and staff. "How do they eat this much food?" she asked near the end of the breakfast shift. She didn't think she'd ever fed that many people in one breakfast session.

Nate laughed. "We work them hard. The trainees burn off almost as many calories as most people consume in a day."

"Maybe. I think it's because a professional chef cooks for them." Everything Nate cooked tasted amazing. "I don't know how you do this all the time. My back, legs, and feet are killing me."

"I've seen the work you do in Perk. Right now, you're exhausted and still recovering from an injury. Your body is using everything it can to heal. Did you eat breakfast before you came?"

"Does coffee count?"

He slid her a look. "You know better than that. Set aside what you want and we'll eat as soon as the dining hall clears out."

"Deal. Did Stella mind the call out?" Sasha slid one of the baking sheets into hot, soapy water, and started washing. There weren't many left to do. Nate cleaned as he cooked, something she tried to do at Perk.

"Nope. She's used to it. Sometimes Durango is deployed in the middle of the night. Other times she's the one with a duty call in the early morning hours."

Sasha paused, her eyebrows winging upward. "In Otter Creek? The sleepiest burg in the world?"

"Not so sleepy at night. Criminals don't sleep. If there's more than one crime scene in Otter Creek, a second detective is called in. Nick, Stella, and Rod trade off answering those calls."

She smiled at the thought of Rod Kelter, another brother-in-law of Ethan's who loved her coffee and pastries. "Do you go with her?"

"If I'm in town. I shoot the breeze with the cops setting up a perimeter. More often than not, Josh is on duty. He loves the night shift. Says it's busy enough to keep him occupied."

"How does he balance working as a town cop and a Fortress operative?"

"We aren't deployed all the time. It's better now that Bravo is stationed here permanently."

"How often do you go out?"

Nate grabbed a towel and dried the baking sheets. "Once a month, sometimes twice, depending on how shorthanded Maddox is. You wondering how often Cade will be gone?"

"Deciding if I need to learn a new skill like knitting to keep me occupied when he's out of town."

"Nick's wife, Madison, is teaching Stella to knit. I'm sure she wouldn't mind teaching you." He studied her a moment. "Durango's wives help each other through our deployments. When Grace married Trent, they invited her to join them. You have a support network, Sasha. Take advantage of it."

Nice that he included her in their number. Would the other women accept her?

A commotion in the hall outside the kitchen drew their attention. Before Sasha could draw a breath, Nate shifted to stand in front of her, gun in his hand and pointed at the door.

The door slammed open. Gerard ran into the room and straight toward Sasha, his face crimson, eyes narrowed.

"This is all your fault." The former operative's shout echoed in the kitchen. "You're the reason I was fired."

Sasha backed against the counter, moving as far as possible to stay out of Nate's way. She needn't have bothered. Between one heartbeat and the next, the chef had Gerard face down on the floor. The man struggled against Nate's hold, screaming curses at him and Sasha.

Men poured into the kitchen from the dining hall. The first one through the door was Cade. Trent's expression darkened when he caught sight of Nate restraining Gerard.

While Quinn Gallagher, one of Nate's teammates moved to help the chef, Cade wrapped his arms around Sasha.

"Did he hurt you?" The cold light in his eyes hinted of retribution in Gerard's future.

Sasha shook her head.

Cade turned as Nate and Quinn hauled Gerard to his feet, still cursing. "How did you get into PSI?"

Gerard smirked.

Trent looked at Simon, who nodded and left the room. "Nate, find out everything."

The smirk faded as Quinn and Nate forced him toward the hall. "Where are you taking me?"

"You think you're tough going after an innocent woman," Nate said. "Let's see how you deal with me."

Blood drained from Gerard's face. "I know my rights. I want a lawyer."

"Do we look like the police?" Quinn shook his head. "You wanted to play in the big leagues. You got your wish."

"Somebody help me." The former trainee's voice rose to a shout. No one interfered. Trent fell into step behind them.

Sasha noticed Josh Cahill leaning one shoulder against the wall, his expression neutral. His teammates, Alex and Rio, stood on each side of him. She twisted in Cade's arms. "What happened? One minute Gerard is spouting off curses and vowing revenge. The next he's scared out of his mind."

"It's Nate," Alex said after the rest of the trainees were herded from the kitchen and into the gym for a session with Josh and Rio.

She frowned. "Gerard's afraid of Nate?" Sasha didn't understand. The chef was one of the sweetest men she'd met.

Cade's arms tightened around her. "Nate's a great guy and an amazing chef. He's also one of the best interrogators in the business. Alex is right behind him."

Surprised, her gaze shifted to Alex. Ivy adored her husband and he treated her with gentleness. Anyone with eyes could see Alex would do anything for his wife.

"The military trained us well, Sasha." Alex took a step toward her, stopped as though afraid she would bolt if he came too close to her. "We need to know if Gerard had anything more in mind than a stupid bid for revenge. Nate will obtain those answers for us."

"What about Josh? Won't this be a problem for a cop?"

"Nate knows how far he can go. He won't cross the line."

Alex watched her, waiting for her reaction to Cade's revelation about him. Did he expect her to reject him? Fat chance of that. He was a friend in the same line of work as Cade. She wouldn't reject either of them. "I should be able to open Perk tomorrow. Stop in. I'm trying out a lemon poppy seed muffin. I'd like your opinion on whether or not it should have a permanent place on the menu. The muffin and coffee are on me for being a taste tester."

The cautious look in his eyes disappeared, replaced by relief. "Can't pass up that deal. I'll be there if you can let me in a few minutes early. Josh has us running at 6:00 tomorrow."

"No problem."

With a nod, Alex went the same direction as Josh and Rio.

"Are you finished in here?" Cade asked.

"Almost. I have two more pans to wash. After that, I need to take care of the serving dishes in the dining hall."

"I'll get them." He kissed her. "Thank you."

"For what?"

"Not rejecting Alex."

"Never."

"Even if you found out he is a world-class sniper?"

Her eyes widened. "Wow. A shooter and an interrogator." Sasha wrapped her arms around his waist. "I know you are Bravo's EOD expert. What other special skill do you have?"

His lips curved. "Tracker."

"Is that how you found me in Crime Town?"

"Partly. I also watched Gerard's team. They ranged themselves close to the building where they hid you."

Nice. Her boyfriend was not only skilled, he was smart.

After another lengthy kiss, Cade retrieved the dishes in the dining room while she finished washing the final two baking sheets. Once the coffee dispensers and serving dishes were ready for use during lunch, Sasha followed Cade to the suite of offices.

At least that's what she'd assumed. Behind one of the doors, Simon sat in front of a bank of screens. On one of the screens, Sasha watched her arrival from earlier in the morning.

"Anything?" Cade moved a chair to the table for Sasha.

"Take a look." Simon indicated a screen in the middle of the array and tapped a few keys on the keyboard.

People came and went from the front entrance of the main building. Trainees and staff members. A female trainee Sasha remembered from Cade's combat class appeared on screen, walking through the lobby. She stopped and turned toward the front door. She opened it, talked to someone Sasha couldn't see. A moment later, Gerard pushed past the startled woman.

"Does he go anywhere besides the kitchen?" Cade asked.

"Nope. He knew where Sasha was. He must have gotten the information from Shelly."

"I'll talk to her." He pushed away from the table and held out his hand to Sasha.

They returned to the gym. Josh, Alex, and Rio turned at their entrance. Although the trainees were engrossed in their hand-to-hand combat techniques, most of them made note of their progress across the front of the gym.

Josh's eyebrow rose as they approached.

"Shelly," Cade said.

"You need Alex?"

"Wouldn't hurt."

Durango's leader signaled the sniper. Alex tilted his chin in acknowledgment and walked toward them.

Cade made eye contact with one trainee and motioned for her to follow him.

When the woman turned, Sasha recognized her from the video surveillance feed. Instead of puzzlement and shock in her gaze, it was fear.

Cade clasped Sasha's hand and led her from the gym. Shelly followed with Alex bringing up the rear. More than one of the trainees watched their progress across the floor with uneasiness in their eyes.

They walked down the hall toward the offices again. Somewhere down the corridor, Sasha heard a muffled shout of pain. When she jerked, Cade squeezed her hand and kept moving. They entered a room with a wooden table, four chairs, and no windows. On one side of the room was a mirror.

Sasha frowned. The room reminded her of interrogation rooms in movies or television programs. That's when she noticed the camera in the corner. She thought about what PSI trained their people to do. Maybe this was where they taught trainees how to resist interrogation if they were captured by the enemy.

Suspecting how skilled these men were, Sasha wouldn't want to be on the receiving end of an interrogation.

"Sit down, Shelly." Cade's voice was almost gentle. He motioned for Sasha to sit in the chair against the wall.

"Yes, sir," the woman whispered. She sat where Cade indicated, her gaze on the table in front of her.

Silence blanketed the room. The longer no one spoke, the more anxious Shelly grew. She fidgeted, her gaze darting to the door, looking for an escape.

Sasha didn't blame her. Her skin was crawling and she wasn't the one about to be questioned.

Finally, Cade flicked a glance at Alex who had positioned himself behind Shelly.

"Why did you let Gerard into the building, Shelly?" Alex asked.

She flinched and eased forward to put as much space as possible between them. "Tony wanted to apologize to Ms. Ingram for scaring her in Crime Town."

Disbelief filled Alex's gaze. "Did you know he'd been released from PSI and Fortress?"

A visible swallow, then, "Yes, sir."

"What's the rule, Shelly?"

"Never to admit unauthorized personnel into a building on our campus."

"Why?"

"Security threat."

"And yet you broke that rule."

"I didn't think anyone would mind. Tony wanted to make things right. He should be allowed to do that."

"The rules are in place for a reason. What did he say when you opened the door for him?"

Shelly's mouth gaped and she glanced at Alex over her shoulder for a moment before facing forward again. "How did you know it was me?"

Alex placed both hands on the back of her chair and leaned down to speak softly in her ear. "Answer my question. What did he say to you?"

The woman glanced at Cade, then Sasha, terror in her eyes.

The sniper slammed his palm on the table, making Shelly jump. "What did he say?" he snapped.

"He wanted to know where Cade's girlfriend was."

"Nothing else?"

"Just what I said before. He explained why it was important to let him in."

Cade placed both palms on the table and leaned toward her. "You're training to be a bodyguard. Why would you put Sasha's life in jeopardy?"

"He didn't want to hurt her, just explain his actions and offer an apology."

Sasha's boyfriend pulled out his cell phone and sent a text. A moment later, his phone chimed. "You don't believe he wanted to hurt Sasha." Cade tapped his screen and turned it so the trainees could see.

Sasha couldn't see the video from where she was sitting, but she heard the audio. The kitchen also had a security camera she hadn't noticed.

By the end of the segment Cade played for Shelly, tears ran down Shelly's face, her hand clamped over her mouth. "Does this look like he wanted to apologize to my girlfriend, Shelly?"

"I'm sorry. I didn't know. That's not what he said he wanted to do."

"He lied to you. Do you always believe everything people tell you?" Alex asked.

"Of course not."

"But you believed Gerard without questioning him even though you knew what you were doing was against protocol. Why, Shelly?"

Sasha felt for the woman. Cade and Alex were good at this. From their line of questioning, there was something they wanted her to admit.

The other woman hung her head.

"You're on thin ice, Shelly," Alex murmured. "If you want to continue working with Fortress, this is your last chance."

She swiped more tears from her face. "I love him."

"If Nate had stepped out of the kitchen at the wrong moment, Gerard could have done a lot of damage to Sasha before one of us stopped him."

A sharp knock interrupted them and Trent opened the door. His grim expression had Cade and Alex straightening. "We have a problem."

CHAPTER TWENTY-THREE

Cade ushered Sasha into the hall, followed by Alex. "What's wrong, Trent?"

"Gerard was flipped."

Alex scowled. "Who?"

"Black Dog."

Black Dog again. For a group new to the black ops community, the company's name popped up frequently in the wrong places.

"What connection does Gerard have with Black Dog?" Sasha asked.

"He was training with us and reporting to the other organization."

"Espionage." Cade rubbed his jaw. "Didn't expect that."

"How did our background check miss his connection to BD?" Alex asked.

"Black Dog recruited Gerard three weeks into his training and paid him cash each week. No record of the transaction so no trail for the Fortress geeks to follow."

"What was he supposed to report? We train bodyguards and operatives as does Black Dog even though they do a lousy job of training their employees."

Trent eyed Cade. "He was to report your movements."

Dread coiled like a snake in his gut. "Does Gerard know why they're interested in me?"

"Nope. He sent the information to an email address provided to him each week. I asked Zane to check into it. He says each address is a throwaway. As soon as the information on you was downloaded, the file and account were erased along with all the cyber tracks."

"Can Z uncover the identity of the person behind those accounts?"

"Doubt it. They're anonymous accounts routed through so many servers across the globe, tracing the origin is next to impossible and will take too much time given the pace of events unfolding in Otter Creek. He'll keep digging if we want him to continue."

Cade thought about it and rejected the idea. Z was too valuable a resource to waste on a fruitless search. "Is Nate still working on Gerard?"

A snort. "Not much point. He's a minnow in a big pond."

In other words, he'd been kept in the dark about Black Dog, given only enough information to complete his mission each week. "Payment?"

"Two hundred per week."

"The reward when Black Dog's objective was achieved?"

"His handler told Gerard if he brought his PSI team with him to Black Dog, he'd receive a big bump in salary and automatic leadership of his own unit."

Alex shook his head. "He hasn't earned his teammates' trust. If he had, they would have walked away from PSI when he and Gary left."

"He doesn't think it's necessary to earn their trust. In his mind, the most skilled member of the team should lead, period."

"Gerard has an inflated sense of his own skills. He would have ended up dead before the year was out."

Sasha slipped her hand into Cade's. "His death would solve Black Dog's problem. He can't demand higher position or pay when he isn't good enough to earn it if he's dead. Black Dog couldn't lose."

The heartlessness of their logic left a cold knot in Cade's stomach. "I want to talk to Gerard." He wouldn't be with him long, but he intended to make his point. Sasha's life might depend on it when Cade deployed with his teammates.

"No marks," Trent warned him. "I don't want Josh riding me if this ends up a police matter."

"Copy that." He turned and cupped Sasha's cheeks. "Stay here. I don't want you in the same room with Gerard. You can handle it, but I can't. Wait for me." When she nodded, he brushed his thumb over her lower lip and strode down the hall.

He gave a short knock to warn Nate and Quinn and stepped into the room. Gerard's face was pasty white, his hands fisted on the table. When he saw Cade, the muscles in his jaw twitched.

Nate's hand settled on Gerard's shoulder, making the trainee flinch. Quinn leaned against the wall, not taking his eyes off the turncoat.

"Did you come to gloat?" Gerard asked, his voice a growl.

Durango's EOD man shifted his hand. Gerard groaned, sweat beading on his face.

Cade watched him a moment in silence. When the trainee dropped his gaze to the table, Cade said, "I'm your target, not Sasha. You want to come at me, I'll pit my skills against yours any day." He placed his hands on the table. "Look at me, Gerard," he ordered.

The man's eyes snapped to his. Fear simmered in their depths.

Good. Exactly what Cade wanted. "If you ever go after my girlfriend again, I'll hunt you down and gut you. No one will find your body. If you want to live, steer clear of her. Am I making myself clear?"

No response.

Cade grabbed Gerard, hauled him from the chair, and slammed him against the wall. He pressed a forearm against the trainee's throat. When Gerard's face reddened, Cade let up enough for the man to gulp air. "What happens if you go after my woman again?"

"I'm dead," Gerard rasped.

Nate shifted and drew the other man's attention. "If Cade is deployed, Durango will watch over Sasha. Leave Otter Creek, Gerard, and don't come back."

"We'll be watching you," Quinn said. "We can find you at any time, and you won't see us coming until it's too late."

Cade stepped back from Gerard who slid to the floor, gasping for air and shaking. "Keep him here for another minute, then escort him off the property," he told Nate and left. He found Sasha with Trent.

Holding out his hand, he led his girlfriend to the kitchen where he had noticed the plate of food covered in plastic wrap. "Want hot chocolate to go with your breakfast?"

Sasha gave him a shaky smile. "How did you know it was mine?"

"Bird portions, Sassy."

"Hot chocolate sounds good. I'm not sure I can eat." She rummaged through the huge pantry and found packets of hot chocolate mix and a mug. After nuking water, she dumped the packet contents into the mug.

While she stirred the mix, Cade reheated her breakfast and poured himself a mug of coffee from a carafe Nate kept filled for the staff. "Come sit with me."

"Don't you have a class to teach?"

"I have a few minutes before I'm on duty." They sat at a table near the gym entrance.

"What happened with Gerard?"

How much should he tell her? Cade didn't want to hide the truth from Sasha. This was the time to learn if she could handle the reality of his job before he fell hopelessly in love with her. "I told him if he targeted you again, I'd kill him and hide his body where no one would find it."

"How did he respond?"

"Before or after I shoved him against a wall?"

She blinked. "After."

"He slid to the floor after I released him. Aren't you going to ask if I meant the threat?"

"You don't say things you don't mean."

Cade captured her mouth with his. "You know me better than Emily ever did."

Her cheeks flushed. "I've made a study of all things Cade."

Delighted with her, he laughed. "That's fair since I've made a study of all things Sasha." Cade's smile faded. "I'm crazy about you, Sasha Ingram."

She cradled his face between her palms. "I feel the same about you. What will Gerard do?"

"He's to leave Otter Creek. We'll keep track of him. If he tries to hurt you again, I'll take care of him. I can't lose you, Sassy. I'd never recover." He pressed a kiss to the center of her palm. "Will you give me a real chance? Will you let me prove I'm worth the risk?"

"You have nothing to prove. I want this relationship to be real as much as you. Eight months I've wanted a chance with you. I'm taking it."

A scorching kiss this time. Cade forced himself to release her and nudged the plate closer. "Eat a few bites at least before my class starts."

Fifteen minutes later, Sasha followed Cade to the gym. He indicated a nearby chair. "You can sit there and watch. If you'd like to participate, I have two trainees who would be good training partners."

"I'd love to learn if they don't mind working with me."

When the trainees arrived, Cade introduced Sasha to Kat and Dixie. The women agreed to work with his girlfriend. "What do we focus on?" Kat asked.

"Escaping choke holds." He planned to teach her defensive moves himself.

After they started teaching Sasha, he began teaching the rest of the class. Soon, the large room was filled with grappling trainees trying to get the upper hand on their partners. Cade corrected holds, adding advanced techniques for those ready.

He noticed one trainee sucker punch his partner. Cade's eyes narrowed. The injured man clamped a hand to his nose as Cade approached.

"Price, report to the infirmary." Matt was on medic duty this morning.

"Yes, sir." With a final glare at his partner, Price left.

Cade rounded on Ford. "What was that?"

"He moved the wrong way."

"I watched the whole incident. Try again, the truth this time."

"He whines about how bored he is, that he's ready for advanced training."

"You tested his reflexes?"

"If he's that advanced, he should have stopped me."

Cade moved into him, his face inches from the trainee. "Your reflexes should have been good enough to pull back at the last second. You didn't. You were more interested in hurting Price. You chose to land the punch."

An insolent shrug was Ford's response.

Cade shifted into fighting stance. "Let's see what you've got."

A hint of glee lit the trainee's eyes. By the end of the class, he was gasping for air and bruised from the blows Cade had landed.

He stepped away from Ford. "You have thirty minutes before your next session. Hit the track and pound out three miles, full speed."

Ford's jaw dropped. "Sir?"

"You have a hearing problem, trainee?"

"No, sir!"

"Move."

The rest of the class fell silent as Ford raced from the gym. He eyed them. "You have time for a water and snack break before your class with Rio. Fair warning. If you're not familiar with all the uses of duct tape, prepare to be amazed." Laughter rippled through the gym as trainees filed from the room.

Kat, Dixie, and Sasha waited for him at the other end of the gym. "How did you do?" he asked Sasha.

"I don't know how skillful I was, but I had fun."

Dixie grinned. "Don't let her fool you. Sasha did great. By the time you finished mopping the floor with Ford, she was breaking every hold we used without thinking about it."

Outstanding. "Thanks for working with her."

"What's the deal with Ford and Price?" Kat asked.

"Arrogance and stupidity on both sides. Got a problem with my handling of the situation?"

The trainees shook their heads. "Price could use similar treatment when he heals," Dixie said. "At the rate he's going, no team will accept him in their ranks."

"Noted. Grab some water and your duct tape."

Both women grinned and left.

"I bet you need water, too." Sasha tilted her head back to look him in the eyes.

"There's water in the infirmary. I want to check on Price."

Cade laid his hand on Sasha's lower back as they walked through the bustling dining hall and down the corridor. The infirmary was empty aside from his friend. Matt glanced up when they entered. "What's the verdict on Price?" Cade asked.

"Broken nose. I set it, gave him pain killers, and dismissed him from classes for the rest of the day. What happened?"

"He paired up with Ford for training exercises. Price complained about wanting more advanced techniques. Ford tested Price's reflexes and didn't pull his punch."

Matt rolled his eyes. "How is Ford? Will I be seeing him in here later?"

"He's running three extra miles at the moment. He'll need ice packs."

Amused, the medic shook his head. "You worked with him after Price left. Did you pull your punches?"

"He's a tough guy. He can take what I dished out." Cade grinned. "He'll feel every blow in a few hours."

"I heard you had some excitement earlier, Sasha." Matt grabbed two bottles of water from the refrigerator and handed one each to Cade and Sasha. "I was in here bandaging a sprained ankle."

"Good news spreads fast."

He smiled. "I'm glad you're safe. What did you do while your boyfriend taught Ford a lesson?"

"Kat and Dixie worked with me on escaping choke holds."

"What did you think?"

"I had fun and they were patient."

A cell phone signaled. All three checked their phones. "It's mine," Sasha said. A smile broke out on her face as she studied her screen. "I can go into Perk after noon. Ethan says I can open if I want, but I'll probably need to spend the afternoon cleaning."

"I'll talk to Trent about taking the afternoon off."

"You need to train with your team, especially now that Bravo is covering for Durango."

True. He hated to let her out of his sight now that he knew she was in danger. Black Dog wouldn't hesitate to use Sasha to reach him. "If one of the members of Durango can go with you, I'll train with my team." Otherwise, no dice.

Quinn agreed to accompany Sasha and help with the cleaning.

"Don't leave the shop for any reason without Quinn. He volunteered to be slave labor. Use him." Cade brushed her mouth with a quick kiss. "I'll swing by Perk after we finish. We'll pick up dinner from Delaney's."

"Sounds great. Don't worry, please. I'll be fine."

CHAPTER TWENTY-FOUR

"*I'll be fine.*" Famous last words, Sasha thought as she stared at the mess in her coffee shop. Black powder had settled like soot over everything. "How could they make this much of a mess?"

Quinn Gallagher, her voluntary bodyguard and cleaner for the afternoon, whistled. "Beats me. If I made a mess like this at the house, Heidi would have my hide. This will take a while to clean."

Hours. She was looking at hours of work. She had looked forward to dinner with Cade and Matt. Her dinner would be a midnight snack. "I hope I have enough cleaning supplies."

"If you don't, we'll call Ethan and have one of his cops pick up what we need. His people made the mess. They can run an errand."

In the kitchen, the black powder wasn't as thick, but still disheartening to see. Sasha wished there were three of her to tackle the job. She tossed her purse into the cupboard and grabbed her cleaning supplies. "I have large rubber gloves you can use."

"Hand them over and let's get started." He pulled out his phone and sent a text, then went to work.

Sasha scrubbed her sink, counters, and cabinets while Quinn mopped the floor. Before starting on the appliances, she heard voices in the dining room.

Customers? She hated to turn them away. Maybe she could offer a discount for their orders tomorrow.

Sasha followed Quinn into the other room and skidded to a stop. The shop was full of trainees and the other members of Durango with the exception of Nate, all armed with gloves, cleanser, sponges, buckets, and mops.

She turned to Quinn. "You arranged this, didn't you?"

The operative lifted one shoulder. "Cade would have done it had he known what you faced. You're one of us now, Sasha. We help each other."

"Thank you." She hugged him, called out instructions and thanks to the new cleaning crew, and returned to the kitchen. When footsteps sounded behind her, she turned to see Kat and Dixie.

"What needs cleaning in here?" Dixie asked.

"The front of the appliances, doors, and knobs. I have to check the pantry for supplies and to see if the police have been in there."

They had. Thankfully, she kept everything in easy-to-clean containers, but the shelves were full of them. Kat and Dixie finished first and joined her in cleaning the pantry. Working with them made the time pass fast.

They were interested in her relationship with Cade. Sasha was careful, not sure how much information was safe. She enjoyed having something positive to discuss.

When they finished in the kitchen, Sasha and the two women returned to the front. The volume of work the operatives and trainees had finished amazed her. Sasha might have a chance to eat dinner with her boyfriend after all.

At six, she shooed her volunteer labor force out the door with the promise of free coffee the next time they were in Perk. Quinn and his teammates remained behind. Between them, they finished the last of the cleaning.

Sasha climbed on a barstool, grateful to sit down. She might beg Cade for another shoulder massage. "I would still be working if you hadn't called in reinforcements, Quinn."

"We're glad to help." He turned as the rest of Durango arranged themselves nearby. "You and Cade, huh?"

"Do you mind?"

His brows drew together. "Of course not. He's a good man who has been nuts about you since he moved to town. I can't think of anyone I'd rather see happy than Cade. He took a bullet for me once. Did he tell you?"

Shock rolled through Sasha. "What happened?"

"Mission over in the Sandbox. I was cut off from my unit. I knew my teammates were coming, but the odds on me staying alive until they arrived weren't good. A Ranger unit fought through enemy lines to reach me. I didn't know a Taliban soldier had me in his sights. Cade dove on top of me to knock me from the line of fire. Took a bullet to the leg saving my hide."

Josh chuckled. "That's the same op when I took a bullet to the thigh."

"That mission changed our lives," Alex said. "After we healed from our injuries, we decided as a unit to leave the military."

"Best decision we ever made." Rio stretched his legs out in front of him. "Delta was hard on our bodies and minds. It was time to pursue other options."

Sasha's breath caught in her throat. Durango was a Delta unit. She'd read about them in books, but never thought she'd meet one. Turned out she knew five. She considered what she'd learned from their wives since opening Perk. They were careful not to give specifics.

Sasha was a good listener, though, and with this new information had a good idea of this unit's capabilities.

"Does Maddox hire units like yours often?"

"If he can," Josh said. "Some former military personnel want to leave that life behind. When Maddox pitched the idea, we decided we all joined Fortress or none of us would."

"Why?"

"We worked together a long time," Alex said. "We have each other's backs no matter what."

"We're more than teammates and friends," Quinn added. "We're brothers."

Before she could respond, a rapid-fire knock drew her attention to the door. Sasha smiled and slid from the stool.

"Who is he?" Josh asked, his gaze locked on the man waiting to be admitted.

"My brother. It's okay. He would never hurt me."

The Otter Creek cop didn't look convinced by her assurance. The rest of his team stood and spread out.

Appreciating their vigilance, Sasha unlocked the door with Quinn at her side. "What are you doing here, Dean?"

His gaze swept the interior of the shop, assessing each operative. "What's going on, Sash? Are you all right?"

"I'm fine."

He looked skeptical at her words. "Who are these men?"

"Friends. If you're looking for coffee or a snack, I don't have anything ready. Stop in tomorrow."

"Heard you had more trouble. What happened?"

She glanced at Josh who shook his head slightly. "Someone broke into the shop overnight. We were cleaning up the aftermath."

He folded his arms across his chest. "You expect me to believe that?" He inclined his head toward the operatives watching the exchange. "These men aren't just friends, little sister. They look and act like bodyguards. What kind of trouble are you in?"

Sasha stiffened. "I haven't done anything wrong."

"Nothing except involve yourself with the wrong man."

Fury boiled in her veins. "Stop."

"You can't tell me you had problems like this before you started dating Ramsey. He's bad news. Kick him to the curb."

Her fists clenched. "And if I don't?"

"I don't want to see you hurt, Sasha, and you will be if you stay with a loser like him. He collects enemies who don't care about collateral damage."

The front door opened again. This time Cade walked in followed by Matt. Cade's eyes darkened when he saw Dean. He moved to Sasha's side. "What are you doing here, Ingram?"

"Giving my sister some friendly advice." Dean shifted his gaze to Sasha. "Don't forget what I said. Cut your losses and ditch this bum. I'd hate to call our parents to tell them you're dead because of Ramsey."

Pain speared Sasha's heart. The brother she'd grown up with had never been bitter and filled with hatred. "Cade used to be your friend. He hasn't changed who he is. Why are you saying hateful things about him?"

"Because it's his fault my wife is dead." Dean stormed from the store.

Sasha turned to Cade and saw he was as stunned by the news of Emily's death as she was. She wrapped her arms around his waist, hurting for him.

"That man has a lot of hate inside." Rio leaned back against the coffee bar. "How well do you know him, Cade?"

"We were best friends until I went to Ranger school. Dean didn't make the cut."

"Watch your back," Josh said. "Ingram is dangerous with that much strong emotion roiling inside."

"Do you know what he does for a living now?" Alex asked.

Cade shook his head.

"Find out." Josh started for the door. "And do it fast." As he reached for the knob, multiple cell phones signaled through the room.

Sasha frowned as all the men pulled phones from their pockets.

Alex was the first one to react. Blood drained from his face. "There's a hostage situation at Otter Creek Community College. Ivy's teaching a class right now."

Josh held up his hand. "Ethan activated Durango and Bravo. Let's go."

CHAPTER TWENTY-FIVE

Cade turned to Sasha. "We have to go."

She nodded as the other men raced from the shop. "My purse is in the kitchen."

While she was gone, Cade turned off the lights and made sure everything was ready for Sasha to open the shop in the morning. His girlfriend ran into the dining area with her purse slung crosswise on her body.

As Cade sped toward the community college, he considered the safest option for Sasha. The college would be chaotic, an easy place for someone to take advantage of the distraction and zero in on Sasha. "You'll be safe if you stay inside the SUV."

Her soft hand squeezed his arm. "Focus on what you need to do. I'll be waiting in the SUV when you're finished."

He squeezed her fingers. "I don't know how long this will take." Cade held her hand a moment before returning his hand to the wheel. He weaved through traffic until it thinned, then floored the accelerator.

When they arrived on campus, he parked in the center of a semi-circle of PSI vehicles. Matt moved his vehicle behind Cade's.

Relief swept through Cade. Although his ride was reinforced, Sasha would have better protection with PSI vehicles surrounding his. He pressed a quick kiss to her lips and exited the SUV.

Cade opened the hatchback and suited up. "Sit tight, Sassy. I'll be back."

"Be careful."

"Yes, ma'am. Don't leave the SUV for anyone but the members of Bravo, Durango, Ethan, or Nick, even if you know them. Lock the doors." He shut the hatchback, waited for the locks to engage, then joined his team at the front of Ethan's SUV.

"The perps are holed up in the Arts building in room 314. Amphitheater setup with the instructor's platform at the front of the room. Ten students. One teacher." Ethan paused, fury burning in his gaze. "Ivy Morgan is the instructor."

Alex was gearing up with Josh at his side, the sniper's face devoid of expression. Oh, man. Whoever was stupid enough to take Ivy hostage would be lucky to survive this night. And Cade wouldn't take odds on that happening.

Alex was a world-class sniper with endless patience and fiercely protective of the woman who owned his heart. He'd become more protective when he learned Ivy was carrying their first child. Any goon who hurt Ivy signed his own death warrant.

"Why activate Bravo and Durango?" Trent asked.

"We have eight perps in that room with ten college kids and a woman due to give birth any day now. Can't afford stray shots. I wanted two medics on scene in case of injuries needing immediate treatment, particularly to Ivy. My cops are good, but they're not good enough for this situation. You're my SWAT teams."

Alex and Josh joined the group of operatives.

Ethan spread a schematic of the Arts building on the hood of his vehicle. He pointed out the two doors of the room in question and the location of the gunmen and hostages. "Four men have the students and Ivy at gunpoint. Two are guarding the doors. Two are watching for approaches to the building from the windows." He pointed to an entrance on the far side of the building. "Enter here to avoid being seen."

"Orders?" Josh said.

"Take them alive if you can. Your priority is the safety of the hostages. As of this moment, you're on a Fortress mission and an inactive Otter Creek police officer. Clear?"

"Yes, sir."

Cade exchanged glances with Matt at those words. The constraints Josh faced as a police officer had been removed.

"My officers will maintain a perimeter. Nearby campus buildings have been evacuated. Do what you have to. However, my budget would appreciate minimal repair bills. Josh, you and Trent put together a plan and bring me into the loop. When you're ready, I'll try to open a dialog with the gunmen. No promises. I've been unsuccessful to this point. We'll act as though we're mobilizing to breach the building in view of those windows and keep them occupied."

Cade frowned. Why had the men taken Ivy and her students hostage, yet not demanded anything? Made as much sense as the bank robbers who dumped the money in the alley behind the bank.

Josh handed Ethan an ear piece. "Turn it on now. You'll hear the plan and its execution."

With a nod, the police chief slipped the communications device in his ear and left to confer with Nick and a number of his other officers.

Durango's leader turned to the operatives. He and Trent laid out the plan and timing. "Comments or suggestions?"

Josh asked. When the men shook their heads, he looked at Alex and Liam. "Find the best line of sight, and get eyes on that room. I want a sit rep yesterday."

"Yes, sir." The two men jogged away.

"Let's move," Josh said to the remaining members of the teams.

With one final glance to be sure Sasha was safe, Cade headed for the entrance Ethan recommended. The door was locked.

Trent pointed at Cade who grabbed his lock picks and went to work. Seconds later, the operatives surged into the building, AR-10s up and ready. Using hand signals, Trent motioned his team to the south stairwell while Josh's team moved toward the stairs at the opposite end of the hall.

On the third floor, Trent activated his comm system. "Bravo in position."

"Copy," came Josh's response. A moment later, he said, "Durango in position. Nate, Cade, prepare the charges."

Both men acknowledged the order. Cade slid the pack from his back and assembled the small bomb.

"Sniper 1 in position," Alex murmured.

"Sniper 2 in position," Liam said.

"Sit rep."

"Two at the windows, watching the parking lot. One in front of each door. Small window in the top quarter of the doors. Their line of sight is limited. Should be able to reach the doors without detection if you stay low," Liam reported. "The other four gunmen are spread out around the students and teacher."

"Hostages?"

"Huddled on the floor in two rows in the center of the seating section twenty feet from the teaching platform," Alex said. "Ivy is in the second row with male students on either side of her." His voice grew thick. "Looks like they're protecting her and the baby."

"Ice in your veins," Josh reminded his friend.

A pause, then, "Yes, sir." In those seconds of silence, he'd wrenched his emotions under control.

"Alex, Liam, acquire your targets. Nate, Cade, go."

The EOD men moved silently from the stairwells to the doors with their teammates keeping eyes and weapons on the room in case the gunmen noticed the activity. Cade attached the C-4 and blasting cap to the door at the front of the classroom while Nate wired the second door.

When he finished, Cade whispered, "EOD 1 ready."

A moment later, Nate reported his door was ready.

"Copy," Josh said. "Sniper 1, report room status."

"No change."

"Ethan, go."

"Roger that." Over the comm system, the operatives heard Ethan give his officers orders to move three police cars closer and break out the rifles while he called the classroom again.

A minute later, he said, "Josh, no dice on the phone call. I'm breaking out the bullhorn. Cutting power now."

"Copy. Bravo, Durango, into position."

The operatives moved to their respective doors, NVGs giving them clear vision in the darkness.

Alex murmured, "Ethan is moving into position." A pause, then, "Gunmen at the doors have turned toward the bank of windows."

"Snipers, EOD, on my count. Three, two, one, now."

Cade and Nate blew open the doors as the snipers shot the gunmen standing at the windows. Josh and Trent tossed flashbangs into the room, then the teams rushed inside.

Gunfire erupted. Shouts of pain and screams filled the classroom. In less than two minutes, five gunmen were dead and the other three were in restraints.

"Ethan, lights," Josh said.

The operatives shoved up their NVGs as light flooded the room.

"Josh." Alex's voice broke.

"You're clear. Liam, stay in position."

"Roger that."

Matt checked the students for injuries while Rio hopped a row of seats to reach Ivy. He motioned for the boy who'd wrapped his arms around Ivy when the shooting started to move aside.

"Are you hurt, Ivy?" he asked.

While the medics tended to the hostages, Cade and Nate checked the room for explosives. The rest of their teams searched the gunmen for weapons.

A moment later, Alex ran into the room. "Ivy!"

"Alex." His wife's voice was thick with tears.

Rio looked up. "No injuries, Alex, but she needs to go to the hospital."

The sniper's face whitened as he handed Josh his sniper rifle and rushed down the side aisle toward his wife. "You said she wasn't injured."

A grin from the medic. "She's not, but your baby is anxious to meet you. Ivy is in labor."

The students cheered and called out encouragement.

Between them, Rio and Alex helped Ivy from the floor and into the aisle where Alex picked up wife, cradling her in his arms as he hurried from the room with Rio on his heels.

Ethan strode into the room with Nick Santana. He took in the situation at a glance. "Move the students, Nick. There's a reception area on the first floor large enough to provide comfortable seating for them. Take their statements."

"Yes, sir."

Using his radio, the police chief requested three officers to accompany the cuffed men to the hospital, then called the coroner. That done, he turned his attention to the carnage. "This room will take hours to process." Ethan rubbed the back of his neck. "I want to transport the bodies soon. Would Zane run pictures of the gunmen to ID them?"

Josh grinned. "Since this was a Fortress operation, he'd be happy to oblige."

"I'll send Stella to the hospital to take photos of the other three. I need statements from all of you before you leave the scene."

Cade flinched. Every cell in his body urged him to check on Sasha. He didn't want to leave her alone much longer.

"Is the room safe for the crime scene techs?"

"Yes, sir." Josh shifted his hold on Alex's .408 Chey Tac rifle. "I'll take the teams' statements at the SUVs. Sasha is on site."

Ethan nodded. "Email the statements to me. If I have questions, I'll track you down. Bring your sniper off the roof. Good job, all of you. The only casualties were five gunmen. No civilian injuries. Thanks for your service to Otter Creek."

Josh signaled the operatives to follow him.

Cade caught up with Durango's leader on the stairs. "We need to update Ethan on Gerard."

A nod. "I'll take care of it after I have the statements. I'm on shift in three hours. With the activity here, I can't be late. Someone has to guard the town while most of the force is here. Let's hope the town's criminals plot mayhem tonight instead of act on it."

They returned to the knot of PSI vehicles. Someone in a dark uniform stood by Cade's SUV on the passenger side. The man glanced over his shoulder and walked away.

"Stop!" Cade broke away from his unit and ran after the man. A fire truck drove by, blocking Cade's line of sight. As soon as the truck moved, he searched for the man, but he'd disappeared, lost in the chaos of the parking lot.

CHAPTER TWENTY-SIX

Cade jogged back to his SUV and found Sasha standing beside the vehicle with Trent and Liam on either side of her. As soon as she saw Cade, she broke away from his teammates and threw herself into his arms.

He wrapped his arms around Sasha. Cade breathed deep, inhaling the peach scent of her hair. "Are you okay?"

She nodded, tightening her grip around his neck.

"What did he want?"

"He claimed you were injured and had asked for me."

"Did you recognize him?"

She shook her head. "He wore the same black fatigues and t-shirts the operatives wear at PSI. His shirt had your logo. If you hadn't warned me to stay inside the vehicle except for the people you trusted with my safety, I would have gone with him. He was convincing."

Cade frowned. Someone could have copied the design of their logo onto a black t-shirt. What if it wasn't a copy? He needed to notify Trent and Josh, then ask Zane to run searches on the trainees and staff.

Another possibility occurred to him. What if the t-shirt came from Gerard or Gary Westbrook?

"Everything okay?" Trent asked.

"We might have another problem."

His team leader dragged a hand down his face. "As if we haven't had enough lately. Talk to me."

Cade discussed his concerns with the Navy SEAL.

"We have to find Gerard and Westbrook, fast."

"Should I contact Zane?"

"Have Z call me with the information. Josh goes on duty in a few hours, and he'll be concerned about Ivy as well as his wife. I'll update him when we know something definitive."

"Yes, sir." Cade kissed Sasha's temple.

"Ramsey, you're next," Josh called.

He kept an arm around his girlfriend as he went to Durango's leader and gave his statement. He followed the rapid-fire report style he learned in the military, a style familiar to the Delta warrior. Throughout the process, Sasha remained quiet.

When Cade finished, Josh dismissed him. "Go rest. I'll expect coffee from my favorite barista early tomorrow morning."

Sasha smiled. "I'll have it ready along with muffins for you and Del."

Durango's leader chuckled. "My wife will appreciate it. She swears she's carrying voracious triplets who never stop eating."

Cade's eyebrows shot up. "Are you expecting multiples?"

A scowl. "I barely survived my sisters."

Sasha laughed. "I hear multiple births run in the family."

He narrowed his eyes. "Take your woman home, Ramsey. She has a mean streak."

Cade saluted and walked Sasha to his SUV, Matt following with his mike bag slung over his shoulder.

"I'll be on your six," his friend murmured. He moved his SUV out of Cade's way.

As he drove, Cade wondered what Sasha thought of the incident in the school. She didn't seem disturbed by how events unfolded in the rescue. Throughout the drive to his home, Sasha remained silent although she kept her fingers laced with his. That had to be a good sign.

He ushered his girlfriend into the house and deactivated the alarm. "Stay with her," he told Matt.

Sig in hand, Cade searched his house for intruders. When sure Sasha was safe, he returned to the kitchen to find her prepping his coffee maker for the early morning alarm. She finished the coffee preparations and set the timer. "I'll give you breakfast at Perk."

Sasha needed to sleep, but he wanted to spend a little more time with her. Yeah, he was crazy about this woman and hoped she was as invested in this relationship as he was.

They rummaged through the freezer and chose meals prepared by Serena Blackhawk. After dinner, Cade turned to his friend. "I'll take first watch."

A nod. "I'll be up in three hours."

When Matt's door closed, Sasha looked at Cade. "I know I need to sleep, but I want to be with you a few minutes before I turn in."

Did she expect him to object? "Come on." He led her to the living room and sat with her on the couch, grateful she was there and safe.

Cade turned on the television to a light jazz station and reduced the volume. They sat in silence for a few minutes, the lights dim, the night quiet and peaceful as the mellow tones of a soprano saxophone dissolved lingering tension in his muscles.

He threaded his fingers through Sasha's hair. "No second thoughts about us?"

Sasha stared. "Why would I have second thoughts?"

"We blew open doors and confronted eight gunmen, most of whom did not survive."

"You also saved eleven people, one of them a good friend. Why won't you focus on that? What you and your teammates did was amazing. Although I didn't see the action, I heard enough from your statement to know you did what was necessary to protect Ivy and her students, nothing more."

The ball of ice in his stomach melted away. "Sasha."

She captured his lips in a sweet, soft kiss. "I respect what you do and the sacrifices you make. The more I learn about you and your work, the more my admiration grows. I have no doubts about us, Cade."

Unable to help himself, Cade fisted her hair and plundered her mouth with his. He poured the depth of his feelings into the kiss, trying to convey without words how much she meant to him. Her rejection now would break his heart.

When they were both desperate for air, he broke the kiss and eased back to see her eyes. He was either about to make the biggest mistake of his life or the best decision ever. Depended on her response in the next two minutes.

"What is it, Cade?" She palmed his cheek with a gentle touch, concern in her gaze.

"Although I hate that you were kidnapped at the bank, I don't regret having the chance to be with you and learn who you are. Sasha, I thought I was in love with Emily. In these last few days, I've realized how wrong I was. What I felt for her is a shadow of my feelings for you."

Man, he was lousing this up. If she was a wise woman, Sasha Ingram would dump him and run for the hills.

"What are you saying?" she whispered, hope a living, breathing entity in her eyes.

Another soft kiss from the woman in his arms. Hmm. Maybe he wasn't doing a bad job after all. "I love you."

Her beautiful eyes widened. "Cade," she murmured.

Was that good or bad? "I need you in my life more than I've needed anyone. Without you, my life will be an endless, meaningless existence. You bring out the best in me, and I don't want to go back to the man I was before you entered my life."

A wide smile curved her lips. "I love you, too. I think I fell in love with you when I woke up and saw you leaning over me after the kidnapping." Her cheeks reddened. "I've been more than half in love with you for months. Seeing your kindness and protectiveness tipped me all the way over."

Minutes later, he eased away from her again, heart racing and breathing rapid. "Will you marry me, Sasha?"

"I would love to be your wife."

"Soon? I've wasted too much time working up the courage to talk to you. I don't want to waste anymore. I want everything with you. A home, a family, a dog. I want it all, but only with you."

"Yes, to everything. Choose a date. I'll be ready."

Cade held Sasha, kissing her and making plans. "Do you have a preference which house we live in?"

"Yours has better security. If it's all right with you, I'll repair mine and sell it."

He wanted Sasha safe and happy. If that meant installing the same security system in her house that he had in his own, he'd do it. Home was Sasha Ingram soon-to-be Ramsey. Without her, anyplace he lived was just a house. She would make it a home, a place of love and laughter for years to come.

"Sounds perfect. Have you heard from Ethan about your house?"

"I forgot to tell you. Ethan called while I was cleaning the pantry at Perk with Dixie and Kat. The police finished their investigation and Elliott Construction has agreed to repair the house for me."

He stood. "Much as I'd love to keep you with me, you need rest. I'll walk you to your room." At her door, he leaned down and brushed his lips over hers. "See you in a few hours." He stole another brief kiss. "I love you, Sassy." With that, he nudged her inside the room before he lost the battle to stay on this side of the door.

Cade double-checked the doors and windows before he returned to the living room and pulled out his phone. Reluctant to wake Zane if he was sleeping, Cade sent the tech guru a text, asking him to call as soon as possible.

Within ten minutes, his cell phone rang. "Zane, thanks for calling. How's Claire?"

"Excellent. What do you need?"

"Two things. Run a check on the trainees and staff at PSI."

A pause, then, "We routinely run scans every month. What am I looking for?"

"Anything to indicate we have a traitor." He summarized the hostage incident at the community college and the man who approached Sasha wearing a PSI t-shirt. "Someone could have copied the logo and slapped it on his own t-shirt."

"But we can't take that chance. Gerard slipped through our security net because he was paid in cash. If the man who fixated on your girlfriend was bought off and paid with cash, I may not find an electronic trail to follow. What else?"

"Find Tony Gerard and Gary Westlake. Gerard showed up at PSI and went after Sasha."

"She's okay?"

"Yeah, thanks to Nate."

"She's your greatest weakness."

"And my greatest strength," he countered.

Soft laughter drifted through the speaker. "I never thought I would hear you say that. You're in love with Sasha?"

"Head over heels."

"She feel the same way?"

"Yes."

"Congratulations, Cade. I'm happy for both of you. I'll search for Gerard and Westlake and send the information. Because of the number of trainees and staffers at PSI, I'll assign those searches to the tech division. We should have results in a few hours if there is anything to find. I also overnighted jewelry to PSI for Sasha. Trackers are embedded in them. She should wear more than one piece to ensure at least one of the tags will transmit a signal. Expect delivery tomorrow morning."

"Thanks, Zane."

After he ended the call, Cade grabbed his laptop and started digging for information on Black Dog. By the end of two hours, he was frustrated. Not enough information to find the answers he sought, answers that would protect his future wife.

Rumors abounded on the dark web about the group, but no one knew the CEO's name. Although their headquarters was in Kentucky, speculation said the mercenary group wanted to relocate to Tennessee.

Cade frowned. Was that why their operatives were nosing around Otter Creek? Ethan would not be happy if that turned out to be truth rather than gossip.

Maybe he had crossed one of BD's operatives or interfered in one of their missions. His teammates and their families would be at risk also if the crime wave in town was connected to Black Dog.

He needed to find the answer before this group took another run at him or Sasha. Next time, they might not escape unscathed.

CHAPTER TWENTY-SEVEN

Sasha woke with a groan and fumbled for her phone without opening her eyes. She mumbled a croaky greeting into the phone.

"Where are you?" an irate voice snapped at her.

Irritation with a major dose of crankiness swelled in her gut. "What time is it?"

"A few minutes past one. Answer the question, Sash. Where are you?"

"I have to be up in an hour to go to work. You couldn't wait until Perk opened to demand an accounting of my movements?"

"Sasha Marie Ingram," her brother yelled. "Answer my question."

"You aren't Mom or Dad. Using all three of my names doesn't work as an intimidation tactic. I'm an adult, fully capable of staying where I please."

"I'm worried about you."

Sasha sighed, recognizing the concern in his voice. His concern was unnecessary. Cade would take a bullet for her in a heartbeat if someone breached his security system. "I'm staying with Cade and one of his teammates." Someone plugged into the town's gossip network would know she was staying in Cade's house.

Muttered curses came through the speaker. "If you care anything for your own life, stay away from Ramsey."

Stunned, she sat up. "Are you threatening me?"

"How could you think that?"

"I didn't hear from you for twelve years. When you showed up, you acted like a stranger instead of my brother. Are you surprised I don't know what to think about you?"

"Stay with a friend. Anyone is better than Ramsey. I'll pay for a hotel room if you'll leave him. You're at risk in his company."

"Knock it off. I won't bring trouble to my friends' doorsteps. I'm safe with Cade and his teammate."

"I can protect you. I'll put you in a safe house. No one will touch you while you're under my protection. Tell me where you're staying, and I'll rescue you."

"I don't need rescuing, and I have a business to run. Whether I work or not, the bills don't stop coming. I love Perk, Dean. I don't want to lose my shop because you have me locked in a safe house until the person behind the attacks is behind bars."

Silence for a moment. "I'll transport you from the safe house or hotel to your job for as long as you're in danger. I'll post guards in and around your shop to protect you."

Sasha frowned. "Guards?" Who did he know who could provide protection services?

"I know some people. Good people. They'll make sure no one hurts you again."

"Cade and his Fortress teammates are taking excellent care of me."

A bark of harsh laughter. "You have a concussion, your shop was broken into, and your house was set on fire. Doesn't sound like they're doing a great job, little sister."

Sasha's hand fisted around her cell phone. At least he didn't know about the incident at the mall in Knoxville or the episodes with Gerard. "Who are these friends of yours?"

"Men who train hard and do the job, no matter what it takes." Pride came through loud and clear in his voice. "That's all you need to know."

Who were these men? She didn't think her brother would tell her more. He'd been evasive except for his demand that she leave Cade's house and trust her safety to Dean. Never going to happen. She trusted Cade with her life and her heart. Dean was a virtual stranger with an agenda of his own.

"I appreciate your concern, but I'm staying."

"You're making a mistake, Sasha. I hope it's not a fatal one." Dean ended the call.

Sasha tossed her phone on the bed and blew out a breath. Great. Her brother had not only awakened her, he'd riled her.

With anger simmering in her gut, going back to sleep was impossible. If Dean was angry because Sasha wouldn't leave Cade, he would be livid when he found out Sasha planned to marry the Fortress operative.

Tough. Although she loved her brother, if she had to choose between Cade and Dean, Cade would win every time.

Sasha gathered her clothes and padded to the bathroom. After a steamy shower, she still felt sluggish and grumpy.

Coffee, she decided. She'd brew the pot she prepped before bed. Maybe the caffeine-laced drink would help her compensate for another short night of rest.

Sasha's lips quirked. Right. She didn't think consuming a vat of espresso would jumpstart her synapses. How did the Fortress operatives function on so little sleep?

She stumbled into the kitchen and pressed the coffeemaker's start button. Sasha waited impatiently for the brew cycle to finish, eyeing the carafe and the stingy stream of liquid dripping into the glass container.

A muffled step had her spinning on her heel.

Matt walked into the kitchen. "Why are you awake this early?"

"A wise man would allow me to drink a large mug of coffee before he engaged me in too much conversation."

The medic chuckled. "Yes, ma'am. Does Cade know about your early morning disposition?"

She scowled.

After another soft laugh, he held up his hands. "Sorry. Couldn't resist. I need to do another security sweep. I'll return in a few minutes."

Sasha glared at the operative's back as he walked outside for a circuit around the house. How could he be cheerful this time of morning? Matt was right. She did have quite an early morning attitude.

Down the hall, a shower turned on.

She blew out a breath. Rats. The last thing she wanted to do was wake Cade early. Sasha must not have been quiet enough. The operative slept light. Perhaps the circumstances made him hyperaware of his surroundings. Would he sleep deeper when she was safe or was this a byproduct of his military training?

She swiveled to face the infernal machine that dripped coffee at molasses speed. Finally, the coffeemaker beeped, signaling the end of the brew cycle.

Sasha grabbed three mugs and pounced on the carafe, pouring steaming liquid into her mug. She climbed on a barstool and sipped, praying the caffeine did its job before she said something she would regret. By the time she finished half her drink, Matt returned and filled a mug.

A minute later, Cade walked in. His gaze tracked immediately to Sasha. Concern filled his eyes. "What's wrong?"

"A phone call woke me early."

Matt poured coffee into Cade's mug and handed it to him. "Bad news?"

Depended on how you looked at it. "More an annoyance. I was so aggravated by the time the call ended, I couldn't sleep."

Cade sat on the stool next to hers. "Who called?"

"Dean."

"What did he want?" Matt leaned against the counter, mug cradled between his hands.

"To know where I was staying. I told him I was with you and Cade."

"I can imagine how that went over," he murmured, his tone wry.

"He insisted I leave Cade and go with him. He promised to set me up in a safe house or hotel, and keep anyone else from hurting me. I turned him down flat. He was not happy."

"Not a pleasant way to wake up." Cade leaned close and kissed her.

When he eased away, Sasha smiled. "That goes a long way toward making up for my rude awakening."

Matt snorted. "Nice. You get a kiss," he told Cade. "I got a bad-tempered rant about not talking to her before she downed a mug of coffee."

Her husband-to-be smirked at his friend. "You don't have the right touch."

At that moment, both of the men's cell phones signaled an incoming text. Cade grabbed his phone and checked the screen. A broad smile curved his mouth. "Ivy had a seven-pound girl. Her name is Savannah Rose. Mama and baby are going great. According to Josh, Alex paced a trench in the floor, snarled at the doctor and nurses, and is absolutely in love with his daughter."

He tapped the screen and turned his phone around for Sasha to see the picture of a dark-haired baby.

"She's beautiful." Sasha hoped one day she and Cade would be sending a text message with pictures of their child. Her gaze lifted to his face. Did Cade want children? He'd hinted as much when he mentioned having a family, but he'd never said specifically. In response to her silent inquiry, he gave her a slight nod.

Warmth filled her. Cade Ramsey would be an amazing father.

"Something I need to know about?" Matt's mug stopped halfway to his lips as he watched their silent interaction.

"I asked Sasha to marry me last night."

"And?"

"She said yes."

The medic set his mug on the counter with a thud. "Man, a guy sleeps for three hours and everything changes." He came around the breakfast bar and clapped Cade on the shoulder. "Congratulations. That's the smartest thing you've done since I met you."

Cade rolled his eyes.

Matt kissed Sasha on the cheek. "I'm happy for you, Sasha. Hope I'm as blessed to have a woman like you in my life someday."

Hmm. The handsome medic needed to open his eyes. From what Sasha had seen at the restaurant the other night, Delilah would be a perfect match for him.

Once they finished their coffee, Cade grabbed his Go bag and his laptop. "Matt, stop by Perk about 10:00. I need to run an errand before we go to PSI."

His friend saluted him.

Sasha waited for Cade to do his security check of the area and his SUV, then joined him.

Minutes later, he unlocked the door to Perk and ushered her inside. Before long, the shop smelled of cranberry-orange muffins, chocolate chip scones, and four types of coffee. Once again, Sasha was impressed by Cade's adeptness in the kitchen.

Thirty minutes before Perk opened, a knock on the front door drew their attention. Sasha admitted Josh Cahill. "Good morning. How big a cup of coffee do you need?"

The operative smiled. "You don't have a container large enough. Just give me the strongest coffee in the largest cup."

"I've got it," Cade said and grabbed a cup and lid.

"I made cranberry-orange muffins and chocolate chip scones. What would Del like?"

"Either. She's not choosy about food."

Sasha slid her hand into a plastic glove, scooped up a scone, and handed it to Josh. "Munch on this while I box the food for you. How are the Morgans?"

"Fantastic. Savannah is sweet and beautiful like her mother." He gave a short laugh. "I feel sorry for any boy who wants to date that girl when she's old enough. Alex will be the most overprotective father on the planet."

She chose four muffins and two scones and readied them for transport. "What about you?"

"What do you mean?"

"Your wife might have a girl."

His smile this time was more a baring of teeth. "I'll be vying for scary father of the year if I have a daughter of dating age. Between the two of us, Alex and I will be dead even on who is more protective. The teenage boys will be shut down hard if they dare lay a hand on our daughters."

Cade handed Josh the coffee. "Who's keeping watch at the hospital?"

Sasha's brows knitted. "Why would anyone be on guard duty? Alex is there to protect Ivy and his daughter."

"Babies go to the nursery at least once a day. If Alex goes with Savannah to the nursery, Ivy will be vulnerable to attack. He won't be able to rest unless he knows one of us is on watch. We'll provide protection while he concentrates on his family."

Josh washed the last of the scene down with a swig of coffee. "Thanks, Sasha. Quinn is keeping watch until noon, then I'll take over for a few hours. Are you going to PSI today?" he asked Cade.

"After lunch. Sasha has students working in the afternoon right now. We'll also send two trainees to keep an eye on the shop and workers until closing."

A nod. "Trent told me about the guy who approached you last night, Sasha. Did you get a good look at him?"

"Unfortunately, no. The light was behind him."

"Recognize his voice?"

She shook her head.

"Pay attention to people around you, including customers who come into your shop. Pay attention to the voices. If you recognize him, let one of us know. Your camera operational?" He inclined his head toward the camera in the ceiling.

"Fortress monitors the shop feed for me. I have another camera in the kitchen."

Not long after the operative left Perk, Sasha opened her doors for business. Within minutes, customers waiting in line were ten deep. Because Cade pitched in, she kept up with demand and filled orders quickly. By the time the morning rush slowed, Cade had already brewed a new batch of the four coffee flavors.

As the last customer left the shop, Cade's cell phone signaled an incoming text. He glanced at the readout. "It's Zane. He has information."

CHAPTER TWENTY-EIGHT

Cade slid onto a stool at the coffee bar and called his friend. "It's Cade. What do you have for me?"

"The men in the truck at the mall work for Black Dog or at least they did. They are currently putting out feelers on the dark web for employment. So far, no takers."

Black Dog again. "I assume you know who they are. Do we have eyes on them?"

"Not at the moment. Do you want me to arrange surveillance?"

He considered his options, decided against it for now. If the men proved to be a problem, Cade would take care of them. "As long as they stay away from Otter Creek, we'll leave them alone for now. Send me the information on them. Still no indication why the mercenary group is after me or Sasha?"

"I picked up more chatter on both of you. Someone is offering a reward for capture. Bounty is $50,000 each. Still don't know who's behind the upsurge in activity."

Terrific. Made protecting Sasha more challenging. "Anything else?"

"Your package arrived at PSI an hour ago. Make sure Sasha is fully protected. I don't like the escalation."

"I'll take care of it. What about Gerard and Westlake?"

"Gerard's in Gatlinburg, Westlake in Knoxville. Gerard is moving around town like he's taking a vacation before he hunts for a new job."

"What about Westlake?"

"He hasn't moved since his arrival yesterday. I sent you addresses for their hotels. Might be wise to chat with them about their wardrobes."

"Send me the link to track their phone signal. I'll talk to them after I finish my training session with Bravo today. Anything popping on the other search?"

"Nothing so far. I have the geeks working on it between requests from the teams on the field." Zane was silent a moment, then said, "Are you in a place where you can talk openly?"

Cade frowned. "For now. I'm in Perk with Sasha. The shop is empty at the moment."

"I looked into Emily's death."

He stiffened, recognizing the warning tone in Zane's voice. Whatever he'd discovered wasn't good. "What did you learn?"

"There's no easy way to say this, Cade."

"Tell me."

"She overdosed on heroin."

Stunned, he dragged a hand down his face. "Accident?"

"Not according to the police report. She left a suicide note telling her husband she was broken inside because of your abuse and couldn't live with the memories any longer."

Would the fallout from that nightmare relationship ever end? His hand clenched around his phone. "I never laid a hand on her in anger, Zane. I don't know why she lied to Dean, but I swear I didn't hurt her." No matter what she'd done when they were together, he treated her with respect. Too bad she hadn't given him the same courtesy.

"Never thought you did. You're not that kind of man."

"Did the police or medical examiner say if the drug use was long term or a one and done?"

"She had track marks."

Heartsick, he sighed. "I didn't see signs of drug use when we were together. No wonder Dean hates my guts. He believes I'm indirectly to blame for her death."

"He's wrong. Look, for what it's worth, everything I'm seeing online says Emily was a manipulative witch who pushed boundaries to achieve her own ends. I'll keep digging, but I wouldn't be surprised to learn she planned the overdose to gain attention. According to the police report, Dean was supposed to arrive home at 6:00 the night she died, but was more than an hour late because of a lockdown at the base. When he found her, she was dead."

Zane was probably right. Cade should have seen it when they were together. Yeah, she used whatever was expedient to get her way. More than once she'd called with an emergency when he was in town. Cade had raced to her side to find her happy and safe when he arrived to rescue her.

He felt like such a fool. Convinced she would outgrow the tendency to cry wolf after they married, he tried to be understanding about her missing him when he was deployed. When his CO had dressed him down, Cade had refused to come the next time she called with an emergency. Jeopardizing his position in the Ranger unit was not an option. That was the beginning of many arguments and multiple accusations that he didn't love her. After that, she had turned to Dean for comfort. Guess Sasha's brother had been more responsive to her calls.

"Keep digging. I want to know everything, Z." His gaze locked on Sasha's. "Including anything you find on

Dean Ingram and his movements from the time I joined my Ranger unit."

"Copy that."

After Zane ended the call, Cade laid his phone on the coffee bar and waited for Sasha's reaction to his last statement to Z. He didn't have to wait long.

"Why is Zane investigating my brother?"

"I need to know as much I can to better protect you." And himself.

"The brother I grew up with would never hurt us. Now, I don't know what to believe. I didn't expect him to try intimidation to make me leave you." She leaned over the counter and brushed his lips with hers. "Do what you have to do."

"I love you, Sassy."

She smiled. "Remember that when I'm grumpy before my first cup of coffee in the mornings."

He could live with that. Cade chuckled as the shop's door opened. He swiveled on the stool to see his best friend. "Perfect timing. Keep my wife-to-be company. I'll be back in a few minutes."

He walked down the street to KT Jewelry. Once inside, he searched until he found the perfect ring, one almost as beautiful as the woman he loved with everything in him.

When Cade returned to the coffee shop minutes later, a small gray velvet-covered box was secured in the pocket of his cargo pants. Matt sat at the counter with Marcus Lang, drinking coffee, while Sasha talked to Paige.

Paige slid off the stool and threw her arms around him. "Cade Ramsey, you don't mess around when you go after something, do you?"

"She's trying to congratulate you on your engagement." Marcus watched his wife with unhidden affection. "She'll have to turn her matchmaking skills in another direction."

Cade patted Paige's back. "If you played matchmaker, you had good instincts. I need a minute with Sasha. Can you watch the shop for five minutes?"

"Of course."

Cade led Sasha to her small office off the kitchen. He removed the box from his pocket and flipped open the lid.

Sasha gasped. "Cade, it's beautiful."

"Not as beautiful as you. Will you accept this ring as a symbol of my unending love for you, Sasha?"

"I will. I love you, Cade."

He slid the ring on her finger and drew her into his arms to kiss her. By the time he released Sasha, Cade's control hung by a gossamer-thin thread. "Have you given thought to when you want to get married?"

"No more than a month."

He stilled. "Will we be able to plan the wedding that fast?"

"My biggest project will be finding a wedding dress. Paige has agreed to hunt for one with me this weekend. I'll talk to the bakery across the square about a wedding cake and the florist to handle the candles and flowers. I imagine Serena Blackhawk will be able to create a punch for us without difficulty."

"You don't want a large wedding?"

She shook her head. "All I want is Paige to be my matron of honor, Marcus to perform the ceremony, and you to have a best man."

"Are you sure, Sassy? I don't want to cheat you out of your dream wedding. If you want a more elaborate wedding, I'll wait." Even if it killed him.

"I'm planning the wedding I want. If you want something different, tell me."

He captured her lips in a gentle kiss. "Whatever makes you happy is fine with me."

"Great. Come on. I want to show my engagement ring to Paige."

All too soon, the lunch rush began and Sasha's part-time helpers arrived. Once the foot traffic died down and Sasha felt she could leave the shop, Cade arranged for Dixie and Kat to provide protection for Perk's workers and patrons.

After the trainees arrived, Matt followed Cade and Sasha to PSI. Before they went inside the main building to meet the rest of Bravo, Cade told Matt and Sasha about Zane's phone call.

"Oh, Cade." Sasha's hand squeezed his in sympathy. "Emily was an unhappy woman determined to make everyone else in her life miserable, too."

Matt gave him a pointed look. "Her death isn't on you, Cowboy."

"I know that in my head. Takes time to believe it as truth. Go find the rest of Bravo. I need to stop by the main office. We'll catch up."

Cade led Sasha to the business hub of PSI. He nodded to the office staff who called out greetings and stared at Sasha with avid curiosity. The blond at the back of the office grinned. "You must be here for your package."

"I am. How are you, Kira?"

"Can't complain. Who's the pretty lady?"

"This is Sasha Ingram, the woman I'm going to marry in a few weeks."

The office went silent as all eyes turned their direction. "The single women in town will be heartbroken," Kira said. The other workers called out their congratulations and returned to their tasks.

Cade nodded his thanks when the office manager handed him the express mailer. He ripped open the package as he walked from the office with Sasha. He took her to an interrogation room and closed the door. With a quick check to be sure the surveillance camera was off and observation room empty, Cade dumped the contents of the package on the table.

He strapped the watch on one wrist, slid multiple thin bracelets on the other, and handed her the pair of gold earrings. While she slipped those through her lobes, Cade fastened the gold necklace around her neck. That done, he sent Zane a text to let him know Sasha was wearing the jewelry.

They found Bravo in the gym running drills with trainees. Trent directed Cade and Matt to the four groups at the back of the room. Soon, they were engaged in instruction and demonstration with the rest of their teammates.

Two hours later, Trent ended the session and sent the recruits to the indoor gun range for weapons training. From there they would be free to do what they wanted while Bravo conducted their own training session with Durango except for Alex. The new father had a pass for the next two weeks.

Before they began the session with Durango, Cade's cell phone signaled an incoming text. A glance at his screen brought a scowl, unsurprised by the information from Zane. These guys weren't going to give up until he stopped them. The question was why were they so determined to grab him and Sasha.

"Something wrong?"

Cade cupped the side of Sasha's neck. "The man who approached you at the community college works for Black Dog. Someone is determined to collect that bounty."

CHAPTER TWENTY-NINE

When Nate broke away from training with Bravo and the rest of his teammates to prepare the evening meal, Sasha went with him. She was tired of thoughts about Black Dog and her brother circling in her brain with no answers. Having a job would keep her brain occupied and keep her from descending further into a pit of frustration.

"What's for dinner tonight?" she asked the chef.

"Taco bar and apple cobbler. We have five-gallon tubs of vanilla ice cream in the freezer to go with the cobbler." He leaned against the counter, arms folded over his muscled chest. "I appreciate the help, but it's not necessary. What's wrong, Sasha?"

"I must have a sign plastered to my forehead." When he remained silent, his gaze locked on hers, Sasha gave in. She didn't think Cade would mind if she talked to any member of the two Fortress teams. "Everything that's been happening to me lately seems to be connected to Black Dog. Zane just told Cade the guys in the truck at the mall were part of Black Dog, too. I don't know if the house fire is connected. I don't know what I did to draw Black Dog's attention, but I wish they'd turn the interest somewhere else."

"Wouldn't surprise me if Black Dog is to blame for the fire as well. Sasha, none of this is your fault. In fact, it's more likely the attacks are connected to Cade."

The thought had occurred to her. She'd been hoping the chef would convince her otherwise. "I don't want to be used as bait to draw him into danger."

"Bait or not, he'll always be a shield for you." His gaze dropped to her left hand. "As his wife, you and your safety will be his first priority. If you have children, his protectiveness will skyrocket. Ask Alex how he feels about security now that he has Savannah to protect as well. You know how careful he is with Ivy. I feel sorry for any male who looks twice at his daughter when she's older."

She frowned. "Has Stella gotten used to it?"

A broad smile curved his mouth. "Stella has a gun and knows how to use it. She reminds me constantly that she's a cop and can take care of herself." He shrugged. "Doesn't matter. She's mine to protect, badge or not. Cade will be the same with you. Protection is in our genes and it's how we're trained. Don't ask us to ease up. You'll waste your breath."

He pushed away from the counter. "Come on. We'll have a dining hall full of hungry trainees soon." Nate pulled hamburger from the refrigerator. He inclined his head toward the walk-in pantry that made her pantry at Perk look like a small closet. "Grab the onion powder, garlic powder, chili powder, cumin, and paprika."

"Just to brown hamburger?"

Nate slid her an amused look. "You're going to make the taco seasoning."

"I usually rip open a packet and dump it."

"Trust me. Once you've tasted this, you won't ever go back to the packet."

Two hours later, she moaned in appreciation as humor danced in Nate's eyes. "You're right. This is amazing."

From the little chatter in the dining hall, the trainees agreed with her assessment. They were stuffing food in their mouths as fast as possible.

"Told you."

"Is it all right if I use your recipe?"

"Sure." His attention shifted over her shoulder. "Cade and Matt are here." He rose. "Thanks for the help this afternoon, Sasha. You're off duty. I'll handle the cleanup."

Wasn't much to clean. Durango's EOD man was an expert in that kitchen. Once again, he'd cleaned as he cooked. Stella was a lucky woman.

Nate stopped to talk to Cade and Matt before returning to the kitchen. Once the trainees finished eating, the operative would store leftovers and wash the serving dishes. Provided there were leftovers. Sasha wasn't sure there would be.

Cade sat beside Sasha while Matt headed for the taco bar. "Dinner smells great."

"Tastes great, too. You'll like it."

"After we finish eating, we'll head to Knoxville. Are you sure you want to go with me? You must be exhausted. Matt agreed to stay with you if you changed your mind."

"And miss an opportunity to spend time with you while you're in town? Not a chance."

"The confrontation with Gary Westlake might be unpleasant."

"I'll be prepared." Sasha gripped his hand for a moment. "I promise to follow orders and stay out of his reach."

Cade pressed a hard kiss to her mouth. "Fair enough." He followed his teammate to the taco bar. Thirty minutes later, he checked his phone, brows knitting.

"What is it?"

"Westlake hasn't moved. He's been in that hotel room for 48 hours. I'd be stir crazy." He stopped by the staff lounge for bottles of water, then escorted Sasha from the building.

Thankful the drive to Knoxville was uneventful, Sasha's muscles loosened when Cade parked in the lot outside the four-story hotel located on the outskirts of the city. The Palm Hotel wasn't modern in construction, but the building and grounds looked well cared for.

"Westbrook is registered in room 422." Cade turned to her. "Last chance to back out, Sassy."

"Pass." She reached for the handle. "I assume we're also tracking down Gerard in Gatlinburg before we head home."

"We should go. I don't want you out here too long."

Cade circled the SUV and opened her door. They walked to the hotel and into the elevator without being stopped. The desk clerk's attention focused on a massive chemistry textbook.

Sasha grimaced. Science had been her least favorite subject in school. Yeah, cooking was science, but she loved her work in a way she'd never felt about her dreaded science courses.

They exited the elevator and located Westlake's room. The do-not-disturb sign hung on the knob. Now what?

Her future husband wrapped his arms around her and pulled her gently against his chest. "I'm checking for surveillance cameras," he murmured against her ear. When she shivered in reaction, Cade chuckled. "I'm making a mental note of that response."

"I need to make mental notes of my own. Do you have a sensitive spot I can explore later?"

"The curve between my neck and shoulder." A moment later, he kissed the side of her neck. "I need you to stand behind me."

Understanding his driving need to protect her, Sasha didn't argue.

Cade knocked on the door. When he didn't receive a response, he tried again. Still nothing. With a casual glance around, he reached into his cargoes pocket and pulled out a pair of rubber gloves and a thin black plastic gadget similar to the one he used to check for trackers. He flipped a switch and the object in his hand lit up. Numbers began to scroll on the small screen.

Sasha watched in fascination as the gadget worked. Seconds later, a green light flashed on the LCD panel, and the electronic lock on the door turned to green. The operative stood to the side of the door and pressed down on the handle.

He opened the door a crack, froze. Cade glanced at Sasha, expression grim. He pulled out his phone. "Stay here. You don't want to go into the room. Grab your phone and act as though you're checking email. I won't be long."

She started to protest until she caught the putrid scent oozing from the room. Oh, man. Her dinner threated to make a reappearance. Sasha had an idea what caused the stench. "Go. Hurry, Cade." She didn't want him caught in that room.

When Cade slipped into the room, Sasha moved to stand near another room two doors down. She grabbed her phone and scrolled through her emails without reading anything.

A minute later, Cade exited the room and removed the gloves.

"Was it bad?" she whispered.

"I've seen worse."

"How did he die?"

"Single gunshot wound to the head. He didn't stand a chance."

In the SUV, Cade called Zane. "Call the cops and report a murder." He explained what he'd found in the hotel room.

"Will his death connect to you?"

"There's a surveillance camera in the parking lot of the Palm Hotel and one in the lobby that recorded my arrival with Sasha. We were only in the hotel ten minutes. I think Westlake died soon after he arrived. I checked the room and body, but I was careful not to leave a trace of my presence in the room."

"I'll call from one of our burners and report a foul odor coming from the room after I wipe your entrance and exit from the security feeds. Did you take pictures of the scene?"

"Several."

"Send me everything you have. You sure you want to track down Gerard?"

"If he's not already dead, tracking him down and warning him might save his miserable hide."

"He's still in Gatlinburg. You might consider calling your teammates for backup this time."

"We'll be fine."

A snort. "Famous last words. I'll expect you to check in no later than two hours from now. If you don't contact me, I'll assume you can't and act accordingly."

"Roger that. Thanks, Zane."

An hour later, Cade parked in front of the Magnolia Hotel. Sasha's eyebrows rose. A definite step up from the Palm. "Nice place." A large fountain bubbled in front of the hotel. She couldn't wait to see inside the place. The decor didn't disappoint. In fact, Sasha wished her furniture was as nice as the hotel's.

They walked hand-in-hand to the elevator and rode to the seventh floor. A familiar do-not-disturb sign hung on the knob.

Sasha's stomach knotted. Hoping they wouldn't discover another body inside the room, she dropped back behind Cade without him asking. He flashed her an appreciative look over his shoulder.

After a careful scan of the area, he knocked on the door. This time, instead of dead silence, a muffled male voice said, "Hold on a second."

At least the man was still alive.

Someone inside the room fumbled with the lock and threw open the door. Gerard's face drained of all color. "Ramsey."

In the room behind him, a woman squealed.

CHAPTER THIRTY

Cade's eyes narrowed. Was the woman in the room Shelly or someone else? For Shelly's sake, he hoped Gerard respected his girlfriend enough to not cheat on her. "We need to talk."

Gerard widened his stance and folded his arms across his bare chest. "So talk."

"Not in the hall."

"It's okay, Tony." A woman emerged from the shadows of the room, a hotel robe wrapped around her body. Shelly. "Let them come in."

Cade gave her a short nod in greeting. Why was she in Gatlinburg? PSI planned a night training session in a few hours. As they entered the room, he made sure his body was between Sasha and Gerard in case he contemplated exacting revenge. They sat at the table while Gerard and his girlfriend perched side-by-side at the foot of the bed.

"What do you want?" Gerard asked, his voice curt.

"Answers."

"I spilled everything I know to Armstrong." A wry laugh. "He knows his stuff. I haven't experienced anything like that in my life and don't want a repeat performance. Although there isn't a mark on me, I still hurt."

"He's Delta trained. The military spares no expense when training Special Forces soldiers."

"Delta? I thought that was a rumor."

"Durango was a Delta unit. They've worked together since basic training. You're lucky Nate didn't kill you when you went after Sasha in the kitchen."

Gerard swallowed hard. "Why are you here?"

"Have you talked to Westlake since you left Otter Creek?"

"Yeah. Why?"

"When was the last time you spoke with him?"

A frown. "What does it matter? We're not your concern any longer."

"Answer the question, Gerard."

Shelly laid a hand on Gerard's arm. When he glanced at her, she gave him a slight nod.

Gerard turned back to Cade, resignation in his eyes. "About 18 hours ago. Midnight on the evening we left PSI. What's going on, Ramsey?"

"Westlake is dead."

Shelly clamped a hand over her mouth, her eyes wide.

Wrapping his arm around Shelly, Gerard's gaze fixed on Cade. "Did you kill him?"

"Sasha and I found him an hour ago. One bullet to the head."

"If not you, then who killed him?"

"Did Westlake work for Black Dog?"

A shrug. "What if he did? He quit Fortress. Shouldn't be a problem for you."

"It is for you. Black Dog is tying up loose ends."

Gerard stared. "Our job was to report your movements to the email address we received each week. That's all. I didn't know enough to tell Armstrong much as I'm sure you know. We aren't a threat to Black Dog."

The guy was an idiot. "You connect Black Dog to me and Sasha. You're a liability. Did you know about the bounty on our heads?"

His jaw dropped. "Bounty?"

Guess not. Cade turned his attention to Shelly. "Why are you off campus? You have night training in a few hours."

The young woman linked her fingers with Gerard's. "I resigned from PSI while your team worked with Durango. Tony and I got married a few hours ago."

Fast work on Gerard's part. As far as Cade knew, Gerard and Wainwright had met at PSI. Cade met Sasha two months before Gerard and Wainwright arrived in Otter Creek. Some might say he moved fast as well.

Cade glanced at Sasha. He knew what he wanted, had known from the moment he met the coffee maven. He wanted Sasha Ingram.

"Congratulations on your marriage," Sasha said.

Shelly's eyes lit. "Thanks."

Cade shifted his gaze to Gerard. "You and Shelly are in danger. Go off the grid. Cash transactions only. Remove the batteries from your cell phones and buy burners. Lay low while I figure out what's happening and stop it."

"How do I contact you?"

"Call the Fortress switchboard. Leave your number with Zane Murphy. No one else."

"Why did you warn me? You could have let Black Dog kill me. You wouldn't have to worry about me hurting your girlfriend in the future. Shelly would be collateral damage."

"I don't need help protecting Sasha from you or anyone else."

Gerard gave a bark of laughter. "No, I don't suppose you do. Were you Delta?"

Cade smiled. "Dress. Sasha and I will wait for you in the hall and walk you out." He needed to check in with

Zane or his friend would send his teammates for an unneeded rescue.

In the hallway, Cade called the Fortress communications guru. "We're okay. Gerard is alive. He and Shelly Wainwright got married this afternoon after she quit the training program."

"Are you and Sasha going home?"

"Not yet. We're waiting for the Gerards to pack their gear. I don't want to leave them here without protection. If Black Dog is behind this, they might have someone ready to strike."

"Agreed. Two-hour deadline unless you send me a message that you're back in Otter Creek."

"Copy that."

The hotel room door opened and the Gerards walked out with their bags in tow.

After settling the bill, Gerard started toward the front door. Cade clamped a hand on his shoulder. "Where did you park?"

"Both of us parked at the side of the hotel."

"Choose the safest vehicle and hand me the keys to the other. I'll have it moved to PSI. You can retrieve it when you're safe."

Shelly handed Cade her keys. "Blue Honda Civic. Tony has an SUV that's sturdier and blends better than my car."

Cade pocketed the keys and led them toward the rear of the hotel. When they reached the door to the parking lot, he glanced at Gerard. "I'll return in a minute. You see how Sasha looks right now?"

The other man's gaze swept over her and nodded.

"She better look exactly the same when I return."

A small smile curved Gerard's mouth. "Yes, sir."

Cade squeezed Sasha's hand and slipped from the hotel into the darkness. He moved from shadow to shadow, scanning the area.

He peered around the corner of the building to the parking lot. Nothing suspicious. Cade returned to the hotel. "We'll go to the lot together. Don't unlock your vehicle until I tell you it's safe. Use what we taught you. Act as though nothing is wrong, but keep a sharp eye out for trouble."

They reached the corner of the hotel. "Which vehicle is yours, Gerard?" he asked softly.

"Black SUV, third row, seven spaces from the west side."

"I'll scan for trackers and explosives. Don't approach until I tell you the SUV is clear."

Cade crossed the parking lot, slipping a hand into his pocket as he neared the vehicle. He activated the tracking detector and circled the SUV. When the light flashed green to show the vehicle was clean, he dropped to the ground and examined the undercarriage for signs of tampering or a bomb. Nothing.

He moved a distance away and signaled Gerard to remotely start his vehicle. Seconds later, the engine fired up. Excellent. He motioned for the others to approach. "You any good at evasive maneuvers?" he asked Gerard.

"Morgan said I was."

Since Alex was trained in evasive combat driving, that was high praise indeed for Gerard. "Pay attention to your surroundings, particularly vehicles that stay with you. Do you know where you're going?"

Gerard nodded.

"Good. Take detours. Don't lead a tail to your hiding place. If you run into trouble, call Fortress. We'll send someone to you." He didn't remind the other man that bad things could happen in a heartbeat. From Gerard's grim expression, the reminder wasn't necessary.

"I'll be careful. I have a lot to lose."

"Are you armed?"

A head shake.

Cade stared. He always carried multiple weapons. If Gerard was serious about a black ops career, he needed to follow the same rule, fast.

He bent to his ankle holster and grabbed his backup weapon. Cade handed it to Gerard along with an extra magazine. "Don't ever leave home without weapons again, not if you want to stay alive to see your first anniversary."

"Yes, sir."

"One more thing. You were employed by the best black ops firm in the market. Black Dog is at the bottom of the food chain. The money's good, but their employees are disposable. Do your homework before taking the next job offer."

Gerard started to ask something, stopped himself.

"Ask," Cade said, his voice soft.

"Would St. Claire consider allowing me back in the program?"

"He's only one of a long line of people you have to convince, including Brent Maddox. He'll be hard to sell on your reinstatement. If you want back in, you'll have to grovel and prove you're ready to learn. You and Shelly need to go. Now."

Gerard tucked Shelly into the SUV, then stashed their luggage in the backseat. He started around the front of the vehicle, stopped and looked back at Cade. "Thanks. For everything."

Cade lifted his chin in acknowledgment. Maybe, just maybe, the kid had a chance in this field after all. If Gerard and his wife applied to Fortress again, Cade would recommend they start training from scratch. They would have to earn the trust of Maddox and the PSI instructors.

He and Sasha waited for the newlyweds to drive away before heading for Cade's SUV. Minutes later, he pulled onto the interstate. "Need anything?"

"A bed."

"Recline the seat and sleep. I'll wake you when we're home."

"I wanted to keep you company, but I'm too tired to stay awake."

"I'll be fine, Sassy. The best thing you can do for me is take care of yourself."

After Sasha planted a sweet kiss on his jaw, she reclined the seat and settled in to rest for the next hour. Cade threaded his fingers with hers, happy to spend time with her even if she was asleep. Being with her settled him, made him content as nothing in his life had ever done.

What was it about her that affected him this way? Whatever it was, he looked forward to spending the rest of his life with this woman.

The drive to Otter Creek was quiet, peaceful. He loved night driving. Most of his missions were completed in the darkness with Bravo. Same had been true with his Ranger unit. He'd become more comfortable in the dark than he was in daylight.

He glanced at Sasha. She needed a decent night's rest before they had to open Perk. Cade didn't know how she maintained the schedule. Sasha could use a full-time worker to share the load. Long-term fifteen-hour days came with repercussions.

Ironic that he was more concerned about her hours than his own. His days were long, especially when he deployed. Sometimes stopping to rest wasn't an option. He and his teammates did what was necessary to survive. In their case, however, they weren't on the job six days a week year-round, unlike Sasha.

Had Sasha thought about staffing the shop while they were away for their honeymoon? Cade's pulse rate increased. Honeymoon. He needed to find a safe place to enjoy being together without work pressures for a few days.

Much as Cade wanted to take Sasha several hours away, he couldn't. If Maddox sent Bravo on an emergency mission in the next few weeks, Cade had to be close to his teammates.

Matt's family owned a lake house thirty minutes from Otter Creek. They had offered use of the place whenever he wanted. He'd broach the idea with Matt before he pitched it to the Rainers.

The lake house was the perfect place. A top-of-the-line security system and good lines of sight around the large cabin. He and Matt could stock the cabin kitchen with food. Cade made a mental note to purchase hot chocolate and packages of tea as well as coffee for her. Since he'd met Perk's beautiful owner, he had paid attention to her drink preferences.

As he followed the asphalt ribbon, he planned surprises to make their honeymoon special. After Durango returned to mission rotation, Cade would take Sasha out of town. Maybe the beach for a week. His mouth curved at the prospect of spending hours on the beach, soaking up the sun and salt air with his wife.

After parking at the back of his house, Cade trailed his fingers down Sasha's cheek. "Sasha, we're home."

In under a minute, they were inside the house. Matt turned from the counter where he was measuring coffee to make a fresh pot. "Welcome back. Did you find Gerard and Westlake?"

He held up his hand to stop his friend's questions, and turned to Sasha. He wrapped his arms around her. "You need to sleep. I have the first watch. If you need something, come to me." Mindful of their audience, he briefly kissed Sasha, then nudged her toward the hallway.

He waited until the door to Sasha's room closed before he said to Matt, "Westlake is dead. Bullet to the head. Not my doing."

"Gerard?"

"Alive when he left the hotel with his new wife."

His friend's eyebrows soared. "Shelly?"

"Yeah. They got married this afternoon in Gatlinburg after she resigned from Fortress."

"Ah. Wondered if she might walk after Gerard was fired."

"I told them to go off the grid. He's to leave burner numbers with Zane. I'll let them know when it's safe to come out of hiding." He hesitated a moment. "I think Gerard may petition to rejoin Fortress."

"Don't know if the boss will go for that since Gerard sold you out and intended to harm your woman. How is Sasha holding up?"

He glanced toward the hallway. "She's beyond exhausted. We need to figure out who's after us and why."

When his cell phone signaled an incoming message, Cade checked the screen. His stomach knotted as he read the information from Zane. Not good. He'd found Gerard and his wife just in time.

He looked at Matt. "The two clowns in the truck at the mall are dead. Both of them shot in the head. Black Dog is cleaning house." And the danger to Sasha had risen to another level.

The medic frowned. "Why would anyone work for that organization? Your life expectancy is pretty short if you sign on with them."

"People think they'll beat the odds."

"The odds are stacked against gamblers." He clapped Cade on the shoulder. "Wake me in two hours. I'll sleep after you and Sasha leave."

The next two hours passed without incident while Cade searched the Internet for references to Black Dog. Still nothing except rumors and innuendo about the mercenary group's leader. Someone had to know this person's identity.

Frustrated, he decided to follow one more thread before he woke Matt. Three clicks of the mouse later, Cade froze. Oh, man. Why?

As soon as the question formed in his mind, he knew the answer. Had known for a couple days but didn't want to believe his own conclusion. Until now, he couldn't find proof. This wasn't much, a thin strand at best. Hardcore proof would have to come from Zane. Cade copied the link and sent it to the Fortress tech guru. If anyone could unearth the evidence they needed, it was Z.

Disgusted and heartsick, Cade shut down his laptop and went to wake Matt. He opened the door to the medic's room and his friend's eyes opened.

"Please tell me there's fresh coffee waiting."

"Full pot."

"You're a true friend, Cowboy." When he didn't respond to the teasing remark, Matt sat up. "What's wrong?"

Cade stepped into the room and closed the door so Sasha wouldn't overhear his next words. "Black Dog's leader is Dean Ingram."

CHAPTER THIRTY-ONE

Matt blew out a breath. "You sure?"

Cade leaned against the bedroom door. "I sent what I found to Z. He'll confirm the information. This will break Sasha's heart."

"Your woman is tough. She'll handle it." The medic swung his legs to the floor. "Give me a minute, then you can go to bed."

By the time Matt walked into the kitchen, fully dressed and alert with his hair damp and the scent of soap emanating from him, Cade had a large mug of coffee ready along with a couple muffins.

"Thanks." After taking several sips of the steaming liquid, Matt inclined his head toward the hallway. "Rest while you have the chance. I'll watch over the house and your girl."

"See you in two hours." Before Cade walked into his bedroom, he listened at Sasha's door. No sounds. Excellent. Maybe she would enjoy more than two hours of sleep tonight. He hated to see the shadows under her eyes.

He draped a quilt over his body and was asleep in less than a minute.

At the two-hour mark, Cade rolled out of bed and readied himself for the day. Before he left the room, Cade unlocked the gun safe and chose a backup piece. Since Gerard hadn't called for help, he assumed the newlyweds were safe.

He walked into the kitchen in time to see Matt pouring coffee into a mug.

"No problems in the last two hours," the medic reported.

"Anything from Fortress?" Cade accepted the mug and sipped the strong brew. Definitely not Sasha's coffee, but it was hot and packed a punch.

A head shake. "You'll be at PSI around noon?"

"That's the plan. Sasha mentioned blueberry muffins and vanilla scones for today's menu at Perk."

"Sounds good. Tell her to hold back a couple of each for me. I'll be at Perk at eight and stay until you're ready to leave for PSI."

Soft footsteps sounded from the hallway. Both men turned.

Just seeing Sasha made Cade's heart turn over in his chest. Man, she lit up a room when she entered. He set his coffee aside and wrapped his arms around her. He could get used to this. Any day starting off with this woman in his arms was guaranteed to be a good one. "Good morning. Sleep well?"

She nodded. "Needed another few hours, but I'll take what I can get. You?"

"I rested."

Sasha gave a soft laugh. "We need a vacation when this is over."

He couldn't agree more. "Ready to go?"

"I need coffee first. My brain cells aren't firing."

"Got you covered." Matt handed her a travel mug. "It's black."

"Thanks, Matt."

"Always happy to indulge my favorite barista." He turned to Cade. "I'll check the SUV."

"Matt wants you to set aside a couple muffins and scones for him." Cade pressed a soft kiss to Sasha's lips, easing away as Matt returned.

"It's clean."

"Thanks." He capped his travel mug, shouldered his Go bag, and escorted Sasha to the SUV.

Cade considered what he'd learned about Dean. Should he tell Sasha? Dread filled his gut at the prospect of hurting the woman he loved. He didn't want to tell her information unconfirmed by Zane in case Cade was wrong.

He'd wait until he had undeniable proof. Dean deserved that much consideration. Cade didn't want to accuse Sasha's brother unjustly.

On the drive to Perk, Cade watched for problems. His skin crawled, never a good sign. Although he scanned the area repeatedly, he didn't see a vehicle following them.

He parked in the alley behind Perk. "Ready?"

"This day is starting whether I'm ready or not."

He met her at the front of the SUV. "Have you thought about hiring a full-time worker, maybe a manager? If you plan to open a restaurant, you need someone trustworthy at Perk while you're busy with the other place."

"Mornings like this, I'm tempted."

Cade held out his hand for her shop keys. "Do you have someone in mind to run Perk when we're on our honeymoon?"

Her head whipped his direction. "Do you know where we're going?"

"I have details to work out before I tell you."

"Surprise me. Just tell me the type of clothes I need to pack."

"Durango will be on leave. We can't go far until Durango is back on mission rotation."

"I don't care where we go, Cade. As long as I'm with you, I'll be happy."

"I'll make it up to you, Sasha. Our real honeymoon will be worth the wait." He unlocked the shop door and stepped inside.

Cade frowned. The alarm wasn't beeping. Had Sasha's workers forgotten to set the alarm? He caught Sasha's hand as she reached to turn on the light. "Wait. Let me check the rest of the shop first. Wait here."

When she nodded, Cade motioned for her to stay by the door. Eyes now adjusted to the darkness, he moved easily through the kitchen to the main room. Not many places to hide in the shop. He checked behind the counter, then scanned the large room. Clear.

He returned to the kitchen and skidded to a stop. The room was empty. "Sasha?" No response.

Alarm roaring through him, Cade went to the walk-in pantry and yanked open the door. Not there. His gaze locked on the closed door to the alley. Outside? Why? Did she forget something in the SUV?

He ran to the door and twisted the knob. A heavy weight shoved against the door and it flew open, slamming into Cade. He stumbled backward, tripped on the leg of the prep table and went down, hard.

Two men dressed in black rushed into the kitchen, weapons drawn and aimed at him.

Cade froze.

"If you want to see your girlfriend alive again, come with us," the bigger of the two men said, his voice deep and raspy. He was so large, he reminded Cade of a mountain man.

"On your feet, nice and slow." The skinny man motioned with the barrel of his Sig.

He could take them. After eyeing Mountain Man again, he amended that to he could probably take them.

However, he didn't know if these men had partners with Sasha.

"All right. Don't hurt my girlfriend."

"Hurry up," Beanpole snapped. "We don't got all day."

Cade rolled to his side and twisted so his back and shoulders blocked the other men's view of his hands. He grasped the side of his watch and pushed the first button, then got to his feet, hands out to his sides.

They shoved him through the doorway into the alley. Cade saw a van idling near his vehicle. The opened side door revealed Sasha on her side on the floor, unmoving.

His heart skipped a beat. No. Cade prayed she wasn't seriously hurt. If he lost Sasha, he would never recover. He raced toward the van. "Sasha!" After climbing inside, he placed two fingers against the side of her neck and breathed a sigh of relief when he felt a strong pulse.

"On your stomach, Ramsey." The driver turned toward him with a gun pointed at Cade. "Resist and your girlfriend dies."

Without a word, he lay flat. Mountain Man yanked Cade's arms behind his back and cinched his wrists together with zip ties, then backed away.

"Use this," muttered Beanpole. "I don't trust him."

Cade heard the distinctive snap of a taser and knew what was coming. Seconds later, pain wracked his body as electricity arced through him, locking his muscles. Man, he hated tasers. Beat getting shot or stabbed, but he despised having zero control over his body.

"Hit him again," the driver demanded.

Cade's body jerked as electricity overloaded his system. Unable to move, all he could do when the flow of electricity stopped was breathe and pray his emergency signal would bring help in time to save him and Sasha.

CHAPTER THIRTY-TWO

Sasha woke to another miserable headache. In fact, her whole body hurt. She frowned. Why was her bed so hard and vibrating? Not a bed. A vehicle. Had she passed out? Was Cade taking her to the hospital?

Memory slowly returned. Cade had been checking the front room of Perk when someone grabbed her, hauled her outside, and threw her in a van. Sasha remembered horrible pain, and then nothing.

Sasha became aware of men's voices in the vehicle, voices she didn't recognize. Where was Cade?

She opened her mouth to call his name, then thought better of it. Better not call attention to herself. Sasha opened her eyes to slits. Cade lay in front of her. He was on his stomach, wrists cinched behind his back, his face toward her.

Was he still alive? Her stomach clenched. He couldn't be dead. She needed to get a grip. Why immobilize Cade if he was dead?

Since the men who took them weren't paying attention to her, Sasha tried to move toward Cade. No dice. Good grief. What had the creeps hit her with? Maybe they drugged her.

She gritted her teeth and made another attempt to move, and this time succeeded in shifting closer to the man she loved. "Cade," she whispered. No response. Sasha wiggled closer. "Baby, wake up." A nudge with her foot. Still nothing.

Not good. She shifted a few inches more until she could kiss him if she wanted. Would he be like Sleeping Beauty and wake if she kissed him? Sasha staunched the hysterical laughter threatening to escape. They were in trouble, and she couldn't afford to lose it now. Cade's life might depend on her holding herself together.

"Cade." Tears stung her eyes when he didn't respond. At least this close she felt his breath on her face.

What would happen to them now? She had her cell phone, couldn't call for help without attracting attention.

At least she and Cade were together. If Sasha convinced the men she wasn't a threat, maybe they'd free her hands. Where were they taking her and Cade? When she called Zane for help, he'd have to trace her cell signal.

Finally, the driver turned off the paved road and onto a rutted gravel track. Every bump and hole jolted her body. A few minutes or hours later, the driver slowed to a stop.

The other two men turned and saw she had moved to Cade.

The big one leered at her. "Well, look who's awake. Wes will be pleased."

Wes? Sasha's breath caught. Their kidnapping was connected to the failed bank robbery? These men must be part of Black Dog.

The skinny one yanked open the van's side door. "I'll grab the girl. You handle Ramsey." He grasped Sasha's arm. "The boss is waiting for you." He pulled her from the vehicle. When Sasha's legs wouldn't hold her weight, he tossed her over his shoulder in a fireman's carry.

Sasha twisted until she could see the van. The big man and the driver dragged Cade from the vehicle and followed.

"Quit squirming," her captor groused, and slammed a fist into her thigh.

Sasha yelped as pain radiated from her thigh down the rest of her leg. She'd worried about her ability to run when her legs gave out. With the punch to her thigh, that option was gone. Besides, she wouldn't leave Cade. They'd have to come up with a different plan. If she could wake him.

She raised up to check on him. The two clowns still had his arms draped across their shoulders and were hauling him into the building in her wake. Why wasn't he rousing?

A moment later, the skinny man carried Sasha into a large building. The interior walls were cinder block and painted an off white. Boring, utilitarian, and institutional were the words that came to mind.

After walking down a long hallway, her captor threw open a door and hauled Sasha off his shoulder with a grunt. He shoved her into one of the two chairs in the center of the room. "Stay or I'll tie you to the chair."

The two other clods dragged Cade inside and tossed him in the chair beside hers. The big one cut the binding around Cade's wrists and secured him to the arms of the chair, then the men left the room.

Sasha scanned the room. There was nothing to use as a weapon to defend herself and Cade. At least two of the men were outside the door. Sasha could hear them talking.

A camera was mounted on the ceiling in the corner. Couldn't tell if it was on. "Cade. Please, wake up." At the risk of sounding pathetic, she added softly, "I'm afraid. I need you here with me."

He drew in a deep breath.

Her heart skipped a beat. "That's it. Come back to me."

His eyelids flickered. "Sasha," he whispered.

"I'm here."

"Hurt?"

How like him to be more concerned about her than himself. "I don't think so. I think they drugged me. I can't control my muscles. I was too weak to stand on my own a few minutes ago."

"Taser."

She blinked. Well, that explained the lack of communication between her brain and her body. "How long will it take for the effects to wear off?"

"Hour. Longer for me."

"Why?"

"Stunned me twice." He grimaced and managed to raise his head to look at her. "Screwed up."

"There's a camera in the right corner in the ceiling. Could they be recording everything we say?"

"Possibly."

"How can I protect you?" she whispered. "Tell me what to do."

He was silent a moment. "I'm the one they want. If you have the chance, run and don't look back. I'll try to cover you."

Sasha scowled. "I'm not leaving you. We go or stay together."

"You promised."

"I know, but I can't run."

"Taser?"

"That, and one of the creeps punched me in the thigh. I don't think my leg will hold up if I run. Think of something else."

Before he answered, the door opened. Sasha's eyes widened when she saw her brother. "Dean, help me."

His lip curled. "I warned you, little sister."

No. Dean was in this compound, walking freely without a guard. That could only mean one thing. "You did this? You sent these thugs after me? They hurt me and Cade. How could you do that?"

His expression grew thunderous. "Who hurt you?"

"Skinny boy at the door. He used a taser on me and punched me."

Dean turned, pinned the now pale man with his gaze. "Is this true?"

"She fought like a wildcat. I figured the taser wouldn't hurt her long term."

"And the punch?"

Skinny man's gaze skated to her, hatred burning in their depths.

"Look at me," Dean snapped. "Why did you hit Sasha when I told you and your partners not to hurt her?"

"She kept squirming while I carried her inside. I was afraid I'd drop her."

Her brother reached behind his back and grabbed his gun.

"Sassy."

Sasha dragged her gaze from her brother, and turned toward Cade.

"Come here," he murmured.

As Dean stalked closer to the skinny man, Sasha leaned toward Cade, pressing her face against his neck. "Cade?"

"No matter what happens, stay there. Eyes closed, Sasha."

As the man she loved spoke softly in her ear, Sasha tried to block the sound of the man's pleas for mercy. Why had she said anything? Her brother intended to kill the man for disobeying his orders. She didn't want to be responsible for the man's death.

"This is not on you," Cade said, rubbing his jaw against her temple in an attempt to comfort her. She felt him struggling against his restraints.

Seconds later, a gun discharged and the man's pleas came to an abrupt halt.

"Stay with me," Cade whispered.

She shifted closer to him when she heard her brother tell someone to clean up the mess and take out the garbage. She realized how little she knew her brother. This Dean Ingram was cold and ruthless, a man she didn't want to know.

Over the next few minutes, Sasha focused on Cade. Finally, it was blessedly silent in the room.

"Bring my kit," Dean said to someone. That person left the room, then returned a moment later. "Thanks. Move Sasha away from Ramsey."

"Leave her alone, Ingram." Cade pressed a kiss to her temple. "You've hurt her enough."

Harsh laughter escaped her brother. "I warned her to leave you. She wouldn't listen."

"I'm the one you want. Let her go."

"No, Cade," Sasha protested. "We're in this together. I won't leave you."

"You won't have a choice, Sash. Scott, do what I told you. If she wants to be with Ramsey, let her watch. This will be over soon enough."

Fear formed a ball of ice in her stomach. What was her brother going to do? Cade was helpless, tied to the chair. She lifted her head from his shoulder and kissed him.

Hard hands gripped her arms and dragged her from the chair and away from Cade.

"Dean, don't do this. This isn't you."

Another bark of laughter. "You don't know me at all, little sis."

Sasha used what Kat and Dixie had taught her. She broke away from the man who had held her and flew at Dean. With her wrists cinched in front of her, she clasped her hands together and landed a two-handed punch to her brother's face.

His head snapped back, but he didn't go down. Dean back-handed her. Sasha flew backward and hit the wall.

"Dean, stop." Cade fought the bonds holding him to the chair, the zip ties cutting into his skin. "You want to punish someone, come after me, not your sister."

Sasha's brother motioned to the man who had let her escape his grasp. "Keep your hands on her this time. If she escapes again, you're dead."

The man dragged her up from the floor and clamped his hands on her upper arms in a bruising grip.

"Is that your answer to everything?" Sasha snapped. "Kill those who fail?"

Dean shrugged. "Good motivation to keep the operatives in line. I don't tolerate failure." He turned back to Cade. "Your turn to die, Ramsey."

"You going to shoot me now, too?"

An ugly smile formed on her brother's face. "I have something much more appropriate in mind for you." He grabbed a small black zippered case from the chair in the corner of the room.

When he unzipped the case, Sasha saw a rubber tube and a syringe filled with liquid. Her blood ran cold. "What is that?"

"Heroin. Your boyfriend is going to suffer an unfortunate overdose."

Although Sasha twisted and fought, she couldn't break free of the hands holding her with a grip of iron. Stall. She needed to stall. "What does Black Dog have to do with this, with you? Why have Black Dog's people been targeting me?"

Amusement lit Dean's eyes. "You didn't know?"

"Know what?"

"Black Dog is my organization. My people are just as well trained as Fortress. When word leaks how my people defeated Maddox's best teams and killed one of his prized operatives, I'll have more work than I can handle."

"Why a fake bank heist and the hostages at the school? What was the point?"

"Testing Fortress's capabilities. I had to know how they would respond." He laughed. "I kidnapped your boyfriend right under their noses. No one will find him until it's too late to save his life."

"You hate me that much?" Cade asked quietly.

"Emily's dead because of you. You don't deserve to live, Ramsey. You took my wife from me. I adored her, but she loved you to the day she died. I vowed to avenge her death. Today I will fulfill that vow."

Dean motioned to the second man in the room. "Hold him still."

"No," Sasha screamed. "Dean, please. Don't do this."

Her brother ignored her pleas and stalked toward Cade. The second man wrapped his arm around Cade's neck in a choke hold, keeping him immobile. "If you fight me, Ramsey, I'll use the drug on Sasha."

"Leave her alone. I won't fight."

"That's what I thought you'd say. See there, little sister? He does care about you more than his own worthless hide."

Tears trickled down her cheeks as her brother tied the tube around Cade's arm, plunged the needle into his vein, and emptied the syringe.

CHAPTER THIRTY-THREE

Horror filled Sasha at the sight of the vile drug disappearing into Cade's vein. If she called Zane now, would anyone reach them in time to save Cade? How long would it take Zane to track her cell signal? The compound was filled with her brother's soldiers. She'd lost count of the men she had seen as she was hauled from the van into the building.

Dean removed the needle and stepped back. "Doesn't seem fair, Ramsey. You'll go to sleep and never wake up. Sasha will suffer like I did when I lost Emily." He pulled a big knife from a sheath on his thigh and strode toward Sasha.

She lifted her chin, glaring at her brother. "Will you kill me, too?"

"I should. You'll suffer from being left behind. I warned you to stay away from him." He reached for her hands, slid the blade of the knife under the zip tie, and jerked. The plastic fell away. "I'm not totally heartless, unlike your precious Cade. I'll let you spend the last few minutes of his life with him. Maybe next time you'll have better taste in men."

That would never happen. Cade was it for her. "And after he dies?" Her voice broke on the last word.

"I'll set you free. Black Dog will go underground, and you'll never hear from me again." He signaled the man holding Cade in place to cut him loose, then the men cleared out, locked the door, and left her alone with the man she loved.

Sasha raced to Cade's side and dropped to her knees beside him. "Cade."

He clumsily wrapped his arms around her. "It's okay, baby."

"How can you say that? You have a lethal dose of heroin in your veins. We have to get you to a hospital." She pressed her lips to his ear. "I still have my phone."

"Good. Help me to my feet. We need to sit under the camera so they can't see what we're doing."

Sasha used every ounce of strength she had to assist Cade. The two of them staggered to the far corner of the room and sank to the floor. She grabbed her phone and called Zane.

"Yeah, Murphy."

"It's Sasha. We've been kidnapped and my brother gave Cade an overdose of heroin. Zane, if you can't find us fast enough, I'll lose him."

"I know where you are. Bravo and Durango are five minutes out. What can you tell me about where you're being held?"

"It's a compound of one story cinder-block buildings. Four buildings are arranged around a grassy area with concrete walkways leading to each. Another one sits off to the side. That one is three stories high. There are guards everywhere."

"Narrow that number down. How many guards did you see?"

"Maybe twenty. There must be more men inside the buildings. One guard is stationed on the roof of each building in the quad. I didn't see the roof of the three-story structure."

"You're doing great, Sasha. Every piece of information will help the teams coming to you. I'm sending them the information as you're giving it to me. Are you injured?"

"Bumps and bruises. They used a taser on us."

"Is Cade injured aside from the taser and the drug?"

"I don't think so."

"Leave the connection open. Do what you can to help Cade. The teams are three minutes out."

Sasha laid down the phone and turned to the man she loved. Her breath caught when she saw him list to the left. "Stay with me, Cade." She wrapped her arms around the operative and pulled him against her, trying to keep him upright.

"Sasha."

"Bravo and Durango are three minutes out."

A slight nod. "Love you," he whispered.

"I love you, too."

"Whatever happens, I have no regrets in loving you. So blessed to have you in my life. Never dreamed I'd have your love."

Tears fell like rain from her eyes. "Tell me all that again tomorrow. Live so we can enjoy our life together."

"Trying."

She held him tighter and prayed his teammates would arrive in time. Sasha stroked his face. His skin was clammy and pale. She sought a topic that might draw him into conversation. "We haven't talked much about children. How many do you want?"

No response.

"Cade."

"Mmm."

"How many children would you like to have?"

"Four, five. Love kids."

"Perfect. So do I." She mentally implored Bravo and Durango to move faster. Cade's words were starting to slur. "Would you like to get our marriage license this week?"

A slight smile curved his mouth. He drew in a shallow breath. "Oh, yeah."

At that moment, gunfire erupted in the compound. Sasha heard men cursing and yelling. Others screamed. Some ran. Others fell with a thud. She heard Dean yelling at one man, then another, rallying his men.

The gunfire came closer. The sound of fists hitting flesh and groans of pain escalated. Finally, a shout came down the hall. "Sasha, Cade."

Matt.

Sasha laid Cade on his side and raced to the door. She pounded with the side of her fist. "We're here. The door's locked."

"Move away from the door."

She scrambled to the side as the door thudded with the force of Matt's kick. With another massive kick, the door flew open and Matt rushed inside. He ran to Cade and rolled him to his back.

"How long has it been since he was drugged?" the medic asked as he quickly checked Cade.

"Maybe seven or eight minutes. The syringe was full, Matt."

He slid his mike bag off his shoulder. "Can you hear me, Cowboy?"

Nothing.

Footsteps pounded down the hallway toward the room.

Matt thrust a hand into his bag and pulled out a bottle and shoved it into Sasha's hand. He leaped to his feet and placed his body between her and Cade, and whoever was heading for the room. "That's Narcan, Sasha. Cade will need more than one dose."

Trusting Matt to deal with the trouble descending on them, Sasha shook the bottle and squirted a dose of the medicine in each nostril.

"Is he responding?" Matt tackled the man who burst inside the room.

"No."

"Again." The medic blocked a blow to the head, countered with a fist in the other man's face. "Hurry, Sasha."

She repeated the dosages and prayed. "Come on, Cade. Fight. Fight for me." Still nothing. His breathing was a little better, but nowhere near his normal rate. "Matt."

The medic used an elbow to strike his opponent in the temple. The other man went limp. Scrambling to his feet, he lunged toward Sasha and Cade. He checked his friend again, scowled. "They gave him enough to drop a bull elephant in his tracks." Taking the spray from Sasha, he administered more of the counter-active drug.

A moment later, Cade groaned. "Sasha."

Joy exploded in her heart. She gripped his hand with both of hers. "Welcome back, love."

Matt activated his ear piece. "Trent, Cade needs a hospital, fast. Narcan brought him back, but it won't hold for long." He listened a moment, then said, "Copy that."

The medic grabbed his mike bag, strapped it onto his body, then picked up Cade and eased him over his shoulder. "We have to go, Sasha. Stay behind me. If I tell you to drop, do it instantly. No one is going to stop me from getting Cade out of here, including your brother. Do you understand?"

"Yes. Go." She shoved her phone back into her pocket and hurried after the medic. Before they'd reached the end of the corridor, Matt fired his gun. Someone grunted and dropped to the floor. Sasha kept her eyes on the back of Cade's head.

Near the exit, Josh Cahill appeared and wrapped his arm around Sasha's shoulders. "Go, Matt," he ordered. The medic broke into a run.

One of the SUVs from PSI idled with Nate ensconced behind the wheel. Seconds later, Matt climbed into the backseat and eased Cade off his shoulder.

Josh lifted Sasha to the front passenger seat. "Go," he told his EOD man, then slammed the door and stepped back.

The SUV surged forward. Nate swerved around two of Black Dog's soldiers who tried to stop them. Once they cleared the compound and skidded onto the blacktop, Nate raced toward town.

He activated his Bluetooth. A moment later, Ethan Blackhawk's voice filled the SUV's interior. "Talk to me."

"I have the packages. We're en route to the hospital. I need a clear path, Ethan."

"Injuries?"

"I don't know about Sasha, but Cade has an overdose of heroin in his system."

Shots sounded over the connection. Sasha frowned. Was Ethan at the compound?

"I'll take care of it. Go straight into town. I'll have my officers block traffic for you. Sasha?"

"Yes, sir?"

"Are you hurt?"

"A close encounter with a taser and one of them slapped me."

"Who?" The chief's voice was hard with an edge she'd never heard from him.

"My brother. He's the leader of Black Dog, the mercenary group that's been causing me and the town so much trouble."

"I'm sorry."

"Ethan, please don't kill him. His death would devastate my parents."

He was silent a moment. "That's up to him."

After he ended the call, Nate said to Sasha, "Ethan will do his best. Sometimes it's not enough."

"I know." She twisted in her seat. "How is he?" she asked Matt.

"Hanging in there."

Another groan from the man she loved. "Pull over," he said, voice raspy. "Sick."

Nate glanced in the mirror at the medic.

He shook his head. "Drive." He thrust his hand into the mike bag and brought out a plastic bag.

Over the next few miles, Cade retched over and over as his body tried to rid itself of the poison. Sasha's stomach clenched in sympathy.

When they reached town, Nate sailed through the intersections. Finally, the SUV raced up the drive to the hospital and skidded to a stop at the emergency room entrance. A medical team ran out with a gurney. In less than a minute, Matt raced beside the orderlies into the hospital, updating a doctor on Cade's vital signs. The team disappeared into a treatment room.

When she tried to follow, Nate put his hand on her arm. "Give them room to work." He led Sasha to a chair close to the room where Cade was being evaluated and treated. "Stay here. I'll be back as soon as I move the SUV." Without waiting for her answer, he jogged to the parking lot.

Sasha wrapped her arms around herself, her focus on the man currently fighting for his life. Cade was strong and in the peak of health.

As she sat, the aftermath of the kidnapping, rescue, and mad dash to the hospital swept through her in a deluge of trembling. By the time Nate returned, Sasha's teeth were chattering.

The operative knelt by her side and draped a warm blanket around her. "This should help," he murmured. "I know you won't like it, but I'm asking a doctor to check you."

Unable to speak because of the chattering, she narrowed her eyes at him.

He snorted. "That's not going to work on me, sugar." Humor lit his gaze. "The eye thing only works for Stella." With that statement, he walked to the desk and talked to a nurse

Within five minutes, Nate was helping Sasha into an examination room. Dr. Anderson walked in.

"Well, my dear, I see you're back to visit with us. What happened this time?"

Nate folded his arms across his chest. "She and Cade were kidnapped and tasered. Sasha has bumps, bruises, and a hefty case of adrenaline dump."

"Let's have a look. Mr. Armstrong, wait in the hall while I check Ms. Ingram."

Nate caught her eye. "I'll be outside the door. If you need me, call out."

Sasha blinked away the tears threatening to overflow and nodded. Minutes later, the doctor declared her to be fit despite the new bruises forming on her skin. Dr. Anderson brought in an ice pack for her cheek, patted her hand, and released her.

She followed him to the hall. "Any word on Cade?" she asked the dark-haired chef standing guard at the door.

"Matt said he's hanging in there." He escorted her to the waiting room.

Paige and Marcus Lang stood as Sasha approached.

"Sasha." Paige enveloped her in a tight hug.

"How did you know I was here?"

"Nate called Marcus. He thought you might need some company." Paige urged her to sit. "Marcus, I think Sasha would appreciate chamomile tea with sugar."

"I'll be right back." The pastor of Cornerstone Church squeezed Sasha's shoulder and left.

Although Sasha expected Nate to go with the preacher, he leaned one shoulder against the wall in the hallway. He was far enough away to give her and Paige privacy, but close enough to intervene if a problem developed. She should have known he wouldn't leave her unprotected.

"Are you okay, Sasha?" Paige wrapped her hand around Sasha's.

"I'm fine." She waggled the ice pack. "A bruise, nothing more. Cade was the target, not me. I was the bait." She still couldn't believe her own brother tried to kill Cade.

"What happened?"

Sasha recounted the events, sure this wouldn't be the only time she was asked to do so. She expected Ethan had many questions for her.

"Oh, Sasha. I'm sorry you had to go through that." Paige squeezed her hand again. "Cade is strong, and he has someone worth fighting for. You."

"I don't know what I'll do if I lose him."

"You'll honor his memory by living your life to the fullest. Let's not anticipate the worst, though. Your boyfriend wants a future with you."

Marcus returned with a to-go cup in his hand. "Chamomile tea with sugar."

"Thanks." She wrapped her hands around the warm cup, savoring the heat. At least the shakes had stopped. Made drinking tea without spilling the liquid easier.

As Sasha finished the last of her tea, Nate straightened from the wall, his gaze focused down the hall. Sasha hurried to the hallway, followed by the Langs.

Matt walked from the treatment room. "It was close, but he'll be okay," he said without preamble.

Overwhelmed with relief, she threw her arms around the medic. "Thank you."

He patted her back. "Do you want to see him for a minute?"

She drew back. "A minute?" If the medical team thought they would keep Sasha from Cade's side, they were crazy.

"The doctor wants to admit Cade for observation overnight. Once he's in a room, you can stay at his side."

"Let's go." She wanted to see for herself he was alive and recovering. Maybe then the tight band around her heart would loosen, and she'd be able to breathe.

CHAPTER THIRTY-FOUR

Cade opened his eyes when the door to the exam room opened. His fingers itched to draw his weapon, but the medical team had insisted Matt take his Sig when they started working on him. Now, he was stuck in this hospital bed in an ugly, drafty gown that left nothing to the imagination if he moved wrong. He wanted to go home with Sasha. Where was she? Was she safe?

Sasha shoved open the door and ran inside the room. Relief swept through him in a deluge.

"Cade." She sped across the expanse of floor separating them. Although acting as though she wanted to throw herself into his arms, something he wanted as well, Sasha held back, reaching down to touch his cheek instead.

"Come here." Cade spread his arms.

She leaned down and hugged him, her hold gentle.

"I won't break, Sassy."

Immediately, her arms tightened around him. "I thought I was going to lose you."

He'd been afraid of that, too. If Cade had arrived at the hospital five minutes later, he wouldn't be holding the woman he adored. He pressed a gentle kiss to the side of her neck, eliciting a shiver from his girlfriend. "I'm fine."

Cade eased her away and pushed back her dark hair. He scowled at the bruise on her cheek. Ingram had nailed his sister good. If he got thirty seconds alone with the clown, Cade would return the favor with interest. "You're all right?"

She nodded. "Matt said the doctor is admitting you for observation. I'm staying with you. Don't even think about sending me home."

"Wouldn't dream of it." He preferred to have her in his sight until he knew the danger to Sasha was gone.

Matt peered into the room. "Orderlies are here to take you to your room."

Ten minutes later, Cade raised the head of the bed and held out his hand to Sasha. "If you need anything, tell Matt. He'll take care of it for you."

"He's your bodyguard?"

Cade flinched. "Not a bodyguard." He wasn't that bad off. Didn't need that level of protection. Maybe.

"But he's keeping watch."

"Fortress operatives protect teammates when they're injured. Otherwise, the injured operative doesn't sleep." He sent a pointed glance her direction. "If I didn't have at least one of my teammates close, I wouldn't rest, especially with you in the room."

She squeezed his hand and moved her chair closer to the bed. "I'm glad you have friends and co-workers to watch your back."

"And yours. Because you're mine to love and protect, you are a priority for them, too."

A sharp knock on the door. Ethan Blackhawk strode in. His gaze dropped to their clasped hands, sharpening when he spotted the engagement ring. His eyebrows rose. "You're engaged."

Cade smiled. "Are you surprised?"

"Only that you took this long. Congratulations."

"Thanks. You here to take our statements?"

The police chief nodded as he pulled out his notebook and pen. "You able to answer a few questions?"

Not really, but he didn't want to put this off. Ethan wouldn't ask if he didn't need the information. "Sasha stays with me. I won't be separated from her." If he had his way, he'd never be separated from her again except when he deployed with Bravo. Yeah, Matt and Nate were still on duty, and he trusted them with Sasha. Regardless, she was his to protect.

"I understand. How do you feel, Cade?"

"Like a bus ran over me a dozen times. Every muscle in my body hurts. Can't figure out why anyone would pump poison into their bodies."

"Most people only take enough to zone out and forget their problems for a while. According to Matt, you had a massive dose of heroin in your system." Ethan turned to Sasha. "Did the doc check you?"

She nodded. "A few new bruises to show for my second kidnapping experience in a week."

"I'm glad you're all right."

"Do you know anything about Dean?" she asked, voice soft.

"In surgery. He took a bullet to the shoulder." Ethan's face hardened. "Ingram drew on Trent. He's lucky to still be breathing." He turned his attention back to Cade. "Tell me what happened this morning."

"How did Fortress know we were in trouble?" He knew how Z had found them. Sasha's jewelry. He hadn't felt the tracking tag under his skin activate. But he couldn't figure out how his teammates were en route when Sasha called Zane.

"Josh was on shift overnight. He routinely does a sweep of businesses on the square. He noticed your SUV parked at the back of Perk but no lights on in the shop.

After spotting the open back door, he called me, then Fortress. Durango and Bravo mobilized and we put together a plan. Tell me what happened, Cade."

He recounted the events from the time he woke until he passed out from the drug overdose. "The next thing I knew, Nate was driving like an Indy car driver to get me to the hospital in time and I was puking my guts out."

Ethan flipped to a fresh page of his notebook. "Your turn, Sasha."

She summarized events from her perspective. "I can't believe Dean would do something like this. I understand why he wanted to form his own black ops group. Cade said my brother applied to Ranger school, but didn't make the cut. Sacrificing lives for his own agenda to murder Cade?" Sasha shook her head. "That isn't my brother."

"Wait." Cade frowned. "The fake bank robbers said a guy named Wes was their boss. Who is Wes?"

"Dean's full name is Dean Wesley Ingram. He must have used his middle name to help camouflage his identity."

The police chief closed his notebook. "What you've given me is enough for now. I want to ask more questions, but I can tell both of you are tired. When will the doctor release you, Cade?"

"Tomorrow." Not soon enough for his taste. Too many security risks in spite of his teammates keeping watch over him and Sasha.

A nod. "Stop by the station tomorrow and we'll go through everything again."

When Ethan left, Matt stepped inside the room. "Nate's on watch in the hall. Do you want me out there with him?"

Cade shook his head. "Pull up a chair. Any news from the compound?"

"Seventeen dead, all Black Dog."

"Injuries on our side?"

"Bullet kissed Simon's side. Rio patched him up."

Cade felt his eyes growing heavy.

"Go ahead and sleep," the medic said. "Your body fought hard against the heroin. Give yourself a chance to recuperate." He eyed Sasha. "You could use a nap yourself. Climb up beside your boyfriend and rest." He stood. "I'll be in the hall if you need me. No one will slip past me or Nate." Lifting his chair, he carried it from the room and left them alone.

Cade tugged on Sasha's hand. "You heard the medic's orders." He scooted over as far as he could and patted the mattress. When she reclined on the bed beside him, he eased her head on his shoulder and let the fatigue take him under.

CHAPTER THIRTY-FIVE

"Are you sure you want to do this?" Cade cupped Sasha's cheek, his thumb brushing her bottom lip. He didn't want this for her, dreaded what would most likely be an ugly confrontation.

"Want to? No, I don't. I need to, though. He's my brother." She turned her face toward him, the shiner Ingram had given her a reminder of the hardship she'd endured.

"All right. I'm going in the room with you."

Sasha placed her hand over his heart. "I appreciate you wanting to protect me, but I don't think that's a good idea."

"Then we have a problem, Sassy. I won't let you go in there alone." He was firm on that. Losing her would gut him, and Cade didn't trust Dean Ingram with the most precious thing in his life.

"He's handcuffed to the bed."

"Doesn't matter. I could slip out of the cuffs in less than a minute and so could my teammates."

"Dean isn't in the same league with Fortress operatives or he'd be working for Maddox. Would Liam come with me?"

Cade's teammate had taken over protection detail early in the evening so Matt and Nate could go home and sleep. Although Cade longed to be there for her, his presence would inflame Sasha's brother and make Dean more antagonistic when he realized his plan to murder Cade had failed.

He walked to the door, grateful Trent had dropped off clothes for him to wear instead of the hospital gown. "Liam." He stepped back to allow his teammate to enter the room.

"What do you need?"

"Sasha wants to see her brother. Ingram has a room on the fifth floor. Ethan cleared Sasha with the policeman at the door. If I accompany her inside the room, I'll set Ingram off." His lips curved. "I'm not on his friend list anymore. I don't want her alone with him."

A nod from Bravo's sniper. "I'll take care of her."

"Leave the door open. I want to hear everything."

Another nod. Liam turned to Sasha. "Ready?"

"Yes. Thanks, Liam."

"Not a problem." Cade's teammate trailed them to the elevator.

On the fifth floor, they walked down the deserted corridor and headed for the policeman at Ingram's door.

"Glad you're okay, Ms. Ingram. That's quite a shiner."

Sasha wrinkled her nose. "Not my best look."

Cade turned her toward him, his touch gentle. "You're beautiful, shiner or not."

"You're biased."

He shrugged. "I'm telling the truth." Cade eyed the policeman. "Is Ingram awake?"

A snort. "If you stand here for more than five minutes, you'll hear him demanding a lawyer and cursing the nurses. He's not in a good mood. You might want to wait a day or two before you visit him, Ms. Ingram."

"Time won't make this better. I'm taking Liam with me."

"Uh, well, the chief didn't clear him. Just you and Ramsey."

"Call Ethan." Cade threaded his fingers through Sasha's. "We'll wait."

The policeman turned his back toward them and made the call. After a quick, hushed conversation, he slid his phone into his pocket. "Go on in."

After a pointed glance at Liam and receiving a nod from the sniper silently promising to take care of Sasha, Cade released his girlfriend's hand. "I'll be here if you need me."

Liam escorted Sasha inside the room, leaving the door to the hallway open. Cade shifted to the opposite side of the doorway where he could observe Ingram in the window reflection.

"Dean, how do you feel?" Sasha asked.

Her brother stared at Liam. "Who is that? You moved on from Ramsey before he's planted in the ground?"

Would she tell him his plan failed or let him find out when he showed up in court to testify? Although Cade hadn't told her to keep the information a secret, Sasha ignored the opportunity to tell Dean. "This is a friend from PSI."

Cade marveled at Sasha's quick thinking. He didn't believe Ingram would be out of prison anytime soon. Still, Sasha protected Liam's identity. If Dean knew Liam was part of the team who had taken Black Dog apart, he might exact revenge when he released from jail. Prison gave people a long time to think, either reflecting on their mistakes and vowing to change their ways, or plotting revenge on their enemies.

"How do you feel?" Sasha eased nearer to Ingram's bed.

Cade moved a step closer to the room before he caught himself. Inside the room, Liam extended his arm to prevent Sasha from approaching the bed. Cade took a breath. Good.

"Like I've been shot," Ingram growled.

"You're lucky you aren't dead," she countered. "The man you drew on is Special Forces. He spared your life for my sake."

A sneer. "Shouldn't have done me any favors. If he'd killed me, at least I'd be with Emily. I'll be behind bars for years, staring at walls. That's no kind of life."

"You made your choice," she said, her voice soft. "Every choice has consequences."

"I guess we'll both be dealing with those consequences for the rest of our lives. Leave, Sash. I don't want to see you again. The sight of you turns my stomach. I expected you to choose blood first. Instead, you chose that low-life Ramsey. At least I have the satisfaction of knowing he's dead."

Cade's hands clenched. Ingram had spewed enough hatred and anger. Whatever Sasha had wanted to accomplish seemed doomed to failure. Cade couldn't stand by and let Ingram hurt her with his words any longer.

He walked into the room with silent steps and stopped at the foot of the bed to stare at Sasha's stunned brother.

"No," Ingram choked out. He crushed the blanket in his fist. "You're supposed to be dead. The heroin should have killed you in less than ten minutes."

Liam eased away from Sasha and moved out of the injured man's sight as Cade threaded his fingers through Sasha's. "Our medics carry Narcan."

Hatred filled Ingram's gaze. "No jail cell is going to hold me. You won't see me coming next time, Ramsey. I'll just shoot you and be rid of you for good."

Cade shook his head. "I doubt you'll ever see the outside of a prison cell. If you do, you'll be an old man." Ethan Blackhawk and his detectives were the best. By the time they finished tearing apart Black Dog, they would have sufficient proof to charge Ingram with murder and conspiracy to murder several times over.

"You had Westlake killed, didn't you?" Cade already suspected the answer, but wanted the information confirmed.

"He was a weak link and a liability."

"Same with the men driving the truck in the parking lot in Knoxville?"

An ugly smile formed on Ingram's lips. "I don't leave loose ends."

Cade didn't know if the remaining scattered members of Black Dog would carry out their boss's orders if the organization was defunct, but he would give Ethan the information and let him do what was necessary.

"Our parents will want to see you. It's been a long time. Will you see them if they come to Otter Creek?" Sasha asked her brother.

"No. Don't tell them anything. Let them assume I'm dead. Get out, Ramsey." He glared at Cade. "Take my traitor sister with you. You're a dead man walking."

As Cade led Sasha from the room, Ingram repeated his threats, including Sasha in his plans for retribution. Cade nudged Sasha into the hall. "Stay with her," he murmured to Liam.

"Cade." Sasha clamped a hand on his forearm. "Don't."

"Do you trust me, Sassy?"

"You know I do."

"Let me do this." A kiss and he turned back into the room.

"Get out," Ingram snapped.

His eyebrow rose. "What do you plan to do if I won't leave?"

"Call security and have you thrown out."

Cade laughed. "That's the worst you've got?"

"Leave."

"In a minute. You want to threaten me, go ahead. But leave Sasha out of it. Know this. If you come after me or Sasha again, I'll kill you without a second thought. I won't tolerate anyone threatening my wife."

Blood drained from Ingram's face. "No. You can't." He turned his face toward the doorway. "Sasha, don't do it. Don't marry Ramsey. He'll be the death of you."

"Enough, Dean." Cade folded his arms over his chest. "I know what Emily told you about me. She lied, man. I never laid a hand on her in anger."

"Shut up." Ingram scowled. "You're the one who's lying to me."

"For what purpose? Look, Em had problems. I didn't tell you or anyone else because she promised me over and over she would stop."

The other man's brow furrowed. "Stop what?"

"She wanted to be the center of my attention."

"Emily had every right to demand that place in your life. She was the center of my world. I would have done anything for her."

"I felt the same until she made up emergencies to make me to come home and be with her. I can't tell you how many times I raced to her house, thinking I would have to take her to the emergency room, and found her safe and happy. My commanding officer ripped me and said if it happened again, he'd strip my rank and send me back into a regular unit. My career was on the line, Dean. I encouraged her to seek help. Instead, she turned to you when I deployed with my unit."

"You expect me to believe that?"

Despite the words and harsh tone from Ingram, Cade saw the doubt creeping into his gaze. "It's the truth. When you told us about her death, I asked a friend to look into the details for me. I don't think Emily intended to commit suicide. You told the police you were an hour late arriving home because of a lockdown at the base. Maybe she was playing another one of her head games and ended up dying accidentally."

Ingram turned his face away, expression grim.

"You were Emily's husband. Access her medical records. You'll see I didn't hurt her in spite of what she told you. I would never mistreat a woman. You know that to be true. I give you my word, I won't hurt Sasha, either."

With that, he turned on his heel and walked out. He'd done what he could. Whether or not Ingram accepted the truth was up to him.

CHAPTER THIRTY-SIX

Sasha wiped tears from her face, heart hurting for Cade and Dean. How could Dean live with himself? He'd betrayed his best friend, stolen the woman Cade planned to marry, and, when he'd lost her, turned that anger and hurt on Cade.

When Cade walked into the hall, concern filled his gaze. "You okay?"

She nodded. How could she say otherwise? Her boyfriend was recovering and Sasha was safe. She wrapped her arm around Cade's waist. "Come on. You need to be back in bed or the nurses will kick me out for being a bad influence."

"I wish they'd kick me out."

"You'll get your wish tomorrow."

Although Cade insisted he was fine, by the time he kicked off his shoes and climbed on the bed, fatigue lined his face. When he extended his hand to her, she stretched out beside him, knowing he wouldn't rest unless she was near.

Sasha curled against his side, head on his shoulder. Within a few heartbeats, Cade was asleep. She envied his ability to drop off instantly.

Sometime later, Trent walked into the room after a soft knock. Cade's eyes flew open, his grip on Sasha tightening as his muscles tensed, prepared to defend her. He relaxed when he saw his team leader.

"How do you feel?"

"Like I've gone ten rounds in the ring with Alex and Josh, and lost."

Trent chuckled. "I'm on shift tonight with Matt. Wanted you to know I was here."

"Grace working?"

"Yeah. She'll check on you when she's on break."

Sasha grinned. "That might be her secondary motive. Her first is to steal a few kisses from you."

The SEAL winked at her. "I won't complain. By the way, your workers are taking care of your shop tomorrow. They said not to worry about anything." He looked at Cade. "Go back to sleep. We have you and Sasha covered."

Throughout the night, the nurse checked on Cade every two hours. When the sun peeked over the horizon the next morning, the noise level in the hallway began to increase.

A few minutes after seven, Dr. Anderson arrived. He checked Cade and declared him too fit to occupy a hospital bed. "You will have lingering fatigue for a few days. I recommend not returning to work until Monday unless it's an emergency."

"Thanks, Doc."

"When the nurse brings your discharge papers, you're free to go. I have real patients to see. Unless you're visiting a sick friend, I don't want to see either of you in this establishment for a long time." With a wave, he left.

Matt peered inside the room. "What's the word?"

"Doc Anderson released me."

"Excellent. I'm ready for food. Why don't we stop at That's A Wrap?"

"Sounds good. Sasha?"

"I'd like that."

"Will you go home afterward?" Matt asked Cade.

"Sasha and I have to stop by the police station and run another couple errands."

Sasha couldn't help but smile when she remembered one of the errands. Obtaining their marriage license.

"Don't overdo it. Your body hasn't fully recovered."

Cade held up a hand. "Dr. Anderson gave the same speech. I'm not planning much for a few days. Anderson won't release me to return to work until Monday."

Matt drove them to the town square. As soon as they walked into That's A Wrap, Darcy hurried around the counter and hugged them.

She glanced around the deli, looking for a place for them to sit. "This place is a madhouse. Go into my office. I'll bring you breakfast."

The quiet was a welcome relief from the noisy crowd in the dining area. Within minutes, Darcy delivered breakfast wraps for them along with coffee, soft drinks, and water.

"I wasn't sure what your stomach could tolerate, Cade" Darcy patted him on the shoulder.

"This is perfect, Darcy. Thanks."

"Take your time eating. I'll check on you in a few minutes."

By the time they left the deli, the dining area was empty. Matt stopped on the sidewalk. "Do you want me to drop you at your SUV?"

Cade shook his head. "I need to walk the soreness from my muscles. And no, Dr. Rainer, I won't overdo it."

"If you don't need me, I'm going home to sleep for a couple hours. Some of us have to work today." With a grin and a salute, Matt drove away.

The walk to the police station took longer than normal. People frequently stopped them to talk. Any other day, Sasha would have enjoyed the conversation. Today, she wanted Cade inside Ethan's office and off his feet.

The desk sergeant looked up when they walked into the station lobby. "Glad you two are recovering."

"So are we," Cade said. "Ethan asked us to come by for more questions."

A nod. "I'll let him know you're here." Following a hushed phone conversation, the sergeant pointed to the double doors. "Through those doors and straight back."

Ethan met them in the center of a room filled with desks and law enforcement officers, including Nate's wife, Stella. Although she was on the phone, she grinned and waved at them.

"Thanks for coming in." Ethan ushered them into his office. "Need anything to drink? We use Serena's Home Runs coffee blend, and the pot is fresh."

Cade shook his head. "We're fine."

"Take a seat." The police chief dropped into the chair behind his desk. "I have your statements ready. Read them. If you think of something to add, we'll change the file. When you're satisfied, you can sign your statements and be on your way."

Over the next hour, Ethan took them through the kidnapping twice more and asked detailed questions. "You're a lucky man, Cade."

"I know." He glanced at Sasha, smiled. "In more than one way."

"When is the wedding?"

"Soon. We're getting our marriage license when we leave your office."

Ethan looked thoughtful. "This time of day, the county clerk's office will be busy. Let me make a call. I might be able to shorten the wait." He pressed the phone's handset to his ear. A moment later, he said, "Casey, it's Ethan

Blackhawk. I need a favor. Cade Ramsey and Sasha Ingram will be in your office in less than ten minutes. Can you move them to the head of the line?" A pause. "Great. Thanks."

He glanced at them. "You're set. " Ethan shook hands with them. "Rest and heal. I'll be in touch soon."

Back on the sidewalk, Cade threaded his fingers through Sasha's and walked toward City Hall. Again, they were stopped frequently. When they reached the clerk's office, the waiting line to see Casey Redgrave stretched the entire length of the hall.

The clerk grinned when she saw Sasha and Cade. "What can I do for you?"

"We need a marriage license." Cade nodded at the blue-haired lady waiting to renew her car tags.

"Yes!" Casey chair danced. "I'm thrilled for you. Congratulations." Minutes later, they stood on the sidewalk with the license.

"Are we going home now?" Sasha asked. Cade was showing signs of fatigue.

"Not yet. We need to stop at the jewelry store."

Not what she had expected him to say. "Why?"

"Wedding rings. I want to take care of it now."

Inside the store, Sasha peered in display cases until a sales assistant was free.

"Choose what you want, Sassy. I'll buy a matching wedding band."

Mindful of his work demands, Sasha chose a plain wedding band that was a little wider and thicker than the standard.

"Perfect." He brushed her mouth with a gentle kiss.

Once he purchased the rings, they checked on Sasha's employees and returned to Cade's SUV. When he didn't start the vehicle, Sasha twisted in her seat to face him. "What is it?"

He reached for her hand. "I don't want to be separated from you aside from deployments. I know we agreed to marry in a few weeks. When I saw you unconscious in the van, I thought the men had killed you and I had lost you. It will be a long time before I'm comfortable with you out of my sight."

The longer Cade spoke, the faster Sasha's heart beat. "What are you saying, Cade?"

"I don't want to wait to get married. I love you, Sasha. I want to spend as much time as possible with you. I want to fall asleep with you in my arms where I know you're safe and wake with you wrapped around me."

Sasha's mouth curved. "I planned to wait until tomorrow to ask you to marry me sooner. Call Matt. Tell him to meet us at Cornerstone Church in two hours."

He froze. "You're serious? You want to marry me today?"

"I need to find a dress. Otherwise, I'd marry you right now."

After a heated kiss, Cade drew back and pulled out his phone. While he called his best friend, Sasha called Marcus and Paige Lang. Paige agreed to meet her at the dress shop. Sasha didn't know what they had in stock, but she'd find something special. Nothing would keep her from marrying the man of her dreams.

Cade slid his phone into his pocket. "Matt's calling our teammates." He looked sheepish. "We may have a few more people than you wanted at the church."

"No problem. Take me to the dress shop. Paige is meeting me there." When he parked in front of the shop, Sasha kissed him. "I'll be fine. Marcus is coming with Paige so I won't be alone. Do what you need to. I'll see you at the church in two hours." Another kiss. "I love you, Cade. Thanks for marrying me early."

He caught her hand. "What about your parents? Will they be angry for not giving them a chance to attend the wedding?"

"I'll talk to them."

Sasha hurried into the dress shop. Two hours and counting to pull this off.

Five minutes after Sasha entered the shop, Paige hurried through the door with her husband close on her heels. "Girl, you don't mess around when you set your mind on something."

"We don't want to wait, not after what happened yesterday."

Paige hugged her. "You don't have to explain. Marcus and I didn't wait long, either. Best decision ever. How long do we have to find your wedding dress?"

"Twenty minutes. After that, I need to go to the bakery and see what's available."

"I'll call the bakery," Marcus said. "You and Paige look for the dress."

Sasha and her friend explained what was happening to the owner of the boutique.

The woman said, "I have just the thing. It's not a traditional wedding dress, but it's lacy and elegant, and the color is perfect for you."

Standing in front of the mirror in the amethyst dress with an asymmetric hemline, Sasha agreed the dress was perfect, almost as though it were made for her.

"Wow." Paige sighed. "You look stunning. Cade will be speechless when he sees you." She handed Sasha a box. "Shoes that match the dress. I found a few other things. I left them at the cash register."

"You're the best." Once she changed into her street clothes, the shop owner covered her wedding dress in gray plastic.

Sasha glanced at the items Paige chose, her cheeks heating. Beautiful, sexy night gowns, and matching lingerie sets. As much as she liked them, Sasha suspected Cade would love them. She purchased everything and turned to Marcus. "Does the bakery have what we need?"

"If you don't mind cupcakes instead of a traditional wedding cake. They're also bringing a punch mix. The church has a punch bowl and many cups to use. I think we have your reception covered."

"Sounds great." To be honest, she didn't care as long as she married Cade.

"Good. I'll call the bakery to confirm. What's next?"

"Flowers," Paige said.

They chose flowers to place around the church, arranged for delivery in an hour, and stopped at her favorite department store to purchase makeup. She didn't know if the fire and smoke had ruined hers or not, but Sasha didn't want to chance it.

By the time they arrived at the church, Sasha had forty minutes to prepare for her wedding.

"Don't worry about anything but you." Paige squeezed Sasha's hand. "I'll take care of everything else."

Five minutes before the wedding was scheduled to begin, a light knock sounded on the door. Paige turned to see her mother in the doorway. She smiled. "You made it."

"Of course." Patsy Ingram wrapped her arms around Sasha. "This is quite a surprise."

"We didn't want to wait, Mom. You know what Cade does for a living. He could be deployed at a moment's notice and gone for weeks at a time."

She cupped Sasha's cheeks. "You don't have to explain, honey. I understand. The way you talked about Cade over the past few months we expected something like this." Patsy laughed. "I had hoped for more than a two-hour notice."

A few minutes later, Paige walked in. "It's time. Cade and Matt are ready."

"Give me a minute with Mom." When her friend nodded and closed the door again, Sasha turned to her mother. "Are you and Dad okay?"

She had agonized over whether to tell her parents about Dean. In the end, she couldn't keep her knowledge a secret. With them rushing to Otter Creek, they would hear about Black Dog and Dean. The town's grapevine was professional grade.

Sadness seeped into her mother's eyes. "We're reeling from the news. We raised Dean to be better than that and feel like we failed as parents."

"No, Mom, you didn't. No one could ask for better parents. Dean is an adult. We all make choices and have to deal with the fallout from our decisions."

"I know, but he's my son. Although I don't want him in prison, jail time is inevitable. What he did was wrong and he'll have to pay for his crimes. It still breaks my heart." Patsy shook her head. "Enough sadness for today. This is your wedding day. We're going to celebrate."

"One more question. Will you go see Dean?"

"You bet we will."

"He doesn't want to talk to you."

"Tough. Your father and I have a few things to say to him, and he's going to listen. Now, I know a young man who's anxious to marry you."

Sasha pressed a hand to her stomach, butterflies taking flight. "Let's go."

When she walked into the fellowship hall, she froze. Over the last forty minutes, the large room had been transformed. The tables were covered with white cloths. Each table had a glass bowl with a floating candle and rose petals scattered around the bowl. At the front of the room, three large tables held cupcakes on elaborate tiers, nuts, mints, and a filled punch bowl.

Serena Blackhawk glanced up from arranging the plastic eating utensils, plates, and napkins. "What do you think, Sasha?"

"This is incredible. Thank you." She scanned the tables again. "We might be eating cupcakes for weeks. That's more than we need."

The police chief's wife grinned. "I don't think so. You look beautiful. Your father's waiting for you at the auditorium entrance."

"Come on." Paige tugged on Sasha's hand. "You're late."

She allowed her friend to hustle her through the fellowship hall and down the corridor to the auditorium doors.

Sasha's father beamed when he saw her. He hugged her, his grip tight. "You look gorgeous, sweetheart. I like your young man. Let's not keep him waiting any longer." He looked at his wife. "Go inside, sweetheart. We'll be right behind you."

Paige opened the doors and motioned for Patsy to walk in, then handed a bouquet of flowers to Sasha. "Cade chose these for you. Don't cry. You'll ruin your makeup."

Sasha blinked rapidly to prevent tears from falling at the sight of the white roses in her hands. The roses were perfect.

Her father extended his arm to Sasha. She became aware of the hum of conversation coming from the auditorium. That sounded like more than Bravo.

Paige walked into the sanctuary at a sedate pace timed to music from a piano.

Sasha's eyes widened. She recognized one of the pieces Darcy Kincaid played when she'd been touring as a concert pianist. Darcy was playing the piano for Sasha's wedding?

Finally, her father started forward. "You have many friends, Sasha. You're a very lucky woman."

She didn't understand why he'd made that statement until they walked into the sanctuary and she saw every pew filled with friends and neighbors from PSI and Otter Creek.

At the front of the church, Cade, Matt, and Marcus, dressed in tuxes, waited for her to approach. Good grief. Cade was drop-dead gorgeous. As she walked toward him, Cade's eyes widened. She winked at him causing him to smile, the joy in his eyes a reflection of the emotion in her heart.

In his eyes, she saw a future filled with laughter and love, family. She put aside the hurt over Dean's betrayal and concentrated on the man she adored.

When she reached his side, Cade captured her face between his palms and kissed her. "You look beautiful, Sassy," he murmured.

"All right now," Marcus said, amusement in his voice. "You're getting ahead of the program, Cade."

Their friends and family burst into laughter.

Ten minutes later, she and Cade placed wedding bands on each other's fingers.

When they faced Marcus again, he said, "I'm happy to pronounce you husband and wife. Cade, you may kiss your wife."

Cade wrapped his arms around Sasha and drew her close. "I love you, Sasha Ramsey. Thank you for trusting me with your heart." He bent his head and kissed her as applause filled the church.

This, Sasha thought, was love. A husband who treasured her as much as she did him. They would face challenges in the days to come. Every challenge gave them a chance to deepen their love and commitment to each other. She couldn't wait to see what the future held for them.

No Regrets

Rebecca Deel

ABOUT THE AUTHOR

Rebecca Deel is a preacher's kid with a black belt in karate. She teaches business classes at a private four-year college outside Nashville, Tennessee. She plays the piano at church, writes freelance articles, and runs interference for the family dogs. She's been married to her amazing husband for more than 25 years and is the proud mom of two grown sons. She delivers occasional devotions to the women's group at her church and conducts seminars in personal safety, money management, and writing. Her articles have been published in *ONE Magazine*, *Contact*, and *Co-Laborer*, and she was profiled in the June 2010 Williamson edition of *Nashville Christian Family* magazine. Rebecca completed her Doctor of Arts degree in Economics and wears her favorite Dallas Cowboys sweatshirt when life turns ugly.

For more information on Rebecca

Sign up for Rebecca's newsletter: http://eepurl.com/_B6w9
Visit Rebecca's website: www.rebeccadeelbooks.com

Printed in Great Britain
by Amazon